THE MAGLEV CONSPIRACY

THE MAGLEV CONSPIRACY

MARY LEONE ENGQUIST & JOE LEONE

iUniverse, Inc.
Bloomington

The Maglev Conspiracy

iUniverse books may be ordered through booksellers or by contacting:

iUniverse
1663 Liberty Drive
Bloomington, IN 47403
www.iuniverse.com
1-800-Authors (1-800-288-4677)

ISBN: 978-1-4759-1862-5 (sc)
ISBN: 978-1-4759-1863-2 (ebk)

Printed in the United States of America

iUniverse rev. date: 05/01/2012

PROLOGUE

THE MAGLEV CONSPIRACY

"The time will come when people will travel in stages moved by steam engines from one city to another, almost as fast as birds can fly, 15 or 20 miles an hour . . . . A carriage will start from Washington in the morning, the passengers will breakfast a Baltimore, and lunch in Philadelphia and supper in New York the same day. Engines will drive boats 10 or 12 miles an hour, and there will be hundreds of steamers running on the Mississippi, as predicted years ago."

—Oliver Evans, 1800

And so gradually began a revolutionary era for transportation. With the completion of the Transcontinental railroad in 1869 both coasts were linked and commodities, industrial products and people were able to move freely throughout the continental United States.

Following World War II, an abrupt change occurred with the railroads as a **(people mover)**. The trains simply became too slow and there was a shift to airlines and bus-lines for a more rapid form of transit.

The average American was more affluent and began to value time much more and was willing to spend more to 'get there' faster. In more heavily populated countries with a less affluent populous the train remained a primary form of transportation.

Some of those countries, like Japan, invested money to increase the speeds of their rail systems. The Japanese 'Bullet Train' (The Shinkansen) was completed in 1964. It reached speeds of over 250 miles an hour.

The Bullet Train concept provided impetus to U.S. inventors to refine and improve on a form of our rail system. With the ever increasing cost of fuel and transportation in general, it became clear that a fast inexpensive and convenient mode of transportation that could move large numbers of people between populous cities and popular points of interest could be viable and very profitable.

A Maglev works on the principles of magnetic levitation where the train hovers over the guide ways with a magnetic field and is propelled at speeds of up to 310 miles an hour.

Germany, Japan, Iran, and China have Maglev trains. The futuristic perception of Maglev and the concept of magnetic levitation have existed for over 100 years.

History is in the making when "The Maglev Conspiracy" is first introduced with action, adventure and romance.

How does an ordinary housewife become involved in one of the most controversy history making events of the 21st century? She meets and falls in love with a man named Gary that is like a future James Bond that she's been longing for all her life who only turns her world upside down and the excitement is almost too much for her to bear. Learning all about the other side of the tracks Lisa never gives in for an easier life. She continues her relationship with Gary, only to find out that he is a top CIA agent.

His involvements' with China had been well kept for years until a leak in the system gets out and part of the drama comes when there is a fight on the Maglev train that was hidden underground.

The chase is full of surprises when a prisoner name Knuckles was paroled by a bad prison Warden who wanted him to find the missing link that went into finding the key that held the future of the Maglev train patents and master plans that were worth billions of dollars and in return Knuckles would get his freedom.

This story will keep you at the edge of your seat with all the adventures of suspense, action, romance, and mystery.

THIS BOOK IS DEDICATED TO:

A small group of men and women who tried working with the Politicians, Senators and Congressman and the State's transportation departments fighting for a Maglev high speed train.

The Guidewinds Project, Inc. is a non-profit company.

Over the last 25 years the company has put together mission statements and environmental impact study reports, and executive summaries. They have research many studies in the transportation fields and letters to the Presidents including and not limited to the Deputy Consulate General of Germany and many Governors, and Senators.

Joe Leone, President of the Guidewinds Project, grew up in Concord and was a 1956 graduate of Mt. Diablo high school. He was very well liked by his teachers and talked about his visions of a high speed train to all that would listen. He then did a two year hitch in the United States Army, with one and half of those years in German and spent 2 years in the National Guards and then two years in the Army Reserves.

He was interviewed for the December 2007 Popular Mechanics magazine to assist staff in understanding high speed rail corridors in the State of Nevada, and California and other parts of the United States.

It was through the Guidewinds efforts of their Senior Vice President who worked hard through the years to get Senate Bill 1307, concerning the high speed rail feasibility study signed. The bill has been enacted as chapter 1104, statutes of 1990 and became effective January 1, 1991. Over the years the Guidewinds project grew to over 25 members. Through trial and errors they had people that had befriended them who decided to steal their ideas and books, sought after their Environmental Impact reports, the Mission Statement, an Executive Summary, and their Business Plan.

ACKNOWLEDGEMENTS

This novel was inspired by countless individuals who without their encouragement I never would have made it pass the first chapter.

My best fan as I was writing this book was my older brother Joe Leone whose wit and charm kept me going. He had his own ideas also for this book so at that point we decided to write this together.

I also want to thank my younger brother Bobby Leone for doing the art work for the cover of this book. You can visit his free on-line Christian comic site at www.HumanBeans.org. I also wish to thank my husband Ed Engquist for all the alone time that I needed to write this book and for his dedication of editing it.

A very special thank you to Robert Hughes from the Great State of Texas for his unbelievable talent and expertise in starting me in the right direction.

I also want to thank Rick Treat from Sutter, California for his encouragement for the project along with all my family and friends who had faith that we could do this.

It is a combination of imagination and unbelievable events that took place in writing this book.

In the back of the book under "Author's notes" are a few things that developed while we were writing this book for your reviews.

PREFACE

The most serious act of espionage happened when one of the CEO members got a threat from a "super power" Country warning the Guidewinds Project not to pursue a demonstration line to test the Maglev trains. The company was told to back off or else! They knew that the Guidewinds group had something far more superior than their trains. This country wanted to sell their trains to the United States.

One day they received an e-mail and a follow up phone call from a foreign country saying that the name **Guidewinds** belong to them. The Guidewinds group knew better because they renamed it after they were threatened by another Maglev company in California.

The truth is that this small group of middle class Americans was up against all odds including other Countries. It was their dream for the United States to be one of the first Countries to have the second generation Maglev high speed train. Many e-mails from the group went out including to all local T.V. channels and the world news channels and not once did any agency return their call or e-mails.

Some local newspapers ran articles about them and the group even received letters of approval from local businesses. The company over the years found the funding three times and offered the States a free Maglev train and all they needed was the right-a-way down the I-80 corridor for the investor's security. The Governors never got to hear their ideas or see them for a presentation including the President of the United States.

At one time Germany was planning on lending the Guidewinds Project money. Due to circumstances that cannot be disclosed the funding was cancelled.

Below are a few more obstacles that this brave company faced.

One peculiar individual that joined the group was asked to meet with the CEO. His job since he was an expert on the computers was to show the Guidewinds web-site to the investors.

He went on to shock the President of the Guidewinds Project, Joe Leone by using a web site that he had made up and saying that he was the owner of the company.

The next shocking event was when they found out that their private secretary that did all the paper work for filings with the State and all the billings had made herself half owner of the company without anyone's knowledge from the Guidewinds Project. She got by with that for over 3 years. She also collected money from the group and fraudulently said it was their fees and she was pocketing the money. No one pressed charges against her but she was fired.

Mary Leone Vice President, Coordinator for the company was responsible in making connections with other Maglev groups in the country that took place. She was responsible for writing letters to the President, Vice President, Senators, and Congressman and making the booklets for all their presentations. Also standing hand in hand with her brother at all meetings and helped in finding the lenders who might help fund their project.

In the meantime the middle man that set them up with the most recent investor double-crosses them. He told them that he wanted to go to a scheduled meeting that they had planned with the State Department of Economic Development.

After the meeting he told them why did he need them? They had nothing and now that he knew who held the patents and he had all their plans and connections what was to keep him from going straight to the Maglev company? Joe Leone, President of the Guidewinds Project saved him the trouble and put him together with the investor and another Maglev project.

No matter what the cost Joe Leone loved his country so much that he decided that the United States needs the Maglev trains more than ever and even if it meant closing his company after more than 25 years against all odds and going through all obstacles.

The Guidewinds Project closed their doors in 2011.

CHAPTER 1

One day you'll realize my love for you,
not false, but true.

These words would come back to haunt me one day. It was a shock when my ex-husband Jake, showed up on my door steps 21 years later and said to me. *"These tapes and letters belong to you"* as he stood there holding a wooden box.

I stood there at the door looking at this older man with his gray hair and how he had aged so much. I looked at him surprised and said, *"What are you talking about?"* I asked as he looked back at me.

"I'm sorry Lisa, but these came in the mail for you back when we still lived in Gilroy and after we got back together again. I then decided to hide them from you. I did not want to lose you again. I did not want you to get involved with Gary again after what he put you through and you being pregnant and all."

"Jake you have no idea I mean no idea what you have done to me by withholding these letters." And then I thought to myself this must be a joke, and why now? My mind was moving pretty fast trying to think how this could of happen.

"After you left me I knew that someday I would return the letters to you when the time was right" Jake said to me.

I was trying very hard at this moment to gasp what he was saying but my mind kept going back to Gary the guy that I was planning to spend the rest of my life with and my one and only true love. I never had the chance to tell Gary that I was pregnant with his child. How we got parted hurt me so much. To lose someone that

1

you love and disappear without a trace. Gary had walked out of my life as fast as he walked into it.

"My God," I said. How this could happen to me? I had missed Gary so much it hurt. Those were good times when I look back. Jake my ex-husband finally was letting go and with my new job it was working out. I had found and met Gary and was so madly in love with him. When Gary disappeared I tried so hard to find him. We had been through so much and the adventures that we had shared together even though dangerous. My gosh! We had been to China and back on a train that was from the future and being robbed and chased and held hostage. God knows everything else. After waiting over months for Gary to return or contact me I gave in to Jake and remarried him so Gary's and my baby could have a name. I felt it was the only right thing to do.

Thinking back on Gary the list goes on in all that Gary and I went through. We had saved more than hundreds of people's lives but little we could do for ourselves. Everything that we did to risk our lives had to be kept secret from our Country. Not even Jake or my child had any clue of what we been subject to and the daring events that took place in our life's.

After going back to Jake and knowing that Gary was gone I never thought that I could ever love again. Now I find out after all these years he had sent me poems and letters. These were all in the wooden box that Jake hid from me for the past 21 years that I was now holding in my hands.

I always remembered that one of Gary's, good points was having a good strong character. He was my lover my mentor and my friend. He was also the most caring and loving man a woman could ask for.

Tirana our daughter was to never find out about her real father and that he was an American hero and everything that happen to us needed to be kept secret. She always thought Jake was her real dad, and he had always treated her like his own and never said a word. I thanked Jake for giving me the letters then I went inside and curled up on my couch and read one of his poems that he wrote me. It said,

'I walk with pride and joy
Knowing my will is of my own.
I walk with joy because my soul is my own
My one and only obligation is to thy self.
I seek not but happiness and joy of one self.
If tomorrow brings me of my choice
Then I can say I did it on my own.
What joy I feel within one self for I am
Finally the master of my will and soul.
No greater joy have I ever known
For now I walk proud and strong.'

When I got through reading this my heart was tearing apart. I thought the rest will have to wait for now, it was so much to think about after all these years.

It all started back in 1986 I had finally filed the papers on Jake, and I was in need of a job. It did not take me long to get a job at a local retail store. I had been told all my life that I was beautiful and that I should have been a model with my blonde hair and slim figure.

They had me working in the deli and I never will forget the first day, I was standing behind a counter in the deli and a male employee was pushing a cart and our eyes met when he leaned over by my station to pick up other cart from behind the deli.

Here was this very handsome man nicely built who had black wavy hair and so nicely tanned, wearing slacks and a brown shirt and stood nearly six feet. He looked like he was in his early 30's, anyway that was my guess. When our eyes met I could feel him giving me the once over and a smile to die for. He did seem kind of shy at first and there was a mystery about him.

"*Hi,*" he says "*my name is Gary.*"

"*Hi Gary, my name is Lisa*" then he leans forward to shake my hand.

"*So is this your first day on the job?*" He asks

"Yes," I told him thinking to myself what a strong and gentle voice he has.

"Do you live around here?" He asked me and before I could answer he told me that he lived about 40 minutes away in a small cabin in the woods.

"Sorry," he said *"I sometimes get ahead of myself."*

"It's alright Gary I live just around the corner."

"Well maybe I will see you around Lisa," while he is pushing the cart and walking away from me. It was like he had lost too much time and needed to get back to work. My eyes followed him until he was out of sight. Wow! I said to myself he is cute.

I went to work the next day hoping to see Gary and I just could not get my mind off of him and maybe because he gave me a little bit of attention or because I felt an instant attraction towards him.

My third day on the job I was doing pretty well in adjusting to my new life. I only saw Gary once that day when he was running down the aisle trying to catch a customer who left a package at the register.

Leaving work that day in the middle of June the weather was warm. When I got outside I could feel the warm air blowing through my hair as I was rushing to my car and I thought that I heard this voice calling my name. I looked behind me and here is Gary.

"Hey, Lisa wait up"

"Oh, Hi Gary"

"You look like you're in a hurry to get somewhere." Gary said with a smile.

"No, I just have an old cat at home waiting for me." Wishing I hadn't said anything so dumb to him.

"Okay Lisa I usually don't move so fast but I sure would like to get to know you better, like maybe over a cup of coffee?"

Now I thought to myself, he wants to take me for coffee? I must have looked dazed for a few minutes until I realized I had not answered him yet.

"Why yes Gary I would love to go" a sign of relief came over his face.

"Do you want to ride with me Lisa?"
"Of course Gary, that would be great"
"Okay Lisa but let me move all the papers off of the seat for you." as he opened his green ford pick-up passenger door for me and picked up the papers then he reached out for my hand and said *"let me help you get into this truck it sets pretty high and with no stair-step."*
"No argument there." I said.

Here I was sitting across from this good looking man who I hardly knew driving me in his truck to get to know me better and my nanny would kill me if she knew I said yes to a stranger. I thought how do I get myself into these situations?

Well, he really is no stranger when we work at the same place. I pushed all these thoughts out of my mind as he made a sharp turn so fast and I slide into his lap, well almost.

"I'm so sorry Lisa, are you alright?"
"I don't feel any broken bones yet." How I could break a bone when his body broke the fall so to speak, I said to myself.

"How long have you been working at the store, Gary?"

Gary answered me without taking his eyes off the road and says, *"I just started a day before you did?"*

Oh no I said to myself, he is a stranger.

"Okay Gary but how long have you lived here?" Hoping that he would tell me many years.

"I just moved here a month ago from Texas" he tells me and reaches over and touches my hand.

I quickly pull my hand away from his, but when I look down he is only picking up a piece of paper that had fallen off the dash when he made that corner so fast and his hand just happen to brush mine. Calm down I told myself here is just a lonely middle age man who wants a nice ladies company and that lady just happens to be me.

It's been a month now and everyday Gary and I have met for coffee after work only this last time we are sitting by a wishing well that was outside by one of the coffee shops. *"Lisa make a wish and throw these pennies in the well and I will also do the same"* Gary said in his strong stern voice.

"Okay, I will make a wish" as I open my hand up to receive the pennies that he was holding for me.

"Close your eyes first and then hold my hand and we will throw them in together." he said. With the touch of his hand I almost forgot the wish that I was making. *"On the count of 3 Gary says, 1, 2, 3 . . ."* I closed my eyes made my wish and we tossed the pennies.

I couldn't help but wonder what Gary's wish was about maybe me? I know that I wished that we could spend more time together.

After the silence he looked at me and said, *"Lisa I make a mean steak and would you like to come over tonight for dinner, would that be possible?"* as he looked at me in a pleading way.

"That sounds like fun Gary, what time should I be there?"

"7:00p.m." he says as he hands me his address.

"Perfect Gary, I will look forward to your cooking."

"Great! See ya tonight" he said in reply.

I went home and started looking in my closet for a nice dress; I want it to be just right. I thought that I should wear my pretty blue plaid sundress; it had a nice neckline, and had small straps that held the dress up and I felt very good in it. Like when you get a haircut or a color it just puts a new lease on you and makes you feel special.

I finished putting on my makeup making sure not to smear it on my clothes, and then I slipped on my heels and then one quick look in the full length mirror. I had a little over an hour now and not knowing exactly where he lived grabbed my keys and out the door I went.

It was a beautiful evening with just a small draft blowing through the car window and I could smell the pine trees the more I drove towards the country. The road was getting more winding has I made my way up the mountain and to think that Gary drives this every day to work. I was impressed.

There it is I said to myself has I drove up a long winding driveway to the front of his log cabin it almost took my breath away when I saw some deer so still in the yard that I thought that they were statues. There were red barrels of colorful flowers and sun screens around them probably to protect them from the wild animals.

"You found me Lisa," came a voice from behind the house and out comes this handsome man carrying an arm full of wood.

"Hi Gary, yes it sure was a pretty drive here." I replied as I hung my head out the car window."

"Glad that you enjoyed the scenery." he says as he's putting the wood down and is rushing to my car to open the door for me.

Dinner was great that night and he did cook a mean steak. After dinner we went on the back porch which had a swing on it.

"Don't be shy Lisa come sit by me" as he took my hand and led me to the swing.

"This is such a beautiful night Gary and your dinner was great." I said.

"Not as great as you being here Lisa." he said and about that time he put his arms around me and kissed me on the cheek.

I must say here I was in heaven until Gary's phone rang, *"Excuse me Lisa, but I must get this call"* with that remark he heads to the pond which is about 8 ft. away with a long phone cord and not too far from the swing. I could barely hear him talk like a few whispers. *"It's okay, it's okay"* he kept saying to the caller *"I will give you a call later."*

"Is everything alright Gary?"

"Yes, it's fine. Just a minor set-back at work." he said, but the look on his face I knew it was more than he's letting on.

Gary comes over by me and gets back on the swing like nothing happen and continues to put his arms around me. He then lifts my chin with his hand and leaned forward and kissed me. We continued to exchange kisses for a few minute as he continued to move closer to me.

"Lisa, I have never felt this way before about anybody. I just had an instance attraction to you. I can tell you anything and feel comfortable. It's just, well you know some things from my past that I cannot even talk about now and I do hope that you understand."

Wow' I thought to myself he really must like me. Then I squeeze his hands and said *"Gary no worries when the time is right you can tell me."* and with that remark we both got out of the swing and stood by each other holding each other tight with his arms around my waist. Not wanting to leave yet I forced myself to say Good-night.

After thinking of this is how it all started I was reminiscing more as it all came back to me. I pulled another letter out of the wooden box which read:

One day when my hair has turned to silver.
My love I can no longer deliver.
My love for her has been ever
She shared her love and affection
Without hesitation.
I'll have enjoyed love and joy without
Reflection
From a women so good and true.
Should my heart falter soon
She tried to bring joy rather than blue.
Lord be good to her, for she is good and true.
She shall enjoy happiness through and through.
Never has a woman gave so much and asked so few.
A women Indeed.

CHAPTER 2

Why do I torment myself by reading the rest of the letters from 21 years ago? Maybe it would have been better if Jake never gave them to me after so many years. Such beautiful letters and they are so special to me but they are just so hard to read them. I know that he wrote them for me so I would know how much he really deeply loved me.

I will save the last one for Gary to read with me and not open it until we are together when we find each other. It was a love that only can happen once in a lifetime. I assumed that is why it hurts so much to read these.

It was a few days before I saw Gary again with his work days being somewhat different than mine. I remember waking up the next morning after having dinner with Gary, as I was pouring myself a cup of coffee and picking up the mornings newspaper and before I made it to the kitchen the phone rang *"Good morning Lisa,"* came this soft voice over the phone *"I hope that it is not too early to call?"*

(Are you kidding, I thought to myself) *"Hi Gary, and good morning to you."*

"Lisa I want you to come over again tonight for I want to explain a few things to you."

"OK, I will be there Gary, just tell me the time?"

"How about 8:00? And bring your swim-suit, in case we want to take a swim in the pond." he said

"OK, 8:00 P.M. it is and thanks for the call Gary" as I hung up the phone and wondered what all the mystery is about.

I thought that the day would never end when I was at work. I only got to see Gary as he was rushing with his loaded cart to the back of the store. I did wonder what all the hurry was to get the cart there so quickly. My mind was going in all directions and what was I getting myself into with Gary? Maybe tonight I will know?

I knew that I was falling in love with him and sometimes you just know who you should be with. The day was long and I was glad to be leaving the store I got a glimpse of Gary as I was walking to my car. Gary was close to the dumpster and a white pick-up truck was there also and it was back to the loading dock. I could not see what was happening behind the truck. Gary and the other man were loading something into it.

I did think that was strange for I never saw the unmarked truck before. Maybe that is why Gary invited me over to talk about the white truck?

When I arrived home from work that day there were a dozen red roses on my front porch and who else would send them to me but Gary. I am not sure but I knew what a thoughtful caring man he was. I put my purse down on the front porch so I could pick up the beautiful roses and looked for a note attached to them, but there was no note, hum, oh well I will thank him tonight.

My trip to Gary's house was almost endless but beautiful with the summer winds blowing the colored leaves around and it looked like a flock of birds dashing in front of my car window as the leaves flew by. When I got closer to Gary's I thought that I could smell smoke and has I made my way down the long winding driveway.

I pulled up at Gary's cabin and saw smoke coming out of the house. Oh no, is the house on fire? I jumped out of my car and went running up to the door with the heavy smoke coming from the house and screamed for Gary, I pulled open the door as a huge whiff of smoke filled my lungs.

Then I remembered what they taught us in school, drop, duck, and cover, something like that. I immediately dropped to the floor and crawled down the hall, please I prayed let Gary be alright.

I could see the flames coming from the back bedroom as I continued to yell for Gary while I was wondering if I would find him before it was too late. I was pushing furniture out of the way and my shoe fell off as I was crawling on the floor but I did not have time to look for it. I then ended up taking off the other shoe so I could move faster.

Parts of the roof were caving in and I was screaming louder for Gary, but no answer. The smoke was getting thicker and the flames could be seen from the upstairs room. One of his cats went running by me. Everything was falling apart. I was choking back the smoke and could hardly take a breath. I could hear the fire sizzling. It smelled of rotten garbage.

A large pillar of smoke cleared the room just enough that I could clear a path to the bedroom and at that moment a beam that was on fire came crashing down on me and pretty soon his curtains went up in flames then before I realized it everything went blank after that, and that was all I remember.

I woke up at the hospital and when my eyes finally focused I could see the doctor. *"You are a very lucky girl to be alive Lisa"* the doctor said to me. He was an older man with a mustache and look like he had lived a hard life according to his features on his face with lines thicker than a banjo string.

About that time two men dressed in black suits came in and identified themselves as crime scene investigators. The doctor looked over at them and said, *"She is not ready to be interrogated yet."*

"When can we come back Doctor?" they asked.

"Come back in twenty minutes and then you will only have a few minutes with her. She is in a lot of pain with all the burns that are on her body."

"You can say that again Doc," I said *"and what I'm I doing here?"* As I look at my body that was all wrapped in gauze.

"Don't you remember what happened, Lisa?"

"Oh No!" I said as I looked in the mirror that was next to my bed. I started crying and then the reality started to set in and then it hit me, oh my God where is Gary? I tried to climb out of the hospital bed, but could not even move my legs. I screamed, **"Where's Gary?"**

"Calm down young lady before you hurt yourself" the Doctor said. *"I will get the nurse for you if you promise to sit still and not try anything crazy"* said the Doctor then I really felt my world was spinning or maybe it was the hospital room.

"Ok, I promise" as I waited patiently for some news on Gary, which I was hoping to get from the nurse. A few minutes later in walks this women she must have been 300 lbs. or more she was dressed in white and had gray hair tied in a bun. She was carrying in a tray of pills and the look on her face reminded me of an old army nurse and one side of her skirt was longer than the other side. It sure looked like that she needed a new seamstress, but this is one time that I would keep my mouth shut.

"Open your mouth now young lady" as she walks towards me like she was getting ready to make a touch-down. *"Take these pills and I promise you it will make you feel better."*

"No, nurse" I said, *"Just tell me about Gary and if he is alright?"*

"Is Gary your husband or are you a family member?" she said as she shoved the pills down my throat and handed me a glass of water.

"Why yes," I said *"I am his sister"* knowing that if I told the truth that I was not a family member then I would get no news about his condition.

She looked at me like she didn't know whether to believer me or not. *"Well alright, Gary is in critical condition but stable and if it wasn't for you, well he could have been dead. From what the paramedics say that you left your car in neutral and it rolled down the hill and hit a car that was out of gas."*

"The driver that was there was waiting for the towing company. He then walked up the driveway to find the owner and then he spotted the smoke and called 911 so you see young lady you are really a lucky girl."

"You were trapped under a beam and when they found you they said you were moaning **'Gary'** *so they looked through the burning house and found Gary unconscious, trapped in the bedroom apparently the way you were headed. You are one hero in my book trying to save your brother like you did."*

I thought to myself, well he is not my brother but I will never tell.

"When can I see Gary?" I asked.

"Gary is in a coma, I am sorry to say." the nurse said. I felt my whole world crashing down around me.

Thinking back on how I lost my own parents in a horrific house fire. I was at my grandmother's house and I always called her Nanny. She was a very beautiful woman for her age and had a great figure to go with it. She was only married once to my grandpa and after he died she wanted no one and crawled into a shell.

The day before Christmas she was watching me while my parents went Christmas shopping and I was to spend the night with nanny. I must have been about 8 years old. The next day my grandma got a call that there had been a terrible tragedy.

Nanny ended up raising me until she died when I was 16 years old. I then got a job and supported myself and never told a soul that she had died. It was easy for we lived on 20 acres with no neighbors for miles and besides my Grandma was a very quiet woman and did not have any friends that I knew of.

I was able to stay at her place. I knew that it was paid for and she had told me that it would be left to me for I was her sole and only grandchild that she ever had. I did not want to be an orphan from the State. I had heard horror stories about foster care and all.

I pulled it off until I turned 18 years old and I graduated from high school. I sold the home and used it to further my education. She always told me that I was bright and would make myself a good future. I have missed her so much. She was a strong woman to live alone and to do the chores she did around the place.

She cut her own wood and stacked it. She milked the cows and grew one heck of a garden. She would shoot the deer if they got near her garden and cut their heads off and use it as trophy's. She loved using the meat to make jerky, and it really did taste good.

That was a good memory but I quickly realized that I was in the hospital and was still waiting to hear when I could go visit Gary. I had already talked to the crime scene investigators and they seem to think that it was arson. But I could not figure out why someone as good as Gary would want to harm him?

CHAPTER 3

Two weeks passed before I could walk again with 10% burns on my body. It was mostly on my arms and legs and through God's grace I was alive and so was Gary. I had many small burns on my face a few scratches and was red from the heat otherwise my face would be okay.

The nurse came in with a wheel chair for me to go down the hall to see Gary. I think she was the first nurse that forced those pills down my throat. I took a second look at her and who else could weigh over 300 lbs.? It was her; I remembered to keep my mouth shut now. She could be pretty mean if she wanted to I knew that first hand and also heard it from the girl next door to my room and she told me to be aware for she had at one time worked as a nurse at the old jail in town.

It was the first time since the fire that I was left out of my room; it felt good to be going down the hallway, even though it was a hospital corridor. It smelled like a convalescent hospital with a strong odor but then who cared? Gary was still in a coma and I wanted to be there for him.

When I was left at the doorway of his room I put my hands on the wheels of the wheelchair and slowly rolled my way back to his bedside. I would have never recognized him with the thin look on his face and all drawn and white. Here was his body all wrapped up and his leg in a swing that hung above the bed, and a cast on his left arm. He had tubes everywhere and a breathing tube down his throat. I could hardly recognize him had I not known who he was.

I reached out and took his hand and said *"Gary, It's me Lisa, you are safe now"* but he did not even flinch a muscle. I notice that he was partially uncovered so I picked up his blankets and covered him up the best I could. The hardest part of this was seeing him in this condition.

I continued for weeks going to his room and talking to him and telling him that I loved him that we would get married someday and have a daughter for him that he always wanted.

I was released from the hospital 3 weeks later but still made my daily visits to Gary.

One day while visiting Gary, I thought back of the memories on that special moment at the coffee shop where Gary had me close my eyes and with him make a wish and threw the pennies in the wishing well and how special it was to me and I thought why not do it again. Nothing that I did seem to help wake him and I was getting discourage as each day went by. Today was a new day and I was more determined than ever for him to wake up.

"Ok Gary," I said as I picked up his hand and held his hand tight with mine and I said to Gary, *"On the count of 3 we will toss the pennies 1, 2, 3, make a wish."* and slowly I said *"Now let's toss the pennies together."* As our hands rose together to throw the pennies I felt him jerk and then his eyes slowly opened and he was trying hard to focus on me. I was astonished and excited. *"It's me Gary, you know Lisa, your sweetheart. I love you. You had been in a fire."*

He then tried to move his lips and I said *Gary please don't talk let me go get the doctor.* I hurried into the nurses' station and yelled *"Get the doctor now! He's waking up and please hurry!"* Then I rushed back into the room.

A few minutes later the room is surrounded by the doctor and two nurses. *"Well,"* said Doctor Warren, as he walked over and started checking Gary's vitals, he was the one who had been overseeing Gary the last few weeks. Then he flashes the light inside of Gary's eyes and says to Gary, *"Now I want you to follow my fingers, good Gary, well now who is the President of the United States?" "Last I heard it was Ronald Reagan"* answered Gary.

"Good" says the Doctor, *"Now what year is it?"*

"Why last time that I checked it was 1986" Gary said in a shaky voice.

"Well son" said the Doctor Warren, *"you have been in a coma for 2 months and we never thought that you would come out of it and your wonderful sister has faithfully been by your side every day possible. You were in a terrible fire that almost got you and Lisa killed, you both were in the house when it was on fire. Someone reported the flames that were shooting out of your home. I did not get the whole story but your both alive and that is what's most important."*

At that point Gary already looked confused. *"It's okay dear,"* I said to him, *"Don't you think Doc that he should get some sleep."*

"Yes, I do Lisa,"

Then as the Doctor left I moved closer towards the bed closer to Gary picked up his hand and held it. Gary smiled and winked at me and what a wonderful moment in my life that was to have my one and only true love back. *"I love you Gary,"* and then gave him a kiss on the cheek. I knew now that I would go home and have sweet dreams.

CHAPTER 4

Gary continued to improve every day for over a couple of weeks and was getting ready to be released from the hospital in a few days and now with his home burned down he had no place to go, I offered him to come stay with me that I had plenty of room with two bathrooms.

"Thank you Lisa, for offering your home for me to stay in."

"Great Gary then I must go home now and get your room ready and I will be back tomorrow to pick you up." Gary nods his head at me and then says *"Lisa before you go I want you to know that Dr. Warren came in yesterday and told me more about what happen and how you went into my burning cabin looking for me. I can never repay you for what you've done for me and how you risk your life."*

"Gary, I would do it again in a heartbeat and please don't mention it, it was nothing." as I leaned over him and gave him a kiss on the cheek, then blew him a kiss as I was leaving the room.

When I arrived home I could not believe my eyes, here on my front porch was another dozen red roses, now this is odd for I know Gary did not send them and I have no one else but wait a minute could they be from Jake? My ex-husband I thought? Well again there is no card in it.

I unlocked the front door and continued to pick up the flowers and brought them inside and got my white crystal vase out. I filled it with water and as I was arranging the flowers in it the phone rings.

"Hello," I said *"This is Lisa."*

"Lisa, where have you been? This is your old hubby Jake."

"Excuse me?" I said.

I thought that my heart would drop about then, *"Jake what do you want? I have not heard from you in 6 months and our divorce should be final soon."*

"Yes Lisa, it is me and I will not sign the papers I still love you and want you back." I thought to myself this is all I need now, another man in my life when I'm in love with Gary

"Forget it Jake, its over" I said *"and it's been over for years. You are just too thick headed to realize it."*

"You can't tell me Lisa, after 10 years of marriage that you are going to call it quits?"

"You listen to me Jake; you called it quits when you had that last affair with that prostitute." My dandruff was getting up now and I felt too tired to argue with Jake.

"I told you before Lisa, it wasn't what you thought."

"Well, you tell me Jake, the two of you I caught in bed you both were naked, now tell me it's not what I thought?"

"Well Lisa, that one is not hard to explain. She wanted me to go to bed with her and I said no way. I thought that she left so I got in bed and then she shows up in our room when I was already in bed. She took all her clothes off and climbed in with me before I could say anything. And about that time you walked into the room. Now what was I supposed to say to you Lisa?"

"You know Jake that story is getting old and I want you to stay out of my life, now do you hear me?"

"Well I have one up on you Lisa that I bet you cannot explain. I just read an article in the newspaper Lisa, that you help save some dude from a fire and what were you doing there to begin with? You tell me now you little woman of the night."

"For crying out loud Jake, it was 8:00 at night and what business is it of yours?" Knowing that this conversation was not going anywhere, I replied *"Good-bye Jake and don't bother to call me anymore."*

"Don't you hang up on me Lisa." says Jake.

"Well, just watch me Jake." as I hung up the phone and I could hear him mumbling as I put the phone down on the receiver and not so gently either.

I then tried to put the call out of my mind but old memories kept coming back. I met Jake when I was in high school and he was a lot older than me and he had a way about him maybe because he was pushy, handsome and charming with his blonde hair that matched mine. I just know that it wasn't long before we became an item.

I sat down to take this all in about what just happen with me and Jake and I felt sick to my stomach. Why after all these months that he even bothers with me? I just want him to let me go on with my life. I now have Gary in my life and he needs me now more than ever.

Just then the phone rang again. I ran to the phone and screamed into it *"I told you not to call anymore!"*

"Sorry, Lisa, it's me Gary" he said in a soft voice.

"Oh Gary, sorry about that I just had a phone call from Jake, and he really upset me. He was bringing up very bad memories and wanted to argue with me."

"Anything that I can help with Lisa?"

"It is alright Gary, I will handle Jake. By the way how are you feeling?"

"I will feel better Lisa when I see you again" he said to me.

"Are you still being released tomorrow Gary?"

"That is what they tell me."

"Ok Gary, I will be in tomorrow at 11:00a.m. To pick you up and I need to stay home today and get your room ready for you and I will put fresh sheets on the bed and maybe more blankets for you. I will give you my room which is the master bedroom since it has the bathroom connected to it and I will take the guest room."

"You're a sweetheart Lisa," Gary said to me *"But I don't want to take your room."*

"Gary, I won't take no for an answer. Now you get some rest." With that remark we both said our good-byes and I hung up the phone.

CHAPTER 5

I just hung up the phone with Gary, feeling so content and knowing that we would be together tomorrow. I headed towards my big rocking chair that sits by the bay window and overlooks my flower bed.

How beautiful they looked to me as I sat down in my chair that sat in the living room. I was taking it all in and just to see all the colorful flowers and my fern plant that is the most beautiful color green that I ever saw. Guess that I never realized how beautiful and appreciated I was until I almost lost my life in that fire.

I was now thinking of what all I had to do and maybe now if I took a shower that it would relax me enough that I could sleep tonight, so I continued to the bedroom and kicked off my shoes and sat at my vanity and started brushing my hair then after a few minutes I then slipped out of my clothes and headed to the shower. The warm water felt so good going over my body. About 10 minutes of hot warm water running over my tired body I knew it was time to turn off the shower and after I stepped out of the shower I heard a *Knock-knock*, someone is at my door now who could that be? *"Wait a minute!"* I yelled down the hallway, *"I will be there in a few."* I through a towel around my hair and grabbed my bathrobe, and rushed to the front door.

I opened the door just enough on my safety chain to see who it was and two strange men busted through my door. Oh no, I said as they broke the chain and came in and knocked me across the room. Before I knew what hit me my body was going into shock. I tried to scream but I was so scared that nothing came out.

"Say one word lady or you will be dead." said the strange man that was dress in black and had a bean hat on and black gloves.

"Hey Knuckles" he said to his friend *"Tie her to the chair that is in the corner of the living room. That will keep her confined for now"* he said. They proceeded to tie me to the chair and took some duct tape that they had with them and tied my feet and then my hands behind my back.

"Oh my God," I said *"what do you want? I have no money, I have nothing of value. You can take the $20.00 I have in my purse, but please just leave."*

"Shut up or we will kill you" said the shorter man in black who was a lot heavier than the other one and a lot meaner.

"Tell us where the 12 red roses are or else" I believe his name was Knuckles.

I tried to remain calm and said that I threw away both boutiques of 12 roses each because I thought that my ex-husband sent them to me.

"You mean you had two sets of roses delivered to you?" The man in black said?

"Where did you toss them at, and tell me no lies or you will be sorry when we kill your boyfriend Gary, guess burning down his house was not enough?"

I thought to myself, I wonder if this had anything to do with what is happening with Gary, at work and how I saw someone that day loading something in a white truck. No way could it be a dozen or so roses that would take a truck to haul them in.

"Lady, I'm talking to you! Where did you put the roses?" as he pulled me by the hair and almost out of the seat that I was tied to.

"Please," I said *"give me a minute. Check my garbage can,"* I said *"Well, lady you better hope that they are there."*

Oh, heck I thought to myself as old Knuckles headed towards my side yard to check my trash, then I really was worried now remembering today was garbage day.

A few minutes later he came running back in the house comes over to me and pulled on my hair again and then says to me, *"Your history woman if you don't get me those 24 red roses back. Your stupid garbage man already came and you better know where the dump station is*" he said to me.

So he says to his partner, *"Should we kill her now or wait and use her for bait with Gary?"*

"Don't rush it Knuckles, we have plenty of time now go ahead and untie her and we will bring her with us besides she's nice to look at."

"Enough of that you square head" the man named Knuckles said. *"You and your women, you have no time and no money to want a women right now."*

"Shut up," he said *"I have all the time and all the money now that we know that Gary is not on our side and there is a high price on his head. When we get him we will get the reward that is on him, ha ha,"* he said. *"Enough now untie the pretty lady."*

I was glad that they were about to untie me but I had no intentions of going with them if I could help it. I said to the kinder man, *"I need to go to the bathroom before you take me with you or your car may have a problem if my bladder does not hold."*

"Hold your horse's sister," he said to me. I was thinking right you're not as smart as you think if only they knew that I did know some self-defense. I know that the sooner you act the better. And I was taught also to plan my escape being hopeful and never to feel hopelessness.

Like they say (*An ounce of prevention is worth a pound of cure.*) also going over in my mind was remembering what nanny, taught me about sending a SOS signal. I would use 3 short blasts, then 3 long blasts, pause, and then repeat. That would work if I was inside my car or a room by myself but never with this situation, that's okay I have a great back up plan now if I could get to the bathroom, I could jump down the laundry chute that goes to the basement then I could escape and so with that in mind I requested again, please let me go to the bathroom.

"Okay." he said *"you lead the way. Now any funny business lady I will have to shoot you."* as I am walk into the bathroom.

"One last word lady, don't lock the door."

My laundry chute was built in the cabinet so they would never know it was there. Well, that is one thing that Jake, did right in building this home like he did. He just forgot to make the locks more secure, instead he put flimsy chains on the door that broke off when I opened the door. If I live through this ordeal, Jake, will get a piece of my mind.

I must hurry I told myself as I closed the bathroom door. I went to the toilet and waited a second and then flushed it, and then went to the bathroom sink and let the water run as I quickly opened up the cabinet and forced myself in the laundry chute. It sure had a smell to it for I had just cleaned it out with ammonia so I also needed to hold my breath. It was a tight squeeze but I managed to get inside of it and down I went with a bang so loud that I could hear them running into the bathroom and yelling *"she's escaping. Quick Knuckles get outside and grab that lady or you will be dead along with her."* I could hear them shouting at each other as I was climbing out.

I hurried to the back door of the basement and all of a sudden I heard sirens and they were coming here. I saw a police man running with his guns out and I stuck my head out of the basement and yelled at him and said *"Help me I have been held hostage and I just escaped through my laundry chute."*

"It's okay" he said to me, *"your neighbor saw a stranger going through your garbage and she decided to call us after about 30 minutes of thinking about it."*

"How many men are in the house?" the police man asked.

"There are two men dressed in black and someone they called Knuckles. They are armed and dangerous." As he got on his car phone and told the other officers.

In the meantime he told me to get in the squad car and I would be safe there and he would leave one of his men with me. *"Thank you officer,"* I said, as I followed him to his car. "I thought to myself thank you my neighbor for never minding your own business you just saved my life and don't even know it." I never again will get upset with her for always watching me like a hawk for she was retired and had nothing to do but to watch every move that I make, this one sure paid off.

CHAPTER 6

About an hour went by as I was sitting in the patrol car waiting for the police to capture the fugitives when I heard some shooting coming from my house and I thought to myself maybe they finally caught them. It was getting dark and there just was enough light from the street that I could see a few shadows from behind the patrol car that I was in.

A few minutes later the officer that was assign to stay with me received a call from his Lieutenant saying we have an escapee, *"Keep her in the squad car for one suspect has escaped and he has fled and is holding a gun and climb the neighbor's fence. His partner is (10-54-possible dead body) from the shoot-out and I believe that the escapee got wounded in the gun-fire."*

"Okay, Lieutenant I will," said the officer.

Upon hearing that news, I was really scared now. What if he comes after me since I know what he looks like? I thought to myself. *"By the way officer which man escaped?"*

"It was the one that they call Knuckles," the officer said to me *"and he has a rap sheet longer than you can imagine. He is wanted in two States for 1st degree murder and armed robbery and is on Americas Most Wanted list and to top it off in his spare time he is a bounty hunter when he's not in prison."*

"Oh, Gee" I said to the officer *"I will never be safe again!"*

"Don't worry your pretty little head off we will give you protection for a few days and they may want to make sure that you have police security until they capture Knuckles." said the officer to me.

24

I thought to myself, I will be on the run and looking over my back for the rest of my life. Yes and just like in the movies only this is no movie.

It is about 4:00 a.m. in the morning now and I was so exhausted when the officer brought me to a town motel for the night and said that he would be outside if I needed anything.

The motel was an old motel 6 and was called *"Shady Rest"* and only a few cars in the parking lot and it was about a mile off the highway.

I went to the bathroom to wash my face and looked at myself in the mirror. I could not believe the bruises on my face and my arms and one big bruise on my leg as I took off my robe that I still had on and stepped into the shower. The officer did get me a change of clothes that he got from the maid at the hotel. It was a white sweat shirt and gray sweat pants that some guy had left behind. It would be better than my old blood stain robe that I had been wearing.

I remembered that I fell asleep after having the shower and putting on the clothes that they gave me. I woke up to the sun shining through the windows that held the thin yellow curtains and realized that it was 11:00 in the morning. Then I remembered that I needed to pick Gary, up from the hospital.

The officer brought me back to my house that morning and when I looked around it look like a cyclone hit it and there was yellow tape that the officer's tape off the crime scene and it was the outline of a body in my kitchen.

That must have been Knuckles buddy, only he was the one that tried not to be so mean to me. I was really feeling sick to my stomach at the blood on the wall and some of my new furniture broken and the bad memories of last night.

I quickly changed into my own clothes so I could get out of here and jumped in my car and headed to the hospital with the security of a squad car.

I walked into Gary's room and found him sitting in a chair and a look of relief came over his face when he saw me *"Lisa I am so sorry, I saw it all unfold on the late news last night. I was so worried about you"* as he put his strong arms around me and held me tight. I could hear him crying into my ear. *"Lisa it is my entire fault and I tried to keep you out of it now you're in so much danger."*

"Now, Gary, it is time that you came clean with me I said. What the heck is going on? What is all the fuss about the red roses that I received and was it you that sent them to me?"

"No Lisa, I believe it was my partner that sent you the roses. There is talk that Knuckles killed him when he didn't tell them where he sent the roses. Knuckles put two and two together and figured that the roses were sent to you since they found out that we have been spending a lot of time together. So that is when they went to your home and broke in and held you hostage.

"Yes, Gary, and that is when all heck broke lose."

"Ok Lisa," Gary said to me, *"where are the red roses?"*

"Alright Gary, let's talk about this after we get out of the hospital. It is too dangerous to stay at my house."

"Don't worry Lisa I have a cabin in Lake Tahoe or I should say my sister does so we can stay there till things cool off."

"Well Gary, they are talking about putting me in a police protection until they capture Knuckles."

"Well Lisa I can watch you better than the local police, remember I am a CIA agent. You need to stay with me." Gary replied

"That may be a good idea Gary; at least I will know that you will watch out for me probably better than the police can."

"No problem Lisa, we both will survive this ordeal. No one will find us in Tahoe, I promise you."

As we were leaving the hospital there were two squad cars parked outside in the Emergency area. Gary said, *"Wait I will go talk to them and you stay here."*

"Okay Gary, try and not to be too long."

I could see him in a distance doing all the talking and all the officers were doing was shaking their heads. A few minutes later Gary was walking back to our car like he was in a hurry, he jumped in without saying a word and put his seat-belt on and started driving us to Lake Tahoe, to his sister's cabin.

CHAPTER 7

It was a long drive to Lake Tahoe from the town of Gilroy, where I lived. Here I am running for my life and wishing that this all was a bad nightmare but at the same time I had Gary, with me.

"Let's talk about this Gary," I said *"please explain to me about the two dozen roses"* while he is driving and looking straight ahead like he hesitated to tell me.

"Okay Lisa, I will tell you what I know. I am an agent for the CIA but also a double agent and like I have mentioned before we are working on this case and I cannot give you all the details. I will tell you that the first set of 12 roses that you received was from my partner and it was only a plant for bigger things."

"When I found out that he had them sent to you I was furious, I did not want you in any danger and you were not part of our plan that is me falling in love with you. There was not much I could do being in the hospital for months and being in a coma. The damage was already done. The second set of 12 roses had one bulb that was plastic and in it was a key and the key was what the fugitives wanted; a key to their freedom."

"What do you mean Gary a key to their freedom? And did you say that you're a double agent for the CIA?"

"Slow down Lisa, and I will explain this operation." laughed Gary. *"Those are good questions and I know that you have every right to an explanation and since you are already in danger I will only give you part of the answers for it will be safer that way for you."*

"Now Lisa, please do not repeat anything that I tell you. It must remain in mind only. There is something bigger than you could ever imagine going down that not even the feds know."

"I will start by saying first Lisa, how much I love you" as he squeezed my hands and took his eyes off of the road for only a minute. It was getting dark now while we are driving to Tahoe, but I needed to know something so while he kept driving he also kept talking to me.

"I was put there as a plant Lisa, when I went to work at the store and actually there were two of us, my partner that sent you the roses and myself. Knuckles, had friends that work here at the store and I was told by headquarters to make friends with them for they would eventually trust me and lead me to Knuckles and his gang."

"His friends are the ones that had a white pickup truck and would come to the store and I would help them smuggle toys and teddy bears that were filled with drugs that came in from a shipment from China. They would know that I was not an honest person and maybe that they would put their trust in me. Things were starting to get hot there at the store; some employees were suspicious of our activities so we had to slow it down."

"You see Lisa, their friend Knuckles and Starfish had been released from prison to be of benefit for their crooked Warden, and knowing full well that these men were dangerous and murderers were giving a job to do and to be released was their chance to gain their freedom. One of my jobs was to capture them and find out who is the big man that they answer to besides the warden. There was more to this than anyone knew, this was my job."

The time went by quickly and before I knew it we are in Tahoe pulling up at his sister's cabin.

"We made it Lisa!" exclaimed Gary.

CHAPTER 8

"Yes," I said *"and look it is so beautiful Gary, and the view of the mountains and wow"* as we walked up the front stairs in the moonlight.

I know" said Gary, *"it is such a great place to spend some time at."*

Then he stops before opening the door and puts his arms around me and held me tight for a minute and says to me, *"I want you Lisa, more than life itself."* He then picks me up and carries me inside as I held my arms around his neck.

Inside were knotty pine walls and an oval braided rug and a small plaid blue love seat which he gently put me down on. There on the wall was a picture of an old bearded man that looks like he was from the 19th century. It hung there right above the rock fireplace that had a beautiful oak mantle shelve, and on the shelf was an antique mantle clock that was ticking loud and you could hear it for it was so quiet there you could hear a pin drop. I could see the loft from the loveseat and the winding staircase in a distance and it was just like you see in the movies.

"Lisa," he says to me, *"here is a wool blanket and stay under it while I go get some wood and start a fire."*

"Okay, Gary" I said as I cuddled in the blanket that he gave me.

"Hurry back Gary" I cried, *"I miss you already."*

"Right on." He says as he gave me the hand single.

I was just getting comfortable feeling safe again when all of a sudden I heard a *"**bang, bang**"* very loud and then I screamed and jumped from the love seat and ran outside and yelled ***"Gary, Gary, where are you?"***

About that time the whole sky lit up and a flash of lightening shot across the sky, and all of a sudden, it's pouring rain. Gary grabs me by the hands and says *"Squat down on your feet, no time to get inside." "Now lean forward Lisa, on your toes, quick now and do not let your heels touch the ground. Close your eyes and cover your ears."* The lighten lit up the sky as bright as day, the electrical storm hit the top of a metal fence and sheared off of the phone lines and barely missed us. We could see it burn the wires.

"Gary, why did we not go inside of the cabin? And why did you have me stand on my toes and not my heels?"

"It was the quickest way to go Lisa, if we got hit by the lightening and you had your heels down it would go through the whole body but with us only going on our toes we were safer."

Gary says to me *"I forgot to warn you about electrical storms in this area they come without warning. July is the worse month here in Tahoe for these kinds of storms."*

"It's alright Gary, it just scared me for a moment and I thought that you had been shot."

"I'm okay Lisa, and nobody will find us here."

He put his arms around me and said, *"Lisa, you are all wet. Get your clothes off and I will get you some dry ones."*

I then proceeded to get out of my wet clothes and I wrap the wool blanket around me and waited for Gary to bring me some dry clothes. Talk about being tired and then to go through all this, I was ready for bed.

CHAPTER 9

It was not but a few minutes later Gary came walking down the stairs carrying an armful of clothes and says *"Here you go Lisa, put these on they belong to my sister and you both are about the same size and she would be happy to help out."*

"Boy, Gary those are some nice clothes, designer jeans? Old Navy, I sure will feel special in them."

"Wear the red sweater, and the designer jeans Lisa, I think that you will look very special in them."

"Okay Gary if you say so." and then I proceeded to get changed. *"Thanks Gary,"* I said as he turned his head so I could get dressed. He then knelt down and proceeded to build the fire. The fireplace looked so cozy with the red brick and marble top.

A few minutes later you could smell the scent of the wood burning in the fireplace and the warmth of the fire and the sound of it sizzling and cracking with just enough light from the fireplace to make it romantic

"You can turn around now Gary, I do feel so much better being in warm clothes now." I softly said to him.

"Wow, Lisa, you look like a million bucks."

"Well thank you Gary"

"Well" Gary said, *"I tell nothing but the truth and Lisa, I still owe you an explanation"* he says as he cuddles on the couch with me. *"I will tell you what I know Lisa."*

"Now let's start with the two dozen roses. It is like this Lisa, my partner knew that Knuckles, was watching you to make his move and he thought that I would slip the key to you instead of leaving it in my

31

home and Knuckles, assumed that the key could be in the roses." he explains.

Gary continues, *"When they first saw the roses arrive is when they broke in your home and held you hostage. They thought that I would give you the key since you and I spend so much time together and it was not safe with me anymore. They never knew that my partner sent other dozen roses to you until they heard it from you."*

"Now Lisa, what did you do with the two dozen roses that my partner sent you?"

"Ok Gary, this is what happen with me. I remember getting my white crystal vase out and filled it with water and as I was arranging the flowers, I got a phone call and it was from Jake, while I was talking to him on the phone, I thought that the roses were from him so I went back into the kitchen and grabbed the roses and threw them in a green Tupper wear box that was used for holding a loaf of bread and put them in my refrigerator."

"And at that point I knew that the phone call would end and so would my memories of him. Then I went back into the other room and hung up on Jake. I thought to myself that I would bury them just like I was trying to bury all the old memories of Jake."

"Lisa, you are telling me that the two dozen roses are still at your home in your refrigerator?" as his voice got filled with excitement.

"Yes, Gary that is where I had left them. I completely forgot about it until I was held hostage. All I could think about was getting away and if I had told them where the roses were they would have killed me for sure so I pretended that they went out in the trash and lucky for me it was garbage day pickup so they had no idea that I was lying."

"Lisa, it is still so unsafe for you and me to go back to your home with Knuckles on the loose." Gary said to me, *"I must go back tomorrow Lisa and try and get the roses and hope that the plastic bulb is still there."*

"I know Lisa," Gary said to me, *"and you do realize that I must leave you here and get the key from the roses. Before Knuckles heads back to your place and searches again. I cannot take a chance Lisa, please understand. I do love you so much Lisa, but both are life's are in danger until Knuckles, is captured and I can retrieve the key."*

"Well, Gary that is pretty heavy stuff!" I exclaimed as I was getting irritated, maybe at myself for I was feeling selfish in wanting Gary to stay with me and not leave.

"I will be out of here at the light of dawn, Lisa so please understand that this is something so serious that it can threaten us forever so we need to take care of Knuckles, number one, and then I can go on to find the hidden patents and master plans that are worth billions of dollars to our Country."

"You mean to tell me Gary that this is not just about the drugs that were shipped here from China that you were involved with?"

"Yes Lisa, it's like I said this was only a front. But I see now that you're getting the picture." Gary said to me.

CHAPTER 10

It was getting so late now Gary said *"You can have the downstairs bedroom and I will take one upstairs."*

I asked not so shyly, *"Gary can I stay with you in your room for I do not want to be alone tonight?"*

"I would like nothing more than you to stay with me tonight Lisa, but there is only one bed upstairs, so tell me will that be alright?"

Well, I thought to myself before I answered Gary, what if I never see him again? I want at least one night with him for I knew that I loved him so much.

"Lisa hello there! Well what do you think?"

"Ok, Gary, I will follow you." As I followed him up the winding stair case I could just think about him holding me in his arms so tight that nobody could touch us.

Gary stopped in front of the bedroom door and kissed me gently on the lips as we walked in the bedroom together hand and hand I could see how beautiful the room was, with Crystal chandeliers hanging from the tall ceilings. The room was painted a soft lavender with pretty flowered wallpaper border right below the ceiling. The bed was a gorgeous four poster bed with carved wood and it looks like Lions legs coming up the headboard.

I thought, yes we will be protected tonight. There was another fireplace and this one was made of rock and part of the room you could smell the cedar from the hand carved cedar chest that was at the foot of the bed.

"Gary," I said *"I want to seize this moment in time."*

"I agree Lisa, we will always remember this night no matter what."

About that time the old antique clock from down stairs started chiming. We both counted the chimes out loud, till it struck 12 o'clock midnight. Gary then leaned over me as I climbed into the bed and gave me a long lingering kiss.

"Gary, you won't believe this but I left my slippers downstairs." Maybe I was trying to distract him for a moment, trying to make this night be the longest night of my life.

"Okay Cinderella, I your prince, will go retrieve them. Now don't go away," as he rushed out of the bedroom and down the stairs. As he was leaving the room I couldn't help noticing his white shirt-tail hanging out and his sleeves rolled up, I wanted to stop him from leaving the room.

A few minutes later he walks back into the room with my slippers and pulling off his shirt. I never notice it much before but his arms were so big and as he put them around me. Now I feel safe, I told myself. The night was beautiful being in the arms of Gary, but when I woke up I looked around for Gary and could not find him so I then pulled the covers back thinking maybe he was underneath the covers.

Gary was not around and then in a panic I grabbed my robe and started looking around the house for him and when I went down stairs to the kitchen over by the coffee pot was a note from him which read:

Dear Lisa, sorry to leave you like this but I am headed to your house to pick up the roses. I hope to be back tomorrow. I do love you my princess, and to help you stay safe you will find a gun in the upstairs closet in the bedroom, it is loaded so please be careful my dear. Love eternally! signed Gary. After reading the note, I must say that I was really upset that he would leave me there without any car and a loaded gun in the closet and does he think that I am CIA also and trained to use a gun?

Maybe that is not a bad idea though I remember that nanny, taught me almost everything that I know, maybe I should refresh my memory. I can hear her now say, *"Okay girl protect your face it's too pretty to mess up with a rifle or shotgun, now find yourself a target, and close one eye and leave one eye open, you got it Lisa, all you have to do now is aim and shoot"* Well I am hoping that I will never have to use this information that nanny fed me.

The coffeepot was still warm from Gary, so I proceeded to pour myself a cup and then I curled up on the love seat that not many hours ago I shared with Gary, and put the wool blanket over me even though he had a small fire going in the fireplace I was still cold.

I remember it being a long day and thinking so much what have I done? My whole life now will be on the run. Is this what I really want? That was easy to answer, whatever it took to be with Gary I would sacrifice.

I pray that Gary will be with me but now that I know who he really is and the job that he must endure will probably not include me in the picture.

Now that I know why they want the dozen red roses I do hope that Gary finds them in my refrigerator. Still so many unanswered questions. I could hardly wait for Gary's return.

I looked around the room as I was on the loveseat and saw the T.V. controls over on the black desk. I went and got the controls and turned the T.V. on. The first thing that showed up was a picture of Knuckles, announcing that he was on the Americas most wanted that he was armed and dangerous, and last seen in Gilroy, California.

Chills went all over my body when I saw his picture and I really needed Gary, with me at this time. What if he finds me here at Gary's sister's house? I tried to put that thought out of my mind. I left the living room and headed upstairs to get a shower and then thought when I get through that I would go outside and check out my surroundings, since we came here in the dark last night. I climb into the shower and let the water fall on my hair and body and it felt so good. I suds my body with the soap and put the shampoo in my hair then rinsing off my hair. I notice that the shampoo had a different smell to it almost like an apple smell and I did sort of like it. I then climb out of the shower and wrapped a towel around me and looked around for some clothes to wear. Gary forgot to bring in my overnight bag in from the car last night.

I proceeded to look in the bedroom closet looking at his sister's clothes and found a blue blouse and in her dresser I found a pair of pants to match and the necessities that I needed. Thank you God, I prayed.

Now it is time to go outside and check out the beautiful surroundings. It was just breathtaking the view that this estate set on. I saw an old barn that was partially painted on one side a deep red and the other side was yellow. I made my way toward the barn and passed an old tractor that looked like it needed an overhaul. It was so quiet there as I walked towards the barn but I had an uneasy feeling the closer that I got to it and something was warning to me stay out of the barn. I thought to myself this is silly I will not let this person named Knuckles run my life so I continued towards the barn.

CHAPTER 11

I was almost to the door on the barn and I heard a flooding of birds on the roof top as I looked up I could see them flying away and not knowing what scared them I pushed open the side door of the barn door and ran inside.

Inside of the barn were about a dozen bales of hay, and a pitch fork and shovel hanging on the wall with horse shoes over every stable. In the corner of my eye I saw a shadow staring down from the loft.

"Who's up there?" I yelled as I grabbed the pitch fork off of the wall.

And all of a sudden from behind jumps a man from the loft and grabs me which he makes me drop the pitch fork and says, *"Hello Ms. Lisa lady, remember me your favorite friend?"* while he stands behind me with his hands around my throat. He then releases his hold on my throat and throws me across the room.

"Oh No!" I yelled *"Not you again, you old knuckle bag."*

"You still have a big mouth on you do you know that" he yelled at me *"And yes, my Lisa, it's me Knuckles, and do you think that for a minute that I was going to let you identify me? You could send me to prison for life or maybe even the death penalty plus you have what I want in the dozen roses. That will lead me to what I want more than anything."*

"You better start talking or I will take that boyfriend of yours and hang him upside down, then put him in the ground 6 ft. under."

"You're sick Knuckles, very sick," I spat at him.

"Shut up" he said to me.

"Not until you tell me how you found me."

38

"*Well Ms. Lisa, what if I told you that a little black bird told me exactly where you were headed.*"

"*And what black bird are you talking about.*" I asked?

"*What the heck lady, I will tell you so you know how stupid that boyfriend of yours is.*"

"*Remember the night that you were in the hospital parking lot and your friend Gary went and talk to the officer?*"

"*Yes,*" I said, "*I do remember that night.*"

"*Well, guess what lady? He told the officer that he was taking you to Lake Tahoe, to his sister's place. I was hiding behind a car in the parking lot near the elevator and I heard every word so I just followed you both to this house and waited till I saw your boyfriend leave this morning and I was just waiting for this moment to catch you, only you made it so easy for me by coming out here to the barn.*"

"*Where was your boyfriend going anyway? When will he be back?*"

"*I have no idea.*" I said, "*And besides he left me a note this morning and I saw it when I woke up and by that time he was already gone.*"

"*You better not be lying to me lady, or I will kill you now.*"

"*You're going to kill me anyway*" I said to him, "*so what do I have to lose?*"

"*I do not believe that you threw out those roses and I know that no women ever in their right mind would through away roses.*"

"*Well*" I said to him, "*if they are from an ex-husband, yes they would. The roses are gone get it through your head.*"

"*Don't get smart with me lady and stop your arguing with me*" as he grabs me by my arms and says, "*Head to the house, I am hungry and want you to cook for me.*"

"*You are one feisty woman I must say,*" He says to me "*and get it through your head, mess with me and I will kill you but I will make you suffer first.*"

By this time I am being pushed to the front porch with him having a tight hold on my arms. We get to the doorway and he pushes me so hard I fall to the floor.

"*Get up and get me some grub now*" he says.

"*Okay, I said give me a chance to get to the kitchen.*"

As I was walking into the kitchen I was praying that there was something I could fix for him and at least it would buy me more time until Gary gets back.

He could see me while I was in the open kitchen as he was turning on the T.V. which he had up pretty loud. I looked in the refrigerator and no food except some mustard and ketchup. I then opened up the doors to the large walk-in pantry from behind a man grabs me and puts his hands over my mouth and says *"Don't scream, Lisa, it's me Gary."*

"Oh my God, Gary, how did you get here?"

"Shush not to loud Lisa," whispers Gary, *"I got a call this morning from my partner saying that Knuckles, was seen in the hospital parking lot and that he probably followed us here."*

"So this morning, when I left I went about one half mile down the road, and hid the car and walked back here and hid in the barn and a few minutes later Knuckles walks in after pacing the house out. It worked out good for me I have been watching the house since I left this morning hoping that he would show up here."

"I saw you walking to the barn and I was hidden behind some old saddles that were in the back and I knew that Knuckles was there but I had my gun aimed at him when he grabbed you from behind."

"Okay Gary I need to find some food for him or he'll be all over me."

"Yes Lisa, hurry before he comes in here and gets suspicious."

"Be sure to shut the doors on this pantry Lisa"

"Okay," I replied.

CHAPTER 12

"Hey, woman, who the heck are you talking to in there?"

"I was talking to a stray cat that got inside through the cellar door when I opened it" I said

"Where is my grub?" Knuckles yelled louder at me.

"It's coming just give me a few more minutes," I said.

I hurried to the freezer that was next to the pantry, and found some hash browns and chopped frozen ham. I rushed it to the microwave and thawed it out for a minute and put it in the frying pan on the gas stove. It was sizzling in the frying pan when Knuckles, surprised me and came out into the kitchen.

"Good thing that you're doing what you're told lady Lisa," he said to me.

"Okay, go get the ketchup out of the refrigerator" I ordered him.

At that point, Knuckles came around the corner of the kitchen bar and grabbed me by the back of my hair and said,

"Don't you ever order me around again, or I will kill you and you got one big mouth lady and you better learn to keep it shut."

I kept my mouth closed at this point as he open the refrigerator door and got the ketchup out. Knuckles went into the dining room and I finished up the hash browns and ham and brought them to him. At the same time I was wondering, *When is Gary, going to do something?*

I was getting a plate out of the cupboard and looking for silverware. I finally found it in the draw with the broken knob on it. I then opened up one of the draws and saw a butcher knife. I quietly wrapped a cloth napkin around the knife and hid it under the plate that I had for myself to the table along with his food.

Knuckles, yelled at me and said, *"Set down now and eat your grub"* as he was shoveling food in his mouth so fast that the hash browns and ketchup were running down his chin.

How disgusting I thought to myself and what a pig he was. It did not take him long to take that last bite of food. I had made sure that he was sitting with his back to the kitchen.

I could see Gary now making his move towards Knuckles carrying a gun and coming up from behind him. Gary, quickly put his arm around Knuckles, neck and said *"If you move, I shoot you"* with the gun pressed against Knuckles head. Boy, I could not believe the surprised look on Knuckles face. I loved it.

"Okay, Knuckles, your days of crimes are over with and you're coming with me back to Gilroy, to stand trial for murder, and attempted murder and kidnapping on Lisa."

"The cops said that it was your bullet that killed your partner and not theirs and the list goes on."

"Yea, you think that you are so smart," he said to Gary in a gruff voice, *there is more people like me out there looking for the key, and they are on to you and Lisa. Your lives will always be in danger. "Ha-ha,"* as he laughs at us.

"Shut up," Gary said to him as he shoved the gun in his back harder.

"Lisa, go in the barn and grab the rope that is hanging on the wall," Gary, said to me.

"Okay Gary, on my way" as I left him alone with Knuckles I went to the barn running and tripped over a stump in the ground and went flying in the air. I must have hit myself on a rock for when I woke up it was dark, and then it all came back to me. I must get back into the house, as I picked myself up and wondered why Gary did not come back looking for me.

I opened up the door to the living room, and saw Gary tied to a chair with blood running down his head. I looked around for Knuckles, but he was not in sight.

I rushed over to Gary and yelled *"Wake up, Wake up!"* He shook his head and came too.

"Lisa, are you alright?" he said to me in a faint voice.

"Yes, Gary, my love but what happened?" as I continued to untie him and took my shirttail to wipe the blood off of his face.

"You had just left the room Lisa, to go get the rope for me, and I moved Knuckles, to the other seat at the table where you were sitting, just in case someone else was in the kitchen I would see them coming in. I told him to put his hands on the table, and I had no idea that you had a knife wrapped in a napkin lying on the table. Knuckles saw it before I had a chance to do anything, he grabbed the knife and slit my wrist and the gun fell and he grabbed that and hit me over the head and that is all that I remember."

"Why didn't he come after me Gary? When he had the chance and I was knocked out cold laying in the yard?"

Gary says *"Probably because Lisa, he figures until he finds the key he wants you alive."*

"In other words Gary I should be safe until then, Right?"

"Wrong Lisa, you and I will never be safe until we capture them, he must of heard us talking about it last night when you were telling me about where the flowers were, and when you're a crook like him, you think like a crook and he was thinking what if she is lying to Gary? What happens if I kill them and the flowers are not in her refrigerator?"

"He wanted to get a head start on us just in case you were telling me the truth. If the flowers are not there he will come back here to get us." I said.

"Don't worry now about that Lisa. Do you recall the story that was in the newspaper a few weeks ago?"

"Which one Gary?"

"Well, it was the one about the outlaw gang, many years ago who robbed the Southern Pacific railroad, and never got caught. Then a few years later the gang waited at the Coleman Switch that was west of town, then when the passenger train stopped to switch tracks is when the three masked men jumped on the train and rob all the people."

"Yes, I do remember some of that Gary, but what does that have to do with you and me?"

"Think about it Lisa, that gang had to of been Knuckles and his gang."

"But they said in the article that it was an inside job Gary."

"Which means Lisa, that there is someone besides the Warden that is interested in the patents for the Maglev train? The key is what they want and they think that it is in the roses. How would they know that if somebody in the department didn't tell them?"

"Boy, Gary this is really getting big."

"Come here Lisa, let me hold you for a moment again," Gary puts his arms around me and then squeezes me tight and holds me just for a minute he then puts his hands on my shoulders and leans me back and stares into my eyes and says, *"Lisa, it's going to be alright."* Then he gives me a kiss and says *"You need to trust me on this one."*

"Well then Gary, looks like it still may be under control, don't you think?"

"Yes Lisa that is what I am trying to tell you . . ."

CHAPTER 13

"Gary lets finish cleaning you up."
"Well no time for that Lisa."
"It will just take a minute. We sure don't want you to get an infection."
"Okay Lisa, but we need to hurry up"
I went to the bathroom and grabbed a clean washcloth, a towel and some first-aid cream. As I put warm water on the washcloth I said, *"Gary, sit down here at the table so I can get you cleaned up and disinfected."*
"Yes Mama," he said teasing me.
I was thinking to myself, how can he joke at a time like this? I looked at his wrist and it was so close to the vein where Knuckles slit him and thank God the cut missed the artery. His head had a slow bleed but because it had not scabbed yet I thought was the reason it was still bleeding.
"Wait here Gary, I need to run and get a band aid." I was now thinking how much that I really loved this man and that I would give up anything for him.
I walked back into the room and said, *"Gary, you will be new in no time."*
"Yes Lisa, I believe you but please hurry we have a four hour trip to catch up with Knuckles, and not counting how much of a head start that he got. I will call Headquarters to send out a squad car and have them also send out my partner."
"Yes good idea Gary."
Within minutes we were in the car and driving towards Gilroy, California I must admit I was really nervous about this and thinking

first we run from Knuckles, and now we are running towards him, now what is wrong with this picture?

Gary held unto my hand as I was driving this time and says *"I love you so much Lisa."* Then leans his head on my shoulders and falls fast asleep. Gary was trying to reassure me so I would not worry so much and could concentrate on the drive.

The four hours seem to go by fast and we only had now a few more minutes and we will be pulling up near my home.

Gary woke up about this time and said *"Sorry that I fell asleep. I must have been tired."*

"You sure were Gary, but look we are almost there."

"Lisa, stay a block away from your place and I will walk the rest of the way."

"No Gary, I want to be with you." I said,

"Lisa, now you listen to me, it is much safer for you if you stay here in the car."

"Okay, Gary I will wait here but if you're not back in 10 minutes I will be looking for you." Okay he said as he was pulling himself out of the car and walking away.

Before I knew it he was out of sight.

Gary must have not been gone 5 minutes and I heard the sirens as they zoomed past me towards my place, not one police car but three went passed me. Oh no, I said to myself as I started the engine of the car and headed towards my home. *What now?* I thought.

I could see the sirens lights flashing in front of my place so I jumped out of the car and started running towards my front door and a police officer said *"Stay back please, this is a crime scene."*

"You don't understand officer this is my place." At this time I was feeling like my whole world was falling apart in front of my face. I pray that Gary is alright and safe. A few minutes later I saw what looked to be Gary, it was so dark I was hard to make out who was who until he got closer, and yes, it was Gary as he ran towards me and grabbed me and said, *"Lisa we are too late, Knuckles killed my partner before the agents got here and is still on the run."*

"Oh Gary, I am so sorry to hear that but did he get the flowers out of the refrigerator?"

"I don't know Lisa, for when I got here the police were here. They said that they found my partner with a stab wound to the heart and he was already dead. The crime scene officers will not let me into the house yet. So we have to be patience. I just saw a new coroner, one that I never saw before walked outside pushing the gurney by me and were taken away his body and when they walked by me I recognized my partners watch for his arm was hanging outside of the blanket." I thought that it was strange that they would remove the body so fast but never the less they must have found all they wanted.*"*

"Gary, why don't you show them your CIA badge, then you could get us inside of my house?"

"Lisa, I am also a secret agent and that would give away my identity to all the officers."

"I understand now Gary" at that point I put my head on Gary's chest and just started crying.

CHAPTER 14

Gary tried to calm me down and said, *"It will be alright Lisa, we will catch Knuckles, they have an all-points bulletin out on him."*

"I hope that you are right Gary, for I am sick and tired of dodging him all the time and I just want our life back."

"Lisa, your right and this is not fair to you."

Gary then puts his arms around me and whispers *"I love you so much Lisa and I want nothing more to happen to you and be with you but please think about what I have said."*

"Okay, Gary, I will but please I want to go inside my house now."

"Wait here Lisa, and I will check with the officer and see when they will be done with the crime scene. Don't forget Lisa, I need to get back into the house also and see if the flowers are still in the refrigerator."

"That is right Gary, what if they are not there?"

"We will find out soon Lisa, now sit over here on the bench and just try and rest." as he puts his jacket over my shoulders to keep me warm, then walks over to the officer and tried to convinced him that it is okay to let us in.

A few minutes later Gary comes over to me and gets a hold of my arm and says, *"Hurry, we will go in the back door and please keep quiet. I must see if the flowers are still there. The officer said no."*

We hid behind a bush until the security guard was called to the side of the house and tried to get in the back door and it was locked, as Gary and says to me, *"Now what?"*

"Gary," I said, *"look above the door sham and you will find a key I always keep there in case I get locked out."*

"Ah, good job Lisa," he says as he runs his hands across the top of the door and grabs the key.

"Lisa, hurry now inside" as he turns the key in the lock and unlocks the door for me. We got inside and walked through the kitchen and saw all the food thrown everywhere.

"What happen?" I said.

"Well if you ask me" Gary said to me, *"Knuckles, was probably in a hurry and started throwing everything in the refrigerator to the outside to find the plastic bulb. Remember Lisa, he did not know for sure what he was looking for and it made him excited and maybe he never found the plastic bulb that had the key in it. Help me pick up all these rose buds and watch for something plastic."*

I looked at the mess of food and rosebuds on my beautiful floor. I fell to my hands and knees and crawled around looking and hoping to find something that was plastic and pushing stuff out of my way.

CHAPTER 15

"Lisa, we must hurry before the cops find us in here."

"I'm trying Gary, but not much time to give it a good search. "Wait *Gary, I found something."* as he is rushing towards me. *"It's made of plastic."* I said all excited as I looked up at him.

"Let me see what you found Lisa," after taking it from my hand. I got up off my knees and Gary, held it up to the light and said

"Lisa, this is only a plastic Easter shell" with disappointment I said, *"I remember that I had the neighborhood kids over and we had an Easter egg hunt a few months ago"*

"Come on Lisa, I hear the cops coming, lets hide in your entry closet," as he grabbed me by the hand and says, *"Now careful my dear" and be quiet."*

Okay, I thought to myself I will try and hold the noise down and compose myself to the fact that we are in one horrible mess again. Here I am in my own home where just a short time ago someone got murdered on my living room floor. The cops are outside not letting me in. I had to break into my own home and now I am getting ready to hide in my own closet with my new lover who just happens to be a secret CIA agent. Now to top it off the **Americans Most Wanted** is after me. Should I have no reason to get excited Right? Wrong!

We managed to squeeze in the entry closet that was pretty small. Gary had his arms around me and the vacuum was hugging me on one side and the clothes were hanging down on us.

A few minutes later we heard the cops come inside and say, "W*here did that crazy woman go that was outside, and that want-a-be detective?*"

"*I don't know Captain, what happen to them, they sure wanted in here very bad. Hum! Better check out all the rooms' maybe they came inside when we were not looking.*"

"*Oh no,*" I said to Gary,

"*Hush*" he said as he squeezed my hand and to let me know to be quiet.

We heard them opening the doors to my other rooms and held our breath that they would not open the closet door where we were hiding.

"*Hey, Detective have you checked the entry closet, no Captain but I am on my way*" as he headed towards the closet that we were in.

Guess we were saved by the bell, for at that moment the Captain got a call from headquarters, and said to the detective

"*Come on detective,*" the Captain said, "*I just heard that Knuckles was seen over on Loganberry Street, let's hit it.*" And they went running out of my home and towards their patrol car. Soon as we heard them leaving we opened the closet door and ran to the living room.

"*I'll be a snake's tail,*" Gary said

"*What?*" I said "*I have heard that before.*"

"*Sure you have Lisa that is an old CIA joke. Hey look!*"

We both saw the outline of Gary's partner drawn on my hardwood floors. "*No time for this Lisa, get to the kitchen again.*"

"*Hey, Gary, look over there by the stove, something is shining there.*"

Gary runs over there and picks it up and finds the plastic rose bulb, "*Yes!*" he yells to me "*We got it Lisa*" and gives me a big hug as he shows me the red plastic bulb. Gary, opens up the plastic bulb and when he was pulling on it something flew down the kitchen drain,

"*Oh no Gary, now what?*"

"*No time to call the plumber Lisa, for we now have a billion dollar key down your kitchen drain.*" But was it the key that went down the drain, or something else? I asked for the plastic was cracked.

51

CHAPTER 16

"Those are good questions you're asking Lisa." as we went to the bedroom so I could packed a few clothes knowing that I may never see my home again. *"Hurry Lisa, I hear the cops coming in the front door."* Gary quickly picked up my suitcase and grabbed my hands.

We ran down the street to get to Gary's truck that was parked a few blocks from my apartment.

"Now Lisa," as we got to the truck, Gary said to me *"Stay down and out of sight we know that Knuckles is looking for us."*

"Okay Gary, I will do just that" as I put my head down in the cab of the truck. *"Where are we going Gary?"* I asked?

"First thing Lisa, we are going to one of my friend's house who is out of the country till next month and I think that we will be safe there and it will give us a night of rest and then we can leave tomorrow morning at sunrise."

"Okay Gary, I want you safe too."

"Don't worry about me Lisa, I still have some unfinished business to attend before I can make many plans again."

"You see Gary," I said to him, *"You will still be in* danger." as we pulled up to his friend's house which was on the outskirts of town. It was a brown house with white trim and must have been built in the '50s for it had the old asbestos siding on it.

A few minutes later Gary walks to the front door and motions me to get out of the truck. I quickly grabbed my suitcase and followed him inside.

The house was nice and tidy and had a contemporary look to it. Gary says to me, *"Let me help you take off your coat Lisa, it does not seem that cold in here."*

"Okay Gary, thank you" and about that time he pulled me to him and gives me a kiss and led me to the bedroom. The bedroom was a soft white with green border and you could tell it was a bachelor quarters from looking around the room and the emptiness it had though I did feel safer here.

"Lisa, I want tonight to be so special that you will never forget it or me and to show you how much I really do love you."

"I love you also Gary," I said to him as he unbuttoned my blouse and pulled it off my shoulders and started kissing my arms and bringing them up around his neck. I moved closer to him so I could feel his every breath and his chest against mine. About that time I started to unbutton his shirt and listen for his heartbeat and I put my ear to his chest and the beats were so fast.

The rest of the evening being in bed with Gary, with his arms around me, made me forget about all the problems facing us.

Before I knew it was morning and I could see Gary's shadow in the bathroom talking on the phone. I got up and put my robe on and went to the kitchen to find some coffee when Gary came out of the bathroom realizing that I was up.

Gary said to me *"Lisa, we've got a problem."*

I said *"I know we have problems,"*

"Lisa, listen to me, that was headquarters and they said that Knuckles was in Gilroy, and 10 minutes later he was spotted in Las Vegas. Now we both know that it is a 4 hour drive and it would be impossible for Knuckles to move that fast, unless . . ."

"Unless what Gary?

"Unless he has a twin brother! Gary exclaims. *"They are checking on it now so we should know soon."*

I said, *"Gary this has to be my worst nightmare ever"* as Gary came over to me and put his arms around me.

CHAPTER 17

We must have been there for a few hours before the phone rang again.

"Hello, hello, yes this is Gary," as he was answering the phone. *"What? Are you sure? How long has he been out? Okay, Bro and what? My partners body as disappeared? How could that be?"* Then he hung up the phone.

"Why do I get a feeling that this is bad news?" I said to Gary after he hung up the phone.

"Well, Lisa you better sit down, it seems that number one, my partners body has disappeared from the morgue."

"Number two, Knuckles has an identical twin brother who just escaped from prison and is more dangerous than Knuckles, His name is Starfish and believe me he is no star."

"The good news is Lisa, headquarters called in more CIA agents to work on the case. We have some of the best men in the organization to help capture the two fugitives."

"And what about your partners' body being missing? And how could that of happened?" I said

"Well Lisa, It seems that the coroner who picked up the body was a crook and kept the body and tries to replace it with other body."

"You're kidding right Gary?"

"No Lisa, it's even deeper than that when they realized that the body brought into the morgue was a woman, not a man. Supposedly when my partner's wife came to identified her husband Felix, my partner well, when they pulled back the covers it was a women."

"That is just crazy Gary, and do you think for a moment Gary that it makes me feel any better? No matter what, I just know that

this whole nightmare will get worse and in the meantime what do they really want?" "Just what I told you Lisa, all they want is the key, that's it I'm sure." Gary said to me.

"You're forgetting one thing Gary; I can identify Knuckles for the murders." You have not said much about your partners missing body either?" I said to Gary.

"I have a theory to that question Lisa. Remember when I was outside before you showed up and the coroner pushed the body by me and I did see my partner's wrist watch on his arm as they went by? We know it was him when they picked up the body. The question is when did they exchange the bodies? And why?"

"Too many unanswered questions Lisa, I am still working it out in my head and in the meantime we have other problems than worrying about a missing dead body but on the other hand it could be other clue in this case.

"Do you have any secret rooms in your home Lisa?"

"Are you kidding Gary, for crying out loud it is a typical home." I cried.

"I think that the woman's body came from your house. Settle down Lisa, everything will work out but I do need you to think where would you hide something that size?"

"Let me think Gary, yes there is somewhere you could hide the body."

"Where is that Lisa?"

"It is in the utility room off the kitchen" I said to Gary, *"I have a chest freezer in there that is almost empty and a body for sure would fit in that and no one would ever know."*

"I will call headquarter Lisa, and have them check it out." Gary heads to the phone and not wasting anytime. About 30 minutes later the phone rings. Gary was quick to pick it up. *"Yes,"* Gary says, *"Thank you sir."* and with that short remark he hangs the phone up.

"Lisa," Gary says to me, *"the freezer is gone and the neighbor saw a moving truck show up."*

"We think that the truck was headed to the underground Maglev freight train station that is somewhere near Highway 80 and exit 48 in Fernley Nevada. Seems the driver got pulled over for a tail light out and could not explain where he had been or was going. They put him in the

clunker for the night. He got released the next morning. My hunch is he had to of been going to the underground tunnel."

"Gary, I have never heard of this before, an underground tunnel with a fast moving train, like something out of science fiction?"

"It is one of the fastest moving trains in history Lisa and holds cars, trucks, and freight so the freezer would not be a problem. It can travel of up to speeds of 300 miles an hour."

"But Gary I never heard about a Maglev train and especially one that can travel that fast and underground? And besides I used to live in that area."

"Lisa, it has been a well-kept secret for too many years. Many, many years ago our Country had two well known Scientist who developed a high speed magnetic levitation train that would run without gas or diesel fuel.

"There was a leak at the science lab and all the patents from the project were first stolen and then sold to China for an unknown amount of money."

"The United States could do nothing and regretted not putting in the Maglev train. In the meantime China used Boeing machines and worked their way under the ocean into the United States, and there a train could circle all the 50 States in America, all underground without any knowledge to the Americans."

"It took the Country years before they realized that there were underground tunnels and Maglev trains running from China to here."

"That was why the underground tunnels got build and by the Chinese."

"It was kept hush, hush because not to cause a worldwide panic."

"Keep going Gary" I said urgently.

"Okay, then Lisa when our Country found out there was nothing that they could do unless they got the patents back and the master plans. Then it became a war between the two Countries and that is why this operation is worth so much money."

"Now the key that may be in your kitchen drain could be worth billions of dollars plus security to our Country."

CHAPTER 18

"This is the reason that everyone wants the key. The key will unlock the underground safe that has the master set of plans for the drawings of the Maglev trains which is worth billions of dollars like I said before."

"My missing dead partner probably sent a fake key in the flowers to your place to trick knuckles and his buddies and thought he could put them off the track while he sent you the second set of roses."

"Knuckles knew that you and I were involved with each other and you would be an easy mark, especially if the key was sent to your place."

"Now the problem is I never had a chance to asked my deceased partner Felix, whether he sent the real key in the second dozen roses and hid the original or, your guess is as good as mine."

"And what is in the plastic bulb that he put in the first set of roses? We will get a plumber out when it is safe to go back to your home."

"But Gary, that does not explain about your partners body being stolen and being replaced with a woman's?"

"Lisa, it is like this, and you need to understand, sometimes in our training we have learned to do all we can to save something like that and there is a possibility that my partner swallowed the key to keep it from being stolen." Gary explains.

"The corrupt police captain realized that, and did not have time to find out, and that is when he rushed the body to the morgue, and then did the switch. My poor partner is probably being dissected as we speak."

"Oh Gary," I picked up his hands to hold, *"please don't think that way, maybe they had another reason for keeping his body?"*

"That's what I love about you Lisa, always thinking with your brain and not your beautiful body."

At this point Gary pulled me closer to him, and whispers, *"I love you Lisa, so much, more than life itself and when this is all over you and I will make up for all of this rotten stuff that has happen to us."*

"That sounds good to me, but Gary, How did you and your partner end up with the key?"

"It's like this Lisa, the Government ordered the department to have a double agent sent to China and steal the key back and bring it to America we just needed to find out where the safe is, and from what we know it's like a scavenger hunt."

"What do you mean Gary?"

"We found a clue that came in a few days ago to the department."

"What was it Gary?"

"Well it was made from newspaper letters glued to white pieces of paper and mailed to our office we thought maybe someone was playing jokes on us but I don't think so. Here I have it here in my pocket; I will read it to you Lisa." As he pulls it out.

"Okay Gary go for it." I said.

(I have a face. It doesn't frown.
I have no mouth. Just a sound.
I have hands that don't wave.
I don't walk. But I move around)

"Do you know what it means Lisa?"

"Why yes, I do Gary," Lisa begins, *"It's a Maglev train, it moves around fast. It must be part of a clue. Like the key may be connected to the Maglev train."*

Gary smiles and says, *"Smart girl you are. That's what I think Lisa, one safe will lead you to another and you keep going till you find it."*

"There were rumors that we had some dirty agents from the inside that were after the key, so to take precautions what better way to keep it safe than to have the CIA most trusted agents protect it with their lives and to keep it from arms way."

"That was Felix, my partner and me, though I ended up in the hospital in a coma and my partner ended up, well you know the rest."

"And God Bless America Lisa that is why I do my job to the best of my ability."

"Wow! Gary." I started to cry when hearing how dedicated that Gary really was. *"Gary,"* I said, *"Please forgive me for all the complaining that I do, my God you are a hero in my book."*

CHAPTER 19

"Okay Lisa, but no time for mush, mush." Gary said to me, as he gave me a big hug and kiss on the cheek. *"I must get to Fernley, Nevada and get to the Maglev train station and see if I can find my partners body just in case he did swallow the key and they brought him there."*

"Well Gary, I am right behind you."

"No Lisa, it is so unsafe for you to be with me besides the train station is all underground, no one knows that it is even there. I just know that it is by exit 48 and Hwy I-80"

"More reason for me to go Gary, I grew up in Fernley, before I moved to Gilroy. I know my way around like you know the back of your hand, and besides I should not be left alone."

"Okay, Lisa, but do you know how to shoot a gun?"

"Are you kidding me Gary? My nanny and I use to go to the desert and take live scorpions for bait and then we would put them on a rock from a jar and say ready, set, go and I would wait for the snakes to come out and scare them off with my shot-gun before they ate the scorpions."

"Okay Lisa, hold that thought, now let's get serious. Fernley, Nevada is about sixty minutes from Tahoe and we are four hours here in Gilroy, which would make about a five hour trip for us."

"Now we just have to figure the fastest way to travel. I will call the department and order a Jet to leave from the San Jose airport and we could be there in less than an hour. I will need to give them this address. Now pack up your stuff Lisa, let's be ready to go when I get a return phone call from the department we can leave."

"Okay boss," I said and then went to find my clothes and jacket so I would be ready.

"Well I'll be a snake's tail." I said to Gary.

Gary looked at me with a smile on his face and he busted out laughing and said *"That is my saying."*

"Right Gary, my nanny told me that years ago, then you tell me that it came from an old CIA joke."

"It did Lisa." he said to me with a smile on his face.

It wasn't long before we got a call from the department saying that they are sending a car out to pick us up and take us to the airport and to leave are truck here.

I thought to myself if this wasn't so serious and dangerous this could be fun and a private jet all to ourselves. Within less than an hour the black limousine was there to pick us up. The chauffeur got out of the car and opened the back door of the car for us. He was kind of scary looking with a bald head and he almost looked like a priest the way he was dressed with a black collar tight around his throat.

Gary says, *"You get in first dear."* as he held my hand and took my purse until I got inside and then he followed me and the chauffeur closed the door. Gary puts his arms around me and squeezes me and gives me a kiss. It felt so good to have his strong arms around me.

We had traveled about thirty minutes and Gary got a concerned look on his face.

"What is it Gary?"

"I'm not sure Lisa, but we are going the wrong way, this is not the way to the airport."

About this time the bald headed man locked our doors and turned around and looked at us with a smile. There was a plate glass between the driver and us and it was bullet proof.

"Gary!" I cried *"We are being kidnapped."*

"Not to worry Lisa, I will figure a way out of this."

I could not believe this was happening, not again.

CHAPTER 20

"Lisa I have an idea," Gary said to me, *"just watch and listen for me when we get out of the car."*

"Okay Gary, but it better be good."

"It will Lisa, just not sure yet but remember I have years of training to get out of messes like this." I guess he must have been trying to reassure me.

It seemed like we drove other 15 miles when we could see the driver talking on the car phone and nodding his head as he talked.

"Lisa, we are headed towards Fernley, Nevada, I just wonder if they know about the two dozen roses?"

"Why, what do you mean Gary?"

"There was rumor that some high officials were going to leak the information that our government knew about this horrific event underground and about them stealing are patents. The United States made a deal with China to build their high speed rail underground next to the Maglev train. China knew that we would not be a threat with a much slower train and they gave us the right-of-way underground but we had to follow their route. Plus the tunnel was already built for the Maglev."

"But Gary, what is the difference between the high speed rail and the Maglev train?"

"Okay Lisa, a high speed rail is run on steel wheels just like the old trains but they go about 150 miles an hour. Now a Maglev train is not on steel wheels, it sits up high on a guide way on magnets and there are no tracks. It can reach speeds up to 310 miles an hour."

"Lisa, when it was first design our famous scientists tried to convince our Government to build it immediately but they said no not interested until it became too late and they know now that we are a third world country in transportation."

"Gary, how sad is that for our Nation, when we had a chance to be bigger and better than any Nation around the world."

"Yes, I know Lisa."

"But what is the rest of this story Gary?" I asked.

"Well, the great scientist that worked on these patents and master sets knew that they would be very valuable someday and when no one would listen to them so they put it in a safe until the Chinese got wind of it and took it from them. The people in our country do not know that we have already built the high speed rail underground and then next to it China built the Maglev train and it's all underground. Side by side they are together."

"Now remember Lisa, that China does have the missing patents for the Maglev high speed train for they are hid in a secret safe in China. We have the key and codes. Our Country needs the patents real bad and without them they do not have the knowledge."

"Well Gary, why don't the scientists make a new set of the patents?"

"They would Lisa, if they were alive. I am sad to say but they both got killed this last year in a horrible traffic accident."

"What happened Gary?"

"Well, they were going down Hwy 1 when their brakes went out and they ended up at the bottom of a canyon. It is suspected that someone tampered with their brakes. So you see Lisa that someone does not want us to have a Maglev train in this Country. Our government now wants more than anything else is to build our own Maglev train and get the patents back."

"Lisa, it's a win-win situation for the Maglev and not the steel rails. We are still back in time with the transcontinental railroad that was first built in the year 1869."

"Gee Gary, this is much deeper than I could have imagined and I have not heard any talk about any of this.

It is like something from the future."

"Yes Lisa, and it is bigger than you and I would have ever thought."

"Well Gary, this still does not explain if the high speed rail was involved, then why would they take the body of your partner to the Maglev underground station in Fernley?"

"Now that is a good question Lisa, and all that I can come up with is they know how much money the patents are worth and they want the key so bad that they will do anything."

"Gary, this is just so much for me to comprehend right now, my God I must be dreaming."

"I wish that it was a dream for you Lisa, and you were out of all this danger."

"How long have we been traveling Gary?" As he looks at his watch and says, *"It's been 4 hours now Lisa"*

"Hey Gary looks like we are slowing down."

"Yes Lisa, he is pulling over now."

"Where are we Gary?"

"We are on Hwy 80 near Lake Tahoe, and he is pulling over here at the rest stop. This will be our chance to escape. Wait a minute the rest stop is closed."

"They are always closed for repair Gary, but of all times."

"If we live through this then the State is getting a letter from me and a piece of my mind." I said to Gary.

"Okay, Lisa but you will need to hold that thought."

"Looks like he is getting off here at exit 89 towards South Lake Tahoe, said Gary, *"he is going around the lake now. Yes, and he is looking for a place to get rid of us I bet."*

"Come on Gary, I'm scared enough."

"Sorry Lisa, I'm just thinking out loud. You need to just follow my lead Lisa, and listen carefully."

"You got it Gary," I said.

The driver then gets on this back road that leads to a cabin and he pulls around to the back. A few minutes later he comes over and opens the door holding a gun. *"Now make one move in the wrong direction and you both are dead meat says the driver. Get out of the car, now!"*

Gary, then gets out and helps me out while the gun is pointed at us. Gary looks at me and says, *"Look over there Lisa, I'll be a snakes tail,"* and the driver looks over in that direction also. I knew what that meant soon as Gary said it.

I had a gun in my purse that I forgot to tell Gary about. I open up my purse and grabbed the gun and remember what my nanny always said to me *"Ready, set, go, shoot the gun and scare the* snakes". Gary is trying to tell me shoot the gun. So with that thought I pulled my gun out and just started shooting in the air. It scared the driver enough that Gary grabs the gun from the driver and pins him down on the ground.

He then throws me the drivers gun and yells, *"Good job Lisa, keep it pointed at him."* While he finds some handcuffs in the front seat of the car and puts them on the driver.

CHAPTER 21

"Hurry up Gary; I'm nervous about making it to the jet in time."

"Just a minute Lisa, I just found some rope on the floor-board, he must have had it here to tie us up. Now make sure you keep the gun aimed at him."

"No worries Gary, I would just love to have a reason to shoot this sniper."

"Well Lisa, I just found the handcuffs, we will tie him to this tree here and call the police to pick him up."

"Great Gary," I said, as he ties the rope around the tree and went towards the driver and said *"Get on your feet Mr. Tough guy and get over there by that tree."* Gary grabs him by his neck and shoves him against the tree. *"Now the shoe is on the other foot."* he says to him. Gary continues to tie the rope around and around the tree until he ran out of rope.

"Okay Lisa, Get in the car and start the engine we still have time to make it to the airport."

Startled I say, *"You want me to drive this big limousine?"*

"Yes, then I can make my calls" Gary said, *"we need to find where the leak is in the CIA someone there double cross the organization and sent this guy to kill us. I just don't know who to trust now with my partner gone, besides one other friend that I will try."*

"Let's go Lisa," says Gary as he jumps in the car. He then starts calling an old buddy that he knew he could trust.

"Hey Bro, this is double agent 10927"

"Need help!"

"My location, yes"

"Okay, Bro" then hangs up the phone.

"Gary," I said *"That sure was quick"*

"I know that Lisa, The jet is still waiting for us so step on the gas we need to hurry."

"Then hold on Gary" as I made a corner on two wheels and headed in the opposite direction.

About that time red lights lit up from behind and sirens came on. Gary says *"Shucks, outrun him Lisa, we cannot trust if he is legit."* *"Snakes,"* Gary says, *"I should have drove."*

"Watch me Gary, I forgot to tell you that I was raised by the toughest nanny in the West who at one time was a race car driver and she taught me everything I know, now watch this Gary," as I put the car in a higher gear and floored it down the steep hill. There were some sharp corners, but no one could make those corners like I did.

"Wow! Lisa your goooooooood" as he tried to hold on to the door handle and could hardly catch his breath as his head flew back because of the G-forces. *"I have never seen anyone drive this way, Lisa"*

"Glad you like it Gary," as I floored boarded it around a very narrow corner and Gary ended up in my lap.

"Now please Gary no time for hanky pansy" as his hands end up on me and he smiled.

But the next corner put him back on his side of the car. Gary then looked in the rear view mirror and said *"Lisa, you lost them. Thank God, now you can slow down girl."*

"Not on your life Gary, we got a plane to catch." At that time I looked over at him and gave him a wink as I did slowdown some.

"Good job Lisa, are you for hirer?"

"Only if you're my employer" I said to Gary

"Lisa," Gary said, after taking a big breath. *"There is something that I never mention to you and its time that you should know since you are in so deep anyway with me."*

"Well Gary, what possibly can I not know?" as I sigh in relief, *"like go ahead tell me."*

*"Well it's like this Lisa, I was involved with a company called **The Guidewinds Project**, and it was Maglev high speed train project.*

Their Maglev train was to go all around the I-80 corridor through all the states. The company was doing very well until the Vice President of the company was threatened by a super power."

"The President and Vice President of the company knew that China had already stolen their master plans from their scientist that invented the Maglev train. I told you before that China did steal the patents on it. That is what this whole thing is about."

"I know that Gary, but what happen to the Guidewinds project and their people?"

"Gee Lisa; I was afraid that you would ask that question. If you really want to know Lisa, and yes you have that right now to know, they all disappeared."

"Gary," I said, *"do you think that maybe they went into the secret witness program?"*

"I hate to say this, but no. We checked and there was no information about them. We also are afraid that they could have been kidnapped, and not knowing is why I was assigned to this case."

"The CIA planted me in the project, in the beginning but I realize right away that these people involved in this project were very legit and just wanted to help with the United State to be ahead in the competition of high speed transportation.

It was to keep them competitive. In other words one step ahead of other Countries."

"How can you be sure Gary that all the Guidewinds people are really missing?"

"It's like this Lisa, when you leave your home with just the clothes on your back, your home fully furnished, cars in the drive-way and money in your bank account, all left behind that would be reason enough to suspect that something is wrong with that picture."

"Gary, this is so unbelievable what can we do to help?"

"Lisa, if you hadn't notice we are hot on their trail."

CHAPTER 22

"We are almost to the airport Lisa" I started to take a right turn towards the airport and Gary yelled, *"No Lisa, go left!"*

"But that is not the way to the San Jose airport" I said.

"I know Lisa; we cannot trust whoever from the organization is the leak so we have new orders now to get to a small landing field at the edge of town and a new smaller jet will pick us up there and take us to Reno, Nevada's International Airport."

"From there we will head south of town to a construction site that will have some trucks and we will take our pick of vehicles for the place is closed today."

"Aha! Got you Gary, now that is good thinking."

"Okay, Lisa you are getting close to the landing field, take that back road here on your right and it will take us straight there."

"Yes Sir," I said as I push the gas pedal metal to metal, *"This sure brings back memories of my childhood."* I said to Gary.

"That is great Lisa, but not so fast we are almost there. Look there is our jet." As I drove closer to it.

"Park over there on the side of that gray building so we don't look suspicious."

"Okay, here we are," I said as we rushed out of the limo and made a b-line to the plane.

It was just getting dark now and we had lost a lot of time. *"We should be in Reno, within an hour."* Gary said.

"Where is the pilot?" I asked Gary.

"He is refueling the plane, Lisa"

"Oh, I see now" as we hurried to get aboard.

The pilot yells, *"I will be there shortly just take a seat."*

Gary gives him the thumbs up as we climb aboard.

All of a sudden we are taking off and what smooth ride as I put my head against Gary's chest and gave a sigh of relieve. I must have dozed off at that point for when I woke up the plane was moving back and forth and it sure was not turbulence.

"Gary wake up we are going down!" I yelled at him.

"Oh my, you are not kidding Lisa," as he jumps from his seat and heads to the front of the plane to see the pilot.

"No Way!" yells Gary, *"the pilot is gone."*

Then Gary and I both look outside and see the pilot in a parachute as he was making a fast escape. He must have put the plane on auto pilot when he bailed out.

At that point I said *"Now what?"* *"Gary, I do love you and will see you on the 'Other Side'"* as I grabbed his hands.

"Not so fast Lisa, I was trained in the air force to be a fighter pilot and I can handle this small plane" says Gary as he got in the pilot's seat.

A big relief came over me at that moment. Is there nothing that Gary can't do? I asked myself as he gets the plane under control and we head towards Reno.

"Good job Gary!" I exclaimed, as we get close to the airport and we started our descent and the airport lights looked like we were heading into a sunset.

"Lisa, fasten your seat belt." Gary, said as we flew in like on the wings of a dove. *"I will put the jet over near the hanger, Lisa"*

"It will be out of sight" as he's maneuvers it to a smooth landing towards the hanger. *"Not much time Lisa; it will take us about 40 minutes to get to Fernley, Nevada from Reno."*

"Okay now, let's get off the plane fast and run towards that baggage car that is in the far south corner. That will help us get across the landing field and closer to the construction site quicker." It only took us a few minutes to reach the baggage cart as we both jumped in.

"Hurry Lisa," a plane is approaching and he is not moving slow and we are on the runway.

"I'm right with you Gary." as he turned the baggage cart to the left to get out of the way of the jet landing. Minutes later we are

on the construction site and I had never seen so many 18 wheeler trucks.

"Let's take that white 18 wheeler over there Lisa, it won't be so obvious." He went over to it and hotwired it. It was not a minute later that Gary yelled! *"Get in Lisa"* as the engine started.

"Gary, where is the ladder? I cannot reach the door."

"Hang on Lisa, I will help you in." as he comes over and folds his hands for me to put my foot in. I have not done that since I was a kid I thought.

"We are on are way Lisa"

"Yes and it sure feels good to have are feet on the ground." I said.

"Gary, one thing I do not understand?"

"And what is that Lisa?"

"How could I live in the town of Fernley, Nevada for over 15 years and never heard of a hidden train station under exit 48 and Hwy I-80?"

"How did they ever build it without anyone knowing Gary, I asked?"

"Well, it's like this Lisa; it was easy for they used a boring machine under the I-80 corridors."

"Believe it or not that Maglev train goes east to west and is built under the casino that has been vacant for years. It goes under an abandoned old truck stop and then under the truck inn. Was it not strange to you that those buildings stayed abandoned and why they never sold? And think about this Lisa, why was the price so high?"

"You're right dear," before I could answer Gary said, *"There was no way that they would have let anyone buy that property. Tell me Lisa, about that old abandon railroad building?"*

"You know Gary that it was sold to the city of Fernley for only $2.00 about 20 years ago. It was strange that the city only had to pay that small amount for it and someone else had a bid for two million dollars on it. The cities excuse was that they wanted it to stay historical and qualify for a government grant for the city. You know politics, Gary."

"Yes, Lisa that explains it, but now you know the real reason. They wanted to keep the old railroad station and move it after the sell and someone here knew that they could get millions if they sold the property and was paid to keep quiet.

And that they did Gary! I bet you anything that the woman's body that was in the morgue, whom they tried to push off as your partners body was the real estate gal that sold the property and she knew the secret to the underground train station."

"Yes Lisa, you are starting to think like me now."

"Well Gary, let me finish."

"Okay Lisa."

"Well, it was getting so hot that they needed her out of the way Gary."

"Very good Lisa"

"But I have other reason Gary."

"Go ahead Lisa."

"Whoever bought it wanted it moved to another location, and they wanted to keep the old railroad station and move it after the sale."

"Where did they move it to Lisa?"

"I heard that it was moved behind the old 'Treecuts Estates' in Fernley."

"That's it Lisa."

"What do you mean Gary?"

"Well Lisa, it's a clue."

"What kind of clue Gary?"

"The Maglev has an automatic program code with a chip in it, I bet my snakes tail that the key is hid in the old railroad station. Why else would they go through the trouble of moving an old railroad building?"

CHAPTER 23

"Something else I need to tell you Lisa," Gary said
"And what is that Gary?"
"The missing key was a mole that was only what the organization wanted everyone to think and I believe that they gave us a fake key Lisa."
"Gary, do you mean to tell me my life is in danger and I am being chased and almost killed for a fake key?"
"No other way to answer this Lisa, but to say yes. But if my partner had any brains he would not try and throw Knuckles, off in your direction. He just did not use his brains, and that is why he is dead today Lisa, but just remember Lisa I love you and never would of allowed him to ever put you in danger but I was in the hospital still in the coma, when my partner, started sending you the roses."
"One more thing Lisa," Gary said to me,
"I don't want to hear any more Gary, I am sick up to my head in disbelief and angry that this all happen."
"Well Lisa, I understand." we were about 15 minutes to Fernley, and Gary started to speed up to speeds of 75 miles an hour.
"Slow down Gary, we are bringing attention to ourselves going this fast."
"I think it's too late Lisa." as we heard sirens and he looked in his rear view and saw a NVHP trooper with his lights flashing.
"Gary, are you going to pull over?"
"Yes Lisa." as he pulls over to the side of the road and looks in the rear view mirror and sees the trooper pulling his gun out as he is walking towards the big rig.
"Gary, what are you doing?" as he pulls his gun out and puts it inside of a newspaper on his lap.

"Just be cool, Lisa. I will do the talking."

"Yes Gary," Lisa says.

About that time the trooper is getting closer and closer to our truck and Gary is watching him still in the rear view mirror as he gets closer to us.

All of a sudden Gary yells at me and says, *"Lisa, get in the back cab on the floor board quickly all heck is going to break lose."*

At this point I did not argue with Gary and made a nose dive into the back cab and covered my head in my lap. A moment later the trooper had his gun pointed at Gary and says, *"Hands up or I'll shoot."*

"You don't recognize me, do you Gary?" Not giving Gary a chance to answer him. *"Guess what? I have been following you two since you landed the jet"* he chuckles. *"I am the famous third brother of Knuckles, we are triplets, ha! ha!"* as he brags to Gary,

"Have you heard the name Thumbs? Well that's me you smart two legged snakes!" he snarls at Gary then he yells! *"Bye bye"* as he cocks the gun.

"Okay" Gary says, *"I have something for you too"* as Gary pulls out his gun from underneath the newspaper and I hear **Bang! Bang!** and shoots Thumbs.

Thumbs falls over dead and lands on the step of the truck. Gary opens the door and pushes the body off of the truck with the force of the door and floors it back onto the freeway, still having 10 minutes left to get to Fernley.

CHAPTER 24

"Gary, how did you know that he was not a real trooper?"

"Lisa, I have seen him before with Knuckles, but just could not place him till he got closer to us and I knew he was bad news."

"Dang, I hope that we get there in time before Knuckles and Starfish escape with my partners body Gary said. Once they are on the Maglev train, we will never catch them."

We are driving about 60 miles an hour and all of a sudden there is a large bang. The whole truck started shaking and weaving across the freeway.

"Gary, what is it? I said. *What is happening?"*

"I think that we just blew a tire, Lisa." As Gary pulls over to the shoulder of the freeway.

"Wait here," Gary said to me as he climbs out of the truck. A few minutes later, Gary gets back into the cab of truck and says, *"Lisa, It is a blown tire but it is the inside tire which we can still run on it."* He starts the engine again and pulls out onto the freeway, *"and besides we are almost to Fernley."*

"Gee Gary! if it's not one thing it's another."

"I know Lisa, but hey, look there is exit 48." as he pulls off the exit and heads to the underground Maglev station, *"Where is that old railroad station that the city bought?"*

"Aha, there it is!" I exclaim to Gary, *"Now pull into that parking lot over there to the right."*

"Let's go to that casino first Lisa, that is next to the truck stop. I believe that would be the entrance to the hidden Maglev station." he says getting out of the truck.

"Okay" I said, *oh shucks, I see a sports car, oh no! It looks like Knuckles, and Starfish, now what Gary?"*

"*Run Lisa,*" as he grabs my hand and heads towards the Casino's door. I could see at the corner of my eye that they were in close pursuit.

"*Gary, how do we get inside of the casino?"*

"*Well Lisa, if my hunch is right, all the codes for the organization are the same.*" as he punches in a code.

"*Thank God, it works*" says Gary, "*follow me into the room quick Lisa.*" as he locks the door behind us. "*This casino has two stories, brand new, and never used. Help me find the door that leads down to the secret Maglev station Lisa,*" he says,

"*Okay Gary, but we need to hurry, I can hear them now trying to get in the casino.*"

"*I know Lisa, hey look over there by that mural it's a picture of the Maglev train. It's in 3D now, look for something that would open up this wall on the picture.*"

Well it did not take Gary, long before he found a symbol of a gas can on the mural.

Gary said hey, "*The Maglev is not run by gas or diesel, it only runs on electricity and magnets on a guideway and not gas*" as he pushes on the picture of the gas can. All at once part of the mural opened to a huge platform of the secret Maglev station.

"*Follow me,*" Gary says to me, "*we need to hurry*" as we were making our way through the passage.

"*It looks like the mural is closing by itself, thank goodness.*" I said to Gary.

CHAPTER 25

"Oh My!" I said in amazement of what I saw was out of the future in this secret train station. I could see two guide ways in the middle of the station each going in different directions with a divider in the middle. They were high above the ground, and one of the Maglev trains were wrapped around a guide way. *"Wow! And no steel wheels like a regular Bart or Amtrak train or high speed rail."*

The color of the train sitting at the depot was white and had red trim and words which read on the side *(The Guidewinds)* *"Now where have I heard that name before?"*

Over on the sides of the station were elevators and escalators, going in both directions up and down. *"I thought that this underground station would be like the one that was in London but it looks somewhat different I said. Have you been to that one Gary?"* I asked.

"Matter of fact I was there last year when they had that fire at the King's crossing at the tube station." Gary answered.

"What do you mean a fire?"

"Well Lisa, that was built many years ago and they built the escalators out of wood. Well one day a commuter threw out a lighted cigarette and caused a bad fire which started on the wooden escalators. There were over 38 people killed inside the tunnel."

"Oh, Gary how sad."

"Yes Lisa, the guy was a transient. Now they have outlawed all wooden escalators."

"Sounds like it was a good idea Gary."

"Yes Lisa it should never happened again."

I pause for a minute and was looking down the long tunnel and then,

"What are you looking at? Hello!" Gary yells at me and says, *"are you okay?"*

"Yes Gary, I just cannot believe this" as I looked over the parked trains inside the station here and how beautiful these Maglev trains are. *"What a sad thing to keep this hidden from all the Americans, Gary."*

"Just wait until you see them in action and how fast that they can go my dear Lisa, and they hardly make any noise."

"I cannot wait Gary for one of them to come in the station here not only to see it moving but also to get away from Knuckles, and his gang. You know Gary; this is like being in the great escape"

"You are right Lisa, only we are the only ones escaping and not the bad guys.

"When will one of the Maglevs be here Gary?"

"Soon Lisa, soon," he said to me. Gary and I were standing behind some seats waiting and hiding out from Knuckles and Starfish, waiting for the trains to come in. It would be just a matter of time before Knuckles and his buddies would find their way in here to the secret station like we did.

I was getting impatient for the train and said *"Gary, how long do we have to wait for the train to show up?"*

"Not long Lisa, they run every five minutes and all the trains are automatic."

"Look Gary, here comes one now, wow! And more wow! I cannot believe this!"

"You are witnessing something that is so secret Lisa, and you can never tell anyone of what you're seeing today."

"I promise Gary, mum is the word." I tried to take it all in. This was like being in a dream but reality hit me real quick when I saw the gang found a way in and I yelled at Gary, *"Gary, they are here,*

"Sit tight Lisa," Gary said to me. *"Let's watch and see what they do, for they do not see us yet."*

"Okay." I whispered to Gary. *"The head-lights from the train in this tunnel are getting so close, Gary,"* I said.

"No worries Lisa, the train is only coming in at 50 miles an hour and this train Lisa, is a 10 car train. The train will stop and there is a 60-second timer before the doors close."

Gary looks back and says *"Lisa, there is Knuckles, and Starfish getting on the train about 5 cars back."*

After Gary said that we both heard a chime and the train door closes. *The train will start in a minute to pick up speed we have to get into the operators cab, "Now! Lisa move it! Quick, hurry"* as we were running towards the train. Gary then smashes a window of the cab so we can get inside of the Maglev train.

After we got inside and the train gained speed I said to Gary *"Now what? Knuckles and his gang are only 5 cars back what do we do?"*

"No problem Lisa, I have a plan."

"And what is that?" I said to Gary,

"I will separate the lead car from the rest of the train.

All these Maglev trains run independent of each other, so when Knuckles and Starfish think that that they are close to reach us, and then guess what Lisa?"

"What Gary?" I said

"They are going to be surprised," he said to me *"They will be left in the train tunnel in the middle of nowhere.*

"Well, Gary it's about time that we pull a fast one on them."

"Now Lisa this operators cab has a x-end at the back of this car and it is a button that will disconnect and separate the cars from the lead train. I will do that and you stay here by the y-end which is all the controls and keep an eye on them but please do not touch them."

"Okay Gary, I hear you loud and clear."

I see Gary, almost out of sight. Each car is really long inside. All of a sudden after Gary, gets to the back, I hear him say real loud. *"I'll be a snake's tail"* and I knew that could only mean one thing something just happened with the original plan.

He then yells, *"Oh my God, is it really you?"*

I could not help myself and I left the y-end just to see what all the commotion is about. He did not have to say a word, I took one look at this body, and I was shocked. It was his partner and oh, *"I don't believe this"* I signed, *"he is alive."* I said to Gary.

Gary says *"Lisa, get him some water quick."* as he's busy trying to untie his partners hands and is down on his knees with his partners head in his lap.

"He is close to death Lisa, we must save him and find out how he got in this operators car and by whom." His partner was in and out of consciousness at that point. I thought that this is crazy, but no time to think.

When I was approaching the Y-end again that was up front of the train. I saw this man that was dressed in a uniform. It was too late he already saw me and yelled, *"Stop or I'll shoot you lady. Raise your hands and do not move."*

"Okay, Mr. don't shoot me, I am just a poor little old lady who got lost."

"You should be able to think of a better story than that" he said to me.

"Who are you anyway," I said?

In a strong voice he said, *"I am a Maglev train supervisor. I protect and run the trains. Now who the heck are you?"*

"I told you who I am" I said. *My name is Lisa.*

He yelled again only loud enough that Gary had to have heard him I prayed.

CHAPTER 26

I was just trying to figure out what I should say next and he said to me, *"Is there anyone else on this train with you?"* And just as I stated to answer him, Gary made a noise from the back.

"Whose back there?" said the train supervisor?

"It's me Gary Brooks," came a voice from the back,

"Identify yourself!" the train supervisor said,

"I'm in the CIA and work as a double agent and we are working on a case." as he shows himself from behind the rear seat in the back of the train holding a gun aimed at the train supervisor.

"Drop your weapon Gary, or I'll shoot your lady friend."

"Okay," he says to the train supervisor, as he is reaching down without notice and pushes the x-end button that releases the cars on the train and then shows him that he is throwing his gun down and walks towards the front of the train.

"I have a wounded partner down and he is in the back of this car and I need some help Gary." said to him.

"Let's see some I.D. first" he says as Gary got closer to him.

"Okay," says Gary as he pulls out his wallet and digs in it for his I.D. *"Here is my badge and I am a double agent and my number is 10927,"* as Gary hands it to him.

"Okay, at ease" said the train supervisor as he studies Gary's I.D. and then puts his gun away.

"Now what can I do for you Gary," he said as he hands him back his card.

"My partner is in need of help. Please we need water and bandages."

"Okay, here is some water over here" and he hands Gary, a glass."

Gary went running to the back to give it to his partner and yelled at me to get the bandages and bring it back to him.

"Okay," I yelled while the train supervisor says *"Come over here and I will give you this first aid kit."*

I went running to bring Gary the stuff he needed to help his partner. *"Is he alright Gary?"* I said. I knelled down beside them, Gary is holding his partners head and giving him water.

"Here Gary, let me help, I have had first aid training in college."

"Okay Lisa, but lets get some more water down him."

"Well, Gary have him take it slow and easy don't let him drink it too fast."

"Yes Lisa I will." Gary said to me

"Look Gary, he is coming around."

"Yes Lisa, and his name is Felix, I just never thought that he could have lived through all he has been through." and about that time his partners eyes open and stare at Gary. Gary then says to him *"Now don't try and talk yet, bro."*

With my first-aid training I told Gary to lie him down so I could examine him. I was feeling his pulse and breathing and checked for broken bones and reassured Felix that he would be alright.

I said, *"Gary get me a wash cloth or something to wipe this blood off with. I saw a butler's tray up by the y-end, there should be towels."* At the same time I rip off the bottom of my blouse to use as a tunic and was wrapping it around Felix's arm.

"Wow! Lisa, I am impressed that you know so much."

I looked at Gary and said, *"'ditto' that goes for you too. Now hurry get me what I need."*

In the meantime the train supervisor was checking all the controls and shouted, *"Hey what happen to my other cars on the train?"*

Gary yelled back to him, *"I had to disconnect them for the men that we are after were chasing us and I needed to get Lisa, safe from them for they wanted her, so the best thing to do was to disconnect the train car that they were in until I could get Lisa safe and then go back and capture them knowing there was nowhere for them to go."*

"Now that was smart thinking." the train supervisor said to Gary, *"but there is one thing that you forgot about,* he said

"And what is that?" Gary said.

The train supervisor pulls his gun out and yells at Gary and me, *"Hands over your heads and no monkey business. I am no more of a train supervisor as you guys are. I work for Knuckles and Starfish and they used themselves as a decoy while I hid in this operators car, and I get the lucky job of killing you two, now turn around so I can put a bullet in your heads."* as he snarled at us.

"Oh Gary what do we do?" I said in a shaky voice.

"Just turn around like he says Lisa, I will figure out something."

"You better hurry Gary." I said.

I could hear him cock the gun at us and thought it's over with. I heard three shots fired towards us, but when I realize that we were not hit by the gunfire, we both turned around and saw the guy lying dead in front of us.

From the back of the train car was Felix holding a gun and had shot the guy in the back before he could shoot us.

"Felix, where did you get the gun?" Gary asked.

"It was in the aisle Gary."

"Oh, that was my gun that I threw down earlier when he first saw us here." Gary said.

"I woke up just enough to see what was going on and I saw my chance when I saw your gun lying there, so I grabbed it and that crook never knew what hit him." Felix said.

"I thought that we were dead ducks." I said to Gary and Felix as I was still shaking in my boots.

CHAPTER 27

"Felix you sure saved our lives and I want to thank you." I said,

"No problem Lisa, I am just so sorry that I had the roses sent to your place."

"Yea Felix, that was dumb" Gary said.

"I knew that they had their eye on Lisa's place and I just thought that they would come steal the roses, and not bother Lisa." Felix replied.

"Did you really send a fake key in the roses Felix? My last call to the department said that it was fake but Lisa and I found the plastic bulb and whatever was in it went down her kitchen sink."

"I never had the key, Felix." said to Gary.

"What Felix? The department gave us a key the day that I was with you."

"That's what I thought Gary, but when you and I separated that day I went home and opened the package and low and behold there was just a note inside that said, 'Decoy' so I assumed they wanted someone in the department to think that they gave us the key."

"But you did send her two dozen roses, to Lisa, right?" Gary said to Felix?

"No, I never sent her two dozen roses, only one dozen."

"You got to be kidding Felix," Gary said

"No! I'm not" Felix said to Gary

"But," Gary said *"what about the plastic bulb that Lisa and I found with the roses?"*

"My roses that I sent to Lisa were just that, one dozen roses, that's it!" Felix said.

"*Now we have too many unanswered questions,*" Gary said, "*# 1, what was in the plastic bulb?*"

"*And # 2. Who sent the other set of roses? And why?*"

"*And we have no one we can really trust in the department. God, help this Country. It all may have something to do with the High speed rail, China, and Maglev, that we do know.*"

"*Well don't forget about Knuckles and Starfish.*" I said to Gary

"*Well Lisa, he is working with that bad Warden from the prison.*"

"*You know Gary, if we could find out who his friends are in the department we may just find the leak!*"

"*Lisa, you are brilliant why didn't I think of that?*" Gary said?

"*You do have a few things on your mind Gary, and we still have Knuckle's, and his brothers to deal with that we left in the tunnel.*"

"*True Gary.*" I said

"*I have a plan Gary.*" said Felix.

"*Well Felix, I am willing to listen to anyone right now. Tell me your plan? We are listening to you.*"

"*First of all Gary, we are almost to Washington. The train will be there in 10 minutes. I want you and Lisa, to lay low, maybe go to a motel for a few days until you hear from me.*"

"*Boy that sounds good to me Gary.*" I said

"*Yes, it does Lisa.*"

"*But what about you Felix?*" I said, "*You're supposed to be dead?*"

"*Knuckles doesn't know that I am still alive Gary.*"

"*Yes Felix and we need to keep it that way.*"

"*I have a friend in Washington Gary, that can give me a disguise and no one will recognize me.*" Felix says to us.

"*Okay Felix, you talked me into it and Knuckles and his gang are still stuck in the tunnel and cannot go anywhere and Lisa and I could use a few days of rest.*

CHAPTER 28

"Gary, look we are coming into the station and it says **Welcome to Washington** as the train slows down and stops.

Gary says to me, *"Lisa, hold my hand in case there is trouble."*

I reached for Gary's hand and he grabbed me real tight as he puts his arms around me, as we were ready to leave the train Gary says to me *"I love you Lisa, with every ounce of strength that I have left and I will guard you with my life. If there is any troubles pretend that you don't know me, okay?"*

"Are you nuts Gary?" I said.

"No Lisa, just in love that's all."

"I'm just a part of this as you are Gary, and I am here for the home run."

"Well, that is fine Lisa" Gary says as we were stepping off of the train.

"Well Lisa, there is other part of this operation that you should know" Gary said to me as we were walking down the side of the Maglev.

"Yes Gary, I'm waiting."

"This is the way it is Lisa," as Gary got real serious with me. *"China will soon have a vacuum tube Maglev that will run at Mach 3, which means 3 times the speed of sound. They have already built underground tunnels going all the way around the world and underneath the ocean. They will own the world."*

"What do you mean Gary, they would own the world?"

"Think about it Lisa, with this technology and speed they could attack our Country anytime or place that they desire. We would never be safe. No more borders to worry about and check points."

"Gee whiz Gary, is there anything else you forgot to tell me?"

"Not right now Lisa, we need to concentrate on how we get out of this underground tunnel. We will continue this when we get to our hotel room."

"Look for a door that looks like a mural maybe it is the same at this end."

"Okay, Gary but don't go too far from me."

"Not on your life Lisa."

"I see an elevator to the left Gary, and it has a mural next to it."

"Good job Lisa, that may be are way out." and we headed towards the elevator.

"Look Gary, there is a picture of a gas can on it."

CHAPTER 29

"*Yes Lisa, I see that, but also look here, there is a map on the wall.*"

It has the old map here of the street called Embassy Row, Thomas Jefferson had plans of cities such as Paris, and Amsterdam, that he brought back from Europe in 1788.

"He never got to name them that but designed and envisioned a garden lined Grand Ave. and it is one mile wide and is now called **The National Mall** I bet this underground train station is underneath the mall! Here in Washington"

"Is that a good thing for us Gary?" I asked

"Of course it is Lisa we will be close to the underground safe that we need to find, which I believe that we are sitting on it as we speak."

"You got to be kidding Gary!"

"No Lisa, it's all coming together now. The dozen roses that my partner Felix sent to you was a fluke, now the second set of roses was a clue."

"How so Gary?" I asked.

"Well Lisa, it's like this, look here there are 12 steps leading to this map and each step has a red rose on it, now follow me Lisa, as we walked up the stairs."

"Now look for something red, aha, see the boutique of red roses painted on the wall? And the red gas can next to them?"

"Yes Gary." I said excitedly.

"Oh Lisa, I think that we found the underground safe. Stay close to me as I push the gas can on this map."

"Gary, you are so smart to figure this out."

"Well Lisa, don't pat me on the back just yet."

"*Gary, I thought that you knew where the underground safe was already?*"

"*No Lisa, we only knew that it was somewhere in Washington.*"

"*Now hold my hand Lisa,*" as Gary pushed the button. A second later the wall started moving and oh, my goodness we are inside and then the wall closes with us inside. I thought to myself, sure hope that we can get out of this tomb when we are ready.

First thing that we saw was a giant portrait of Col. Leone hanging on the wall; It was almost like a billboard it was so large. All the walls were lined with ruby and silver and bricks made out of gold. It was just so beautiful, I almost was speechless and so was Gary.

In a distance we saw the safe that was surrounded by bars, and the next thing we saw was unbelievable, leading into the safe was a guide way for the Maglev train, it was almost like a train guide way to nowhere.

As Gary and I took all this in and a few moments of silence, Gary busted out laughing and laughing.

"*Gary, what do you find so funny?*"

"*Lisa, I think that we screwed up!*"

"*What do you mean Gary,*" I said?

"*We just left the Maglev train that could automatically take us to this underground safe; it's a highly classified code that we put in the computer on the Maglev trains console. Then the train will automatically go to this underground safe and open it with a click of the button.*"

"*But we need the code. I bet the code was sent in that second set of roses that you got and is in the plastic bulb that went down your kitchen drain back in Gilroy,*" Gary said to me.

"*We got to get back to Gilroy immediately.*" Gary said excitedly.

CHAPTER 30

"Let's get out of here now Gary, it gives me the creeps, even though it is beautiful and someone spent a lot of money on this operation."

"Do you think that China had this build Gary?"

"Well Lisa, It wasn't the high speed rail people. Not much doubt in my mind that China had this built besides who else would have enough money for a project of this size?"

"Follow me Lisa; I think it's this way."

"Okay, Gary, but wait a minute my shoe is coming loose" I bend down to tie them and I looked over to my right I saw a man hiding behind the benches over by the stair case. I acted like that I did not see him and I motion to Gary with my hands.

He got the hint right away and moves and waves his hands to tell me to get in front of him. I followed his instructions as he headed behind the benches and grabbed the man by his neck and said to him, *"Make one mistake and your dead."*

He then pulls the man to his feet and pushes him into the wall and he falls to the ground. Gary pulls his gun out and points it at him. The man had on a long overcoat on that was brown and faded and wore a red beanie cap that was pulled down over his eyebrows. He had trousers on him that were stained with dirt and very long on him. Gary yells at him to get up.

"Okay, comes a soft young sounding voice" We both look over at him surprised to find out he was a small Chinese man dressed in men's clothing.

"Who are you young man?" Gary says to him. *"And what are you doing here?"*

"You are a long way from China," Gary said.

He looked at Gary and said in low voice, *"I just wanted to see the National Mall and look for my Father, my name is Hua,"*

Knowing some Chinese Gary says, *"His name means mean's magnificent!"*

"Magnificent" I said, *"in what way?"*

The young boy says to me, *"Hua, Shanghai, Hangzhou"*

"Lisa, he is saying that he is from Shanghai. He seems to have enough english to understand our questions."

"Okay Gary, then how does this tie into the Maglev?"

"Don't ask any more questions Lisa, I have enough to ask Hua."

"Lisa, go to that snack machine over there and get this young man something to eat."

"Okay Gary," I head over there and dug some change out of my pocket. I found some chips in the vending machine for him and brought them over and gave them to him. He pulled the bag open and held it up to his mouth and swallowed them so fast I thought that he would choke.

"Get him some water Lisa, I saw a water bottle down behind that garbage can."

"Okay, its coming." as I ran over and picked up the bottle of water.

Gary, gave him a chance to inhale the chips and water. I said to him, *"We will not hurt you Hua, we just need some answers, alright? How did you get down here Hua,"* Gary asked?

"I followed some Americans, and hid in the Maglev box car and before I knew it I was here in Washington D.C. we flew fast like a bird."

"How long have you been here?" Gary asked him.

"Maybe two weeks." he said

"No wonder you are hungry. Now tell me son, what you know about Maglev trains?"

"Nothing" he said, *"besides I now know that the Maglev trains fly faster than birds on a feather. My father never came back from your Country when he was over here last month and I came here to look for him and knew he had been to the National Hotel. There is a saying*

in my country *"A tree node may have at most one parent. A node with two parents is the root of the tree, and a node with 1 child is a leaf on the tree"* I am the only leaf left to our tree until my father comes back."

"We will help you get out of here." Gary said to Hua follow us.

CHAPTER 31

"Look over there Lisa, there is a ramp going downhill. Let's try that route."

"Okay Gary," I said *"I am right behind you two."* The ramp went down gradually and had a handrail that I could use. We went down for a few hundred feet and then I said *"Look over here Gary, there is a well that has a hand pump and wheel on it. Why would they have a well inside of a secret tunnel Gary?"*

"It is here probably to transport water inside of the guide ways. I have read some information on this and this also means that they could carry water to any place in the nation. I also bet anything that this well is tied into the ocean. Like I said Lisa, they will own our County along with all the others."

"Okay Lisa and Hua, stand back while I turn the hand pump and crank the wheel."

We both took a few steps back, and Gary went to the well and cranked the wheel. All at once the huge door swung open. We all stood there and were looking around the room which looked like we were in another underground room. Someone came up from behind us and said something in Chinese and Hua said, *"It's a guard and he told us not to move or he will shoot us."*

"Thanks Hua," Gary said.

"Now he is telling us to throw down our weapons," Hua, said to us. *"Do what he says Gary, for they will shoot and ask questions later."*

Gary proceeded to drop his gun.

The guard said a few more words to us in Chinese and Hua said *"You better turn around he wants us to face him, but do it slow."*

"Okay," Gary said *and I agreed.*

We all are now facing the guard

93

CHAPTER 32

A few minutes later they hauled us off to this dark dungeon room and locked the big brass door behind us and I can remember Hua, saying *"Do not be afraid Lisa."*

He must have realized how nervous and scared I looked. Maybe like the way he was looking when Gary, was pointing the gun at him earlier.

"It is a saying in my country Lisa," Hua, said to me, *"Always look towards the stars it will gave you answers. The moons will show you the way out."*

Not knowing what the heck he was talking about, I just nod my head at him in agreement.

There were only 2 cots in there and a toilet. I was praying that we would get out of there before we had to use any of them. It was very dark and cold in this room with only the brass bars and no windows. Gary had put his arms around me to keep me warm which did help me ease the cold. We stood there and I just could not help myself except to cry on his shoulders. *"It's alright Lisa; we will get out of here."* Gary says.

"Where have I heard that before Gary?"

I Guess I should have never said that to Gary, I could tell that it must have hurt his feelings.

"Sorry Gary, I have a big mouth sometimes."

"It's alright Lisa, I understand."

Hua yelled, *"Here they come Gary, just play it cool and I will do all the talking."*

"Go Bro," Gary said to Hua!

Here comes two guards dressed in olive green two piece suits, and carrying their rifles over their shoulders, and then comes another two guards with guns. The guards starting yelling at us and saying *(hu you Hai Ding)* in Chinese, I whispered to Hua, *"What are they saying?"* and he says, *"They are asking me if I am harboring a fugitive?"*

"Meaning us, Lisa" said Gary, *"and what are they saying now Hua?"*

"I just said to them 'Sum Ting Wong,' meaning that's not right."

"Now I whispered again, to Gary, "Do something before they shoot us."

"Watch this Lisa; I'll see if I can speak some Chinese to them."

"Oh no, forget it Gary."

"No Lisa, I can do this and get them away from Hua and he cannot translate to us anymore for they are pushing him in the corner." All of a sudden Gary yells at them and says *"Chin Tu Fat,"* to the guards.

They stopped interrogating Hua, and looked at us and started laughing and laughing at us. Gary looked over at Hua and said, *"Why are they laughing at us?"*

Hua said, *"Do you realize what you just said to them Gary?"*

"Not really Hua!"

"Well you just told them that you think that they need a facelift. They thought that it was funny."

"Fa Kin Su Pah," meaning (Great) Gary said to them.

Well Hua told Gary, *"At least that came out right."*

"Now no more Gary, or you will get us in 'Dum Fuk'"

"And what does that mean Hua?"

*"It means **stupid man**."*

"Just get us out of here Hua" Gary says

"Okay," Hua answers and says, *"Please just get me back to my people."*

Now the guards are moving in closer to us and Hua says to them, *"Wai So Dim,"* meaning (It's very dark in here).

"Kum, Kum," they said to us and made us follow them to other room. After we were all in there they had us sitting at a table, and they took Hua and put cuffs on him and led him away.

"Oh no," I said to Gary, *"Now what do we do?"*

CHAPTER 33

We watched as Hua, was being taking away. They left only one guard who was on the outside of the room now and we were left alone inside with just a table and four chairs.

"*Gary,*" I said "*I cannot help but think about what Hua said to me in the other room.*"

"*And what was that Lisa?*"

"*He told me that it was an old saying in his country, and said* **(Always look towards the stars, it would give you answers, and the moons would show you the way out.)**"

"*Gee, Lisa, that is too simple, he was trying to tell you something.*"

"*What do you mean Gary?*" I said.

"*It's part of an old Chinese proverb, that often have a hidden if not double meaning.*" Gary said to me.

"*Wow! Gary, I had no idea.*"

"*You know Lisa, what he said to me when you were behind us going down that ramp?*"

"*No Gary, what?*"

He said "**(Drinking the water of a well, one should never forget who dug it**.) *In other words he was saying to me, always be grateful to those who help you succeed.*"

"*Now we just need to put this all together Gary,*" said to me.

"*If you wish to know the mind of a man, listen to his words.*" Gary said

"*Meaning, you can tell much about something just by what they talk about.*" I said to Gary

"That's it Lisa, we need to put our heads together now. Look around this room and tell me what you see Lisa."

"I see a dirty ceiling, but hey look at the ceiling Gary, those specks look like stars, don't you think?"

"Yes, Lisa and the three light fixture looks like moons."

"Remember the moons will show you the way out?" Hua, said to me, *"right Lisa?"*

"Yes, Gary I remember."

"Lisa, help me bring the chairs over here underneath the light fixtures. We will put the chair on the table now Lisa, hurry before the guard gets in here."

Gary was on the table and feeling the three light fixtures that looked like a set of moons, and as he felt them he whispered, *"Lisa, look the light fixtures are moving, hey it's a way out. Climb on the table Lisa and I will lift you up and into the opening."*

A minute later I was crawling into this opening, and Gary after getting me up there then proceeds to pull himself up with a little help from of me when I grabbed his hands and pulled him up. We both could not believe where we were! We were back in the underground Maglev tunnel and boy luck was with us for a Maglev train just pulled up. We ran towards it and it was heading west, so we knew that it would take us back to Fernley, Nevada.

It was about one hour into our trip and we heard a noise coming from the baggage car that was right below the lounge room on the train.

"You wait here Lisa; I will go and investigate the noise."

"Gary, what will you use for a weapon?"

"No worries Lisa, I have a black belt in karate and hold a credential in martial arts."

"There you go again Gary, holding out on me.

"Quiet Lisa, now I will return in 5 minutes and if not lock the lounge door,"

"Oh Gary, you worry me so much." I told him as he gives me a kiss on the forehead and heads down stairs.

He was not down there 3 minutes and I heard a bang, bang, and I heard Gary, yell at me and said *"All is okay Lisa, and then he starts laughing real loud. Lisa, come here you will not believe this.* " so I hurried down the short stair case and here was this lady, in a red dress and a red scarf over her head and one wrapped around her neck. She was standing in the corner like she just saw a ghost. I thought to myself boy! poor thing she sure is ugly I said to myself. I looked over at Gary, and said. "*What is so funny Gary?*" as he continues to do an assessment on her, she did not seem to be able to muddle a word, or maybe the cat got her tongue

"*Lisa, what is different about this lady?*" Gary says.

So I looked her over real well and then it hit me. "*This lady has a man's watch on.*" I said to Gary.

Lisa, I think that we just found Felix, remember he was headed to get a disguise and told us to go to the hotel for a few days.

"*What Gary?*" I said.

"*The watch gave her away or I should say him away.*"

Gary, yelled at him and said "*Felix, Felix, is it really you?*" He pretended not to hear Gary, and finally Gary said, "*I had enough now Felix, tell me what happen to you?*"

I guess it was a few minutes later and he started to speak, in a very soft tone. "*Gary, I did not want anyone to see me like this.*"

"Well, *tell us what happen to you.*"

"*I went to my friends place to have a disguise made up since I was supposed to be dead. I told them I had to look real different, and they kept saying 'real different' and I would answer them yes, 'real different' and I cannot afford to be whom I am.* "Well to make a long story short *they had me get undressed and had me lay on the table and that was all I remembered until I woke up and when I did I had a set of boobs, and found myself castrated.*

"*I wanted to kill them, well guess what? I took a gun and shot them both, now they cannot reverse the operation. So I found this underground tunnel saw the train and crawled inside of it and wanted to die.*"

"*One good thing Felix, your wife already saw a dead corpse of a woman at the morgue when they wanted her to identify you as deceased.*"

"*Well for now Gary, if I showed up at my house looking like I do, she would shoot me herself.*"

"Don't worry Felix, we will find you a doctor to reverse the damage."

"Thanks Gary,"

"No thanks needed my friend."

We brought poor Felix upstairs to the lounge and gave him a stiff drink. Gary tried to comfort him as he cried repeatedly about being a woman.

"You know Felix; it will come off easier than it went on."

Felix agreed and seemed to calm down.

"When we get back I will call this surgeon that I know and I am sure Felix that he can make it right."

CHAPTER 34

"Well Gary, I wonder just what Knuckles and Starfish are up to trapped in that tunnel?"

"You know Lisa, that's a very question. I just hope that the Department is on their way to capture them before they figure out a way to escape from being trapped in the tunnel on that Maglev train."

Little did Lisa and Gary know what was happening with Knuckles and Starfish.

Back in the tunnel Knuckles tells Starfish. *"Gary thinks he has us trapped in this tunnel. Boy, I have news for him."*

"And what's that?" Starfish says to Knuckles.

"Well Gary thinks that without a lead car we cannot go anywhere, Ha ha!" says Knuckles to Starfish. *"That is what everyone thinks."*

"What do you mean Knuckles?"

"Well, being in prison all those years did not go to waste. The Warden gave me many updates and reading material that he got from China and Germany about Maglev trains and how they operate and I had years to study them."

"This is what I know." Knuckles says to Starfish, *"I will show you my brother how it works."*

"I'm watching." says Starfish.

"Okay" Knuckles says, *"We are on the y-end of a Maglev center car and there is a control panel inside, that means that I can control the Maglev train at full speed. I can program the on-board computer and set it to 40 and then the train will take us to Washington D.C."*

"You got to be kidding Knuckles?"

"No way, Hosea!"

"Now Starfish this is what we have to do. Look over there to your left and you will see an automatic cabinet, it's a power panel box. Now make sure that all ATP power switches are off. Got that Starfish?"

"Yes Knuckles, but slowdown will you?"

"We have not even gotten started yet you dumb Starfish, you knuckle head, you piece of a fish."

"Off with the name calling Knuckles, or you can do this yourself."

"Okay, but we better hurry Starfish for there is not much time left you, doe doe!"

"Now select the ATP power switches and make sure that they are on, do you hear me Starfish?"

"Ya, Ya now what?" Starfish asks.

"Now make sure Starfish that you leave the key switch off."

"Just a minute Knuckles, you don't have a key to this Maglev train, now do you?" says Starfish.

"Just don't worry your ugly little, or I should say big head off." says Knuckles.

"I will hot-wire the key switch Starfish, when we get ready. Now there is a little more to this, now listen to me very carefully for I will only have time to say it once." Knuckles said to Starfish.

"Okay, now you must remember Starfish, that the Maglev train is in (wake-up mode) for only 30 seconds until you press length verify display. Are you with me Starfish?" Knuckles asks.

"Ya, Ya now what?" asks Starfish.

"Okay, to get this Maglev train going, the next step is key on (after I hot-wire it) which would be (MCS) which stands for Master Control Switch to auto reset. Now you will need to press (hold door close bar), then press verify T.L. just for (5 seconds) then I.D. destination 40 and train length (9). Now Starfish, do you understand everything I have been telling you?

"Yes, you old beaded fart." he says to Knuckles.

"Well guess what Starfish? There is one more important fact that you must do."

"And what is that you Knuckle-head?"

"*One more remark like that Starfish, and I am leaving you alone in this tunnel because I will not need your sorry body anymore, ha! ha!*" says Knuckles.

"*Now Starfish, let's get serious and please hear this loud and clear you must leave the data log off.*"

"*What do you mean Knuckles?*"

"*Dude, a data log records everything that the train does, even when its off, now if the computer shows its off, well dude its really on. Got that dumb shit?*"

"*Now let's get this done and then I will explain more since your brain is so small.*" Knuckles says to Starfish.

CHAPTER 35

"Now, one other thing Starfish that you need to know."

"And what is that?" He asks Knuckles again?

"Okay, there is a chance that the computer can go off line." Starfish

"Well, that is just great! Then what should I do?"

"Starfish how can you be so stupid? all you have to do is reboot it" Knuckles says.

"What do you mean reboot it Knuckles? This isn't my home computer, dude"

"Just pretend that it is Starfish, now what would you do if your home computer quit working?"

"That's easy Knuckles; I would throw the whole dumb computer out the window. In fact I have done it before that's if I don't shoot it first."

"Your more than nuts Starfish, no wonder you have the name Starfish, you are certainly not a star and you smell like fish all the time."

About that time Knuckles and Starfish are facing each other and Starfish, makes a fist and swings at Knuckles, and hits him so hard it knocks him down on his knees. Knuckles, proceeds to get up off the floor and comes back with a head lock around Starfishes' neck and says, *"One more move like that and you're dead."*

"We are running out of time Knuckles says." as he releases the head lock and pushes Starfish across the room.

"Now listen to me Starfish, if this Maglev train computer goes off line you only have a few seconds to do something. I want you to reboot it by re-selecting the leader ATP which is (auto train performance) now do you got this Starfish?"

"Yes, Mr. Knuckles, Go on."

"*Okay, then simultaneously you push the Togo of the leader and back-up off. Now make sure that the lock-up guard is up, and then go to leader and select-new leader.*"

"*I would give my eye teeth if I could have a new leader at this time.*" Starfish says to Knuckles.

"*Well Starfish, it ain't going to happen. Now listen boy,*" Knuckles says, "*remember #1 Is the leader, #2 Is the back-up. #3 Is the leader. Then repeat over.*"

"*That is just great Knuckles, and you expect me to remember all of this?*"

"*No I don't Starfish, you would be lucky to remember your name.*"

"*Then why are you trying to teach me all this confusing stuff? Knuckles.*"

"*Because there ain't nobody else on this train, you dummy.*"

"*Quit calling me names, you hear?*" said Starfish.

"*Whine, whine you knucklehead,*" Knuckles, says to Starfish.

"*One more thing Starfish that you need to know,*"

"*And what is that?*" says Starfish.

"*Okay,*" Knuckles says, "*now if you have a blank LCD screen which is (Liquid Crystal Display) you will need to:*

#1. Check the contrast control knob. Then I want you to:

#2. Ensure AMTC (automatic train control)

#3. Then check the ATC automatic train control circuit breaker, and make sure that it is on.

"*Now Starfish that's all you have to do.*"

"*You are kidding, aren't you Knuckles?*"

"*Now Starfish, would I be kidding about something as serious as this?*"

"*I guess not Knuckles, but I have one question for you.*"

"*What is that Starfish?*"

"*Where the heck will you be when I am doing all of this?*"

CHAPTER 36

"I sure hope that I have taught you enough Starfish to run this train?"

"Just don't hold your breath Knuckles. I still want to know where you will be and why you cannot help me?"

"Do I have to draw you a picture Starfish?"

"Give me a break Knuckles. I have been putting up with you since you were born. Mom always told me that you had the brains, and I had the looks."

"What Starfish? Did mom really tell you that?"

"Yes," she did Knuckles *"Well guess what Starfish? She told me that I had the brains and the looks and that you would not amount to anything whatsoever. She even told me that she made Dad get clipped because you were so ugly and she did not want anymore and with us all being triplets she figured she had enough brats."*

"You sure know how to run down our Mama, God rest her soul." says Starfish.

"Wait a minute Starfish, do you hear something?"

"If you would be quiet I might be able to tell you Knuckles. Yes, Knuckles, look it's another train. What do we do now?"

"You learn how to pray you knuckle-head."

"Yea, maybe we are on the wrong side of the fence, Knuckles?"

"Jiminy Christmas Starfish, it doesn't take a rocket scientists to figure that one out."

"Quick Starfish, Key on, key on!"

"Starfish go ahead and hot-wire it." says Knuckles.

"Okay, here is the (MCS) which is the master control switch. The destination 40 is already in. It's not working Knuckles."

"Did you press verify T.L. and hold for 5 seconds?"

"Yes, I did." said Starfish.

"It's about time Starfish that you got something right!"

"Ha ha, we are moving Knuckles."

"Okay Starfish, get out of my way." says Knuckles as he looks behind at the train car that was following on the other track.

"They will never catch us Starfish. We are moving at 360 miles per hour and they can only do 150 miles per hour."

"Why can't they go fast like us?" Starfish says.

"Well it's like this Starfish, the dumb fool agents got on the high speed rail instead of the Maglev."

"I saw the steel rails next to the Maglev guide ways when we stopped in the tunnel yesterday."

"I guess they use it for testing." Knuckles said.

"Testing what though Knuckles?"

"They just gave up on it, and for that reason is why it was kept secret and hush, hush."

"Our job for the prison Warden is to get the key for opening the safe that contains the patents and deliver the master plans. He has a chance to make billions of dollars."

"Does that mean Knuckles that the warden is working for China or the States?"

"Well your guess is as good as mine."

"Who cares anyway? Besides I plan on double crossing the prison warden and get the patents first and leave the country where they will never find me, hee,hee."

"What about me Knuckles?"

"Just do what you're told and you can come with me."

"Hey Knuckles, I just saw a shadow from the back of the train,"

"Quiet Starfish, I will look."

"Don't bother." comes a voice from behind and walks down the aisle with loaded pistol in each hand pointed at Starfish and Knuckles. *"Now put your hands above your head."*

"Okay, we will." as they stared at the stranger.

"Who the heck are you?" Knuckles says to the stranger.

"Wait a minute." Knuckle says, *"You're the famous Col. Leone, I have seen your pictures all over the place."*

"What Knuckles," Starfish says. *"Who is he?"*

"Why he is a very famous man in the underground world and is responsible for most of the Maglev's history. He can take a Maglev train and turn it inside out. "He also mentors all the big shots in the world and is a CIA agent and a crooked one at that and believe it or not he has a rap sheet longer than us."

"Shut up." the stranger said as he puts both guns in one hand and reaches down the inside of his pants leg and pulls out two knives and throws them at Starfish and Knuckles at the same time and said *"Make my day, if you can."*

CHAPTER 37

"What are you trying to do kill us" says Knuckles to Col. Leone as the knife got the arm of his shirt pinned to the wall

"I will do the talking and expect you both to listen to me for I will only say this once." Col. Leone says.

All at once Starfish started yelling, *"I'm bleeding! I'm bleeding"* With the knife sticking out of his leg.

"You'll be alright" Col. Leone says, *"Its only near miss and if I wanted you dead, don't you think I would have thrown that knife through your heart?"*

"What do you want from us?" Knuckles says to Col. Leone?

"Now if I told you Knuckles, that would be giving it away, right?"

"Probably so," says Knuckles, *"but tell me one thing Col. Leone.?"*

"Okay, I will give you one question," he says *"what is it?"*

"Who was on the other train? And why did they take the high speed rail instead of the Maglev train cars?

Col. Leone looks at Starfish and says, *"Well that is two questions, but I will give them to you."*

1. The FBI and the CIA Departments were on the train.

2. They took the high speed rail, because they are idiots and maybe they wanted me to look bad. Anymore stupid questions?"

"Yes, one more question." Knuckles says to Col. Leone.

"What do you want with us?"

"Besides you two being on the most wanted list in America, and now the Chinese are after you there is a nice price head on you both." says Col. Leone.

"But don't you have enough money?" Starfish says!

"It's not about money." the Col. Leone replied.

"You just said that we are worth a lot of money." Knuckle says.

"Now listen to me boys, and listen carefully." Col. Leone is losing patience with them. *"Your old prison Warden was busted for releasing you guys and for some other crimes. I just happen to know that he released you so you could get to the patents before Gary does."*

"You will be working for me now and not the Warden. Do you have that?" Col. Leone said to them both.

"You mean to tell us Col. Leone that your one of us?"

"Don't put yourselves up there with me you thugs." says Col. Leone

"Now you will do as I say, you will be put on the other train and put in security for a while. I want you both to be kept out of sight until Gary thinks you're both dead and no threat to him or that Lisa gal for they are headed back to Gilroy."

"I think that they will lead us to the code to get into the safe where the patents are kept. You two have just been in the way, slowing them down.

"Now we are almost to Washington D.C. my partners will put you back on the other Maglev and get you to our underground prison. You will be held there until I need you. Got that?" Said Col. Leone

"Guess it's better than you killing us." says Starfish.

"Shut up." says Knuckles, *"before he changes his mind."*

It was not long before Knuckles and Starfish were put on the other Maglev train and headed to prison, and little did they know that they may never get out but only if Col. Leone needed them.

CHAPTER 38

"Look Lisa, we are coming into Fernley, Nevada already."

"Wow! Gary, this is amazing how fast that we got here and all the way from Washington D.C."

"Yes, now we need to get some transportation to Gilroy, California."

"No plane this time Gary?" Lisa asks.

"No time Lisa, we can drive there in about 4 or 5 hours and besides no one knows what we are up to, not even Knuckles and Starfish."

"I wonder if your department picked them up yet from the tunnel where we stranded them?" Lisa asks Gary?

"Now that we are back to Fernley, let me give them a call." Gary said.

"Headquarters, this is #10927 Gary Brooks, reporting in. What is the status of the project tunnel?"

"What?"

"They got away?"

"How is that possible?" A few minutes later Gary hung up the phone and was shaking his head in disbelief.

"Gary, what happened and how could they get away?"

"Lisa, the department screwed up."

"What do you mean Gary?"

"Guess that Knuckles and Starfish figured out a way to start the Maglev and Headquarters told the CIA and the FBI to follow the Maglev. They did not know a difference between a Maglev and a high speed rail. Well guess what? The agents made the mistake of jumping on the high speed rail which only goes about 150 miles an hour and compared to the Maglev that goes double the speed. So Knuckles, and Starfish made fools out of the Department."

"They got away, but the odd thing is when the Department sent a vice squad to the hidden train station the Maglev train showed up but no Knuckles and Starfish. Strange but the department is checking to see if there are any more train stations they might of stopped at on the way from Washington D.C to this station."

"That is just terrible news Gary," Lisa said

"You are so right Lisa, but we have a job to do. Getting back to your place and finding that plastic bulb that may be stuck in your kitchen sink."

"Lisa, let's go to this truck stop here in Fernley by the exit and maybe we can stop a trucker and seize his truck."

"You want us to steal another truck Gary?"

"Yes, Lisa we need to hurry and no time to fool around. But first Lisa, grab that dress that you brought along that looks real sexy on you. It will be up to you to stop a trucker."

"Come on Gary, please think of something else."

"No Lisa do as I say, now take off your clothes and I will help you get ready."

"Okay Gary," I said as I pulled the dress out of my overnight bag. Gary helped me pull off my clothes and put the red dress on that was silk and had a V-neck.

"Gary, what are you doing to my dress?" as he ripped my V-neck down to my waist almost.

"Got to let them hang out Lisa, to get their attention and with a figure like yours we will be on our way pronto."

"Okay, now Lisa, let's get off this train and get up above ground we will be by exit 48 then I want you to stand on the corner and pull your dress up."

"What are you asking me to do Gary?"

"You heard me Lisa, Just above the knees and just enough to tease them."

"After they stop I want you bend over and then you tell them that you hurt your ankle and need their help to get into the truck. Then when they get out of the truck I will come from behind the brushes and knock them out."

"Gary, you are sick!"

111

"*No Lisa, this works every time, haven't you seen this done in the movies before?*"

"*Okay, Gary, anything for you.*"

Gary stood back and looked at me when he finishes ripping my dress and says, "*I will take care of you later and that is a promise and you look so beautiful Lisa, but please remember to smile for them.*"

"*Okay*" I said.

We made are way up to the outside and Gary, rushed me over by the truck stop and said "*Look Lisa, he is just leaving now get over there and do your stuff.*"

"*Ok, ok*" I said, not wanting to flaunt myself but wanting to please Gary.

Oh my, I told myself as I went over to the side of the road and lifted my dress above my knees. The truck driver squealed his brakes to stop short of me and hollows "*Hey young lady, Need help?*"

"*Yes please.*" I said as the truck driver got out of his truck so he could help me. Gary came up from behind and hit him over the head and out he went.

CHAPTER 39

"Gosh Gary, is that poor man going to be alright. You hit him pretty hard on his head."

"Don't worry Lisa, he will remember that he took one look at you and thought that he died and went to heaven."

"Come on Gary, be serious"

"Yes, Lisa now get in this 18 wheeler truck quick before he wakes up." as I climb into this huge truck I could not help but feel sorry for this old timer.

"Gary, I am glad that you pulled him off to the side of the road so other truckers would not hit him."

"Lisa, not to worry, that trucker will be okay."

"Gary, I am glad that the roads are still good and no snow."

"Yea Lisa, going over this summit in a semi-truck in the snow is pure torture. China is so much a head of us with their trains that carry freight, passengers and 18 wheelers. The Chinese have been doing it for years."

"How did they get so smart Gary?"

"They didn't really Lisa, our American scientist had invented it and China was smart enough to steal it from us. They knew that our government was not interested in it until it was too late."

"No wonder the Maglev patents are worth billions of dollars."

"Yes Lisa that is why they are after us knowing that we may have the key. I really believe Lisa that they will not try and kill us before we give it to them, so what I am trying to say is we are safe until then."

"You know Gary that does not make me feel any better at this moment."

"I know Lisa," Gary said to me.

"Just 30 more minutes Lisa, and we will be at your place and it will just be getting dark. We will park this truck down the street at that dead end where that old warehouse is and no one will see this truck for a while."

"Sounds good for me Gary, I am really tired and need some rest."

"You sure deserve it Lisa Brooks."

"What did you say Gary?"

"I said Lisa Brooks."

"Is that a proposal Gary?" I asked.

"I love you Lisa, Yes I want to marry you when things settle down and you are a very brave and smart women Lisa, to go through all of this and still have your sanity."

"Why Gary I am just as insane as you are." as I teased him back.

The time went by fast and here we are already. Gary proceeds to park the truck and then we both jump out and race to my place around the corner. *"Oh Gary, it is so good to be back home after all we have been through in the last few days."*

"Yes, I agree with you Lisa."

We just got inside the door when I looked around, I could not believe what they did to my home. It had been ransacked and stuff was everywhere my clothes and my dresser draws at been thrown and tossed around the room. All my stuff in the kitchen was on the floor and broken in pieces.

"Gary" I cried, *"How could they?"*

"It's alright Lisa; we will clean it up in the morning and then call the plumber."

"I really want to get to bed." I said to Gary

"That is what I was thinking." Gary said to me, as we made are way towards the bedroom and kicking stuff out of the way and that was a challenge in itself.

CHAPTER 40

"Well, at least the bed is in one piece." I said to Gary,.

"Yes Lisa," Gary replied. *"It looks like everything from the bedroom ended up in the living room."*

"Yes, but that bed sure looks good" and about that time I just collapsed on the bed and that was it before I fell asleep and all of a sudden it was morning. It looked like Gary put a blanket over me while I was sleeping.

Gary was still sleeping like a baby so I crawled out of the bed real quiet and went into the kitchen and put on the coffee and then started cleaning up the mess.

A few minutes later I get a phone call, *"Hello"* I said, *"Hello, hello"* well there was no answer so I hung up the phone. A few minutes later Gary, comes walking out of the bedroom rubbing his eyes, and says *"Lisa, who was on the phone? That is what woke me up."*

"Oh, Gary, it was nobody. I just picked up the phone and kept saying hello and then they hung up on me."

"Lisa that only can mean one thing and that is they wanted to see if you were home."

"I am sorry now that I answered it Gary."

"It is alright Lisa, they would of found out later."

"Listen though I want you to get me a wrench and a pair of pliers. I will disconnect the elbow under your kitchen sink and just maybe that plastic bulb got stuck in it."

"Okay, Gary let me check in the bottom kitchen drawer. Ah, here they are Gary," as I handed them to him.

Gary gets underneath the sink and says, *"Hand me the wrench Lisa."*

"Here it is Gary," as he reaches for it.

"I need the pliers now Lisa."

"Okay Gary, here they are."

A few minutes later he had the pipe apart and found the plastic bulb lodged in the elbow. Gary, leans on the side of the sink to pull himself up and says, *"Look Lisa there are some numbers carved inside of this."*

As I looked inside of the bulb I could read it very faintly but it was there. *"Is that the code Gary?"*

"I think so Lisa; it reads 180E48 is that what you see?"

"Yes, Gary I believe that is what it reads."

"But what about the key Gary?"

"I think that there is a good possibility that it is in Fernley, Nevada Lisa, if you look at this code 180E48 which I think means 1-80 Exit 48."

"Your right Gary, but how does that help us find the key?"

"We just need to get back to Fernley and do some investigating. We need to pack up now Lisa."

"Well Gary, I am having a cup of coffee whether you like it or not."

"Go ahead Lisa, I will wait for you but pour me a cup also."

"You sure drive a hard bargain Gary," I said as I put coffee in his cup then brought him the creamer.

"You are a jewel Gary" said to me and then came over and gave me a kiss on the forehead.

"Lisa, soon we will be one. Just you and me and nobody to chase after us or wanting us dead."

"We will buy us a house in the suburbs that is yellow with a white picket fence and flowers and shrubs everywhere. Maybe a few pet dogs that wag their tails when we come home from work."

"Well that all sounds good and dandy Gary, but what about kids?"

"What about them Lisa?"

"Well Gary, you do want children don't you?"

"Yes Lisa, I would love to have a little girl that looks and acts just like you."

"Oh Gary, that is so sweet to say that."

"Well I mean it." Gary says to me.

CHAPTER 41

We finished our coffee and I went into the bedroom to gather more clothes and put them in a bigger suitcase.

"*Gary,*" I yelled from the bedroom, "*Please wash the cups and turn off the coffee pot and make sure you put the grinds into the garbage, okay?*"

"*Yes sir,*" he yells at me sarcastically.

I just laugh to myself and thought he sure is a keeper.

It wasn't long before we found Gary's truck that he had park a few blocks away from my house the last time we were here and I was surprised that they didn't haul it away after all this time.

"*Hey!*" Gary yells as we are walking towards his truck. "*It is still here Lisa.*"

"*Yes Gary, and thank God we have regular transportation now and we will not stick out like a sore thumb.*" I said to him as we approached the truck.

"*Right Lisa,*" Gary says, as he open the truck door for me and I climb inside of it. It was a long drive back to Fernley, Nevada but we had quite the conversation about our future. Just all positive stuff and I was feeling like a million dollars by the time we made it back to Fernley. I must have fallen asleep because Gary, said "*Lisa wake up we are here. We got to get down into the secret Maglev station here and put that code into the computer on the Maglev trains console. Then the train will take us all automatically to the underground safe.*"

"*But Gary, how do we unlock the safe? We have no key.*"

"*Not sure yet Lisa, but I have a hunch that it will be close by.*"

"*Sure hope that you're right Gary!*"

"We shall see," Gary says as we were climbing out of the truck.

"Let me carry your suitcase Lisa." as we rushed towards the secret Maglev station. We found the wall mural again that was in the casino and pushed the gas can fixture on the mural and then made are way in the passage."

"Look Lisa, there is a Maglev train over there that is across the guide ways follow me."

"Okay" I said as I followed behind Gary

"Now remember Lisa, that there is a 60 minute timer, make sure to be inside of the Maglev before the Maglev train door closes and it's for safety reasons, and especially since there are no drivers and all the trains are automatic.

"I'm right behind you Gary," I said as we boarded the Maglev train.

"Okay, here goes Lisa" as he punched the code numbers into the Maglev trains console. *"Look Lisa, it works!"*

"Wow," I said to Gary *"this is awesome to finally be headed to the secret safe."*

"Yes Lisa, so true and all we have to do is wait." Things were going great for a while as the train was traveling so fast.

"But wait Gary, what is happening?" as the light outside got darker and darker.

"It's alright Lisa, looks like the Maglev took a different route."

"What do you mean Gary?"

Gary looks in front of the lead train and says, I*'ll be a snake's tail.*

"Oh No!" I exclaimed, *"That can only mean one thing, we are in trouble."*

"It will be alright Lisa; I think that we are now in an airless tube and traveling about 620 miles per hour. You remember little Hua? Lisa. He said the reason that he followed his brothers inside the secret Maglev station was to see if he could find the airless tubes."

"Yes." I replied.

"Well it looks like we found them before he did and I bet it is leading us to the underground safe."

"But where will we end up Gary?"

"Well Lisa, I hate to tell you this but I think it's taking us to China?"
"Oh my," I said *"to what extent is all this true?"*
"Just look at it this way Lisa, who else do you know that could find a secret Maglev station and a secret code, and end up in China?" Gary said to me.

"Too funny, I thought to myself and he must be joking"

CHAPTER 42

"Gary please stand-by me for there is this weird feeling that I am feeling."

*"Lisa it is only the **G-force** that you are feeling for we are traveling so very fast."*

"I sure do not like this feeling Gary", I said

"You will get used to it Lisa besides the new jets now travel over 700 miles an hour and there is something to be said about that."

"Your right Gary," I said as I snuggled up closer to him. (I thought to myself that everything will be alright and that we will have this mission over with soon.)

"Gary it only seems like an hour when the Maglev took us inside of this vacuum tube that we are in and now it looks like we are moving so very fast."

"Lisa, I think that we are in the Bohai Sea, you can see the ocean through the cracks of the air-less vacuum tube."

"Excuse me Gary?"

"Well Lisa, it looks like this train will bring us near Laolongtou, and that is the eastern beginning of the Great Wall which extends into the Bohia Sea in China."

"How do you know all this Gary?"

*"Well I found this map over here and it actually shows where this airless vacuum tube goes. I am beginning to think that the secret safe may be in China, and hidden in the Great Wall. There is also a Chinese proverb that says **He who has never been to the great wall is not a true man.** In other words Lisa, it means if you do not visit the Shanhia Pass, you will not understand the true military power of ancient China."*

"*Well Gary, I do remember another old Chinese proverb.*"

"*Really Lisa and what might that be?*"

"*I heard it while we were held hostage by the Chinese gang and one of them said 'A bird does not sing because it has answers. It sings because it has a song.' "I had no idea what they were talking about for they were leaving the room as they were talking about this Gary.*"

"*Good ear Lisa,*" Gary said.

"*Maybe they were talking about Hua?*" I said to Gary?

"*That could be Lisa, and I did feel so bad leaving Hua there with them. I sure hope that they did not kill him. He was a good boy.*"

"*Yes he was Gary. I sure wish that Hua was with us now since we are headed to China.*"

"*Me too*" Gary said to me, "*and a little something else Lisa that I would like to tell you but I did not say anything before, not wanting you to freak out.*"

"*Gary I am beyond freaking out so tell me and believe me I can handle anything.*"

"*Okay Lisa, I know I told you earlier that we are traveling at 620 miles an hour.*"

"*Yea, I remember that Gary*"

"*Well Lisa, would you believe that we are going 3000 miles an hour?*"

"*Oh that's all?*" I said and then fainted.

"*Lisa, Lisa wake up it's alright.*" Gary said to me. "*It was a joke!*" (But Gary knew that it was not a joke but did not want to lose me there in an air-less vacuum tube and thousands of feet under the ground.)

A few minutes later I did come too. "*Oh Gary, I just had a very bad dream.*"

Gary held me in his arms and said to me. "*I do love you so much Lisa, now please stay with me.*"

"*Well like I have somewhere that I can run too Gary.*"

CHAPTER 43

"Hey look Lisa; we are coming out of the vacuum tube thank God."

"Where are we Gary," I asked.

"Well looks like we are near Laolongtou, and this must be their Maglev station and the beginning of the Great Wall."

"Gary, look at all the people there must be 100's of them, men, women, and children."

"What are they doing Gary?"

"I don't know Lisa, but look we are passing the station. The train is going to take us to the hidden underground safe. The crowds are not even looking at us and it looks like they are just staring ahead."

"Yes Gary, just like zombies, this is unbelievable. Where are they going?"

"Good question Lisa, but we have enough of our own problems now. I do know that the great wall was eventually abandoned after the wall proved unsuccessful to keep out the Mongol Nomads. They did do fortifications established in new areas from the Qin Walls. Now these walls are 25ft high and 15 to 30 ft. wide at the base made large enough for marching troops or wagons, or . . ."

". . . Maglev trains." says Lisa.

"That is right Lisa; someone knew many years ago that someday China would own the first Maglev train, even if it meant stealing the ideas from Americans."

As we approached the Great Wall, the Maglev slowed down and a huge rock wall suddenly moved and clearing the passage so the train could get in. I could see in the distance that at one time there was an old abandoned guard station and watch towers that stood by but then it looks like they have been rebuilt from the Qin walls. Things are looking up I thought has the train came to a sudden stop.

"*Quick Lisa, follow me the doors only stay open for 60 seconds before they close again.*"

"*I'm right with you Gary, lead the way.*"

We just stepped off the train and looked around the huge underground station that brought us to the underground safe. All of a sudden we are surrounded by troops yelling, "*Dui Tou! Dui Tou!*"(*Enemy, Enemy*)

"*No, no we are friends.*"

"*Lisa, its no use they don't understand you.*"

They came over to us and tied our hands behind our back and with guns pushed in our backs they led us away to a dungeon. We were brought to this cold stone room with a throne setting in front of us. All of a sudden this small Chinese man came over and stared at us and said to the guards, "*Shu Ren, Shu Ren!*" (*Friends, friends*).

Gary and I looked at each other and all of a sudden this small Chinese man came over and we looked at each other in amazement, we both recognize Hua, at the same time.

"*Hua,*" said to us "*I had to make sure that it was you before I could tell them that you were my friends.*"

"*Thank God Hua,*" Gary said and I agreed as I shook my head.

Hua looked over at the guards and said to them, "*They came from Guo Wai.*" (*Abroad*) "*On the Ju Xun Lian*" (*fast train*) "*They are my Shu Ren*" (*Friends*) "*They Jie Yue*" (*saved me*). "*From Dui Tou.*" (*Enemy*)

After Hua said that to them they all left the room. Hua went ahead and untied us from the rope and said that he was so sorry.

"*It's alright Hua,*" Gary said, "*but how did you escape from the Chinese gang?*"

"*You will know soon my friend.*" Hua, said to us. "*You will be taking to a nice room tonight and giving a bath and fresh clothes and then you will be invited to the sanctuary my friend.*" With that he left the room.

Gary and I both were speechless and just smiled at each other as we waited for the guards to come back.

"Here they come already Gary," I said.

Two guards not pointing guns and two Chinese women behind.

"Gary, what are the Chinese women for?"

"You will find out soon Lisa" as we made our way out of the dungeon and walked about 2000 ft. and came to these double gates. The gates automatically opened up. What we were about to see next was literally beautiful it was a round room with a huge hot tub spa in the center. It had marble floors and walls, and all gold faucets and beads of multicolor hanging down with golden bells and beautiful green ferns with water falling off of them like a mist flowing through the plants. I could hear the sound of a waterfall in the other side of the room.

A few minutes later about 4 more Chinese girls came out and all they did was smile and started to take off all of our clothes. I looked over at Gary, and he gave me a really big smile. I could hear some kind of music playing in the background. A minute later the girls were washing our bodies with lavender and a sweet smelling soap. I have to admit, I've never been given a bath before it sure felt good. I think that Gary thought the same thing as I looked over and saw how much he was enjoying it.

CHAPTER 44

The baths lasted about 40 minutes and I do admit that they were awesome. They dressed Gary, and me in red and blue silk robes and cotton socks for are feet.

"I think that we looked pretty good in these robes." I said to Gary.

"Yes Lisa, we look almost like the Chinese."

We hugged each other and could smell each other with the clean smell of scent.

It was not long before two Chinese women came for us and we followed them into the Sanctuary. They are known for being a safe house which sounded good to us. It was just the most beautiful setting that I had ever seen with incense, candles, and metal trays with holes in them setting on a marble table.

A statue of Guan Yin and Taoist Deities stood on the right and left of us. They were known all over East Asia. I remember that from my history class in high school. We were waiting for Hua, who a few minutes later walked in. He was dressed in a gold robe with a crown on his head.

"Lisa," Gary whispered to me, *"he is the Emperor of Shanghai."*

The candles were being lit by two Chinese boys about 12 years old.

"Gary," I said, *"what is that middle candle for?"*

"Lisa that is called a wish candle and it sets there in front of the incense burner."

"Watch they are lighting it now," I said to Gary.

A minute later Hua got up and said to us. *"Confucius says, to have friends come from afar is Happiness, is it not?"*

About that time all the Chinese women and guards bowed to him. Not knowing what to do we just sat there and took it all in. Wow! Who would have thought that Hua was the Emperor.

Hua says to us, *"My friends I have a story to tell"* as he continues, *This is a short story called,* **Pot Calling The Kettle Black** *and goes as follows, Mencius said to King Hua, Let's use fighting's of a battle as an example. After a fierce engagement, the soldiers threw down their armament and retreated. Some soldiers retreated 50 paces, other 100 paces. Those retreating 50 paces laughed at those who retreated 100 paces. What do you say? The King replied, no. Even if one does not retreat 100 paces, it is retreating nevertheless."*

Then Hua stood up and says, *"We both have retreated we shall work together for the Ju xun Lian" (for the fast train)* we all lower are heads and agreed and bowed to each other.

"He wants to work with us Lisa."

"Yes," I whispered *"I figured that one out,"* As we were ushered to another room now.

CHAPTER 45

We were anxious to get to our room. We both needed some sleep for we had been up for 24 hours. I also was feeling a little weird since the airless tube and Maglev that we were in was traveling at speed of over 3,000 miles an hour, it was just the idea of that would make anyone feel different. There were red velvet curtains hanging all around with tassels of gold and silver. A very tall poster bed and canopy top that had the red velvet on it. There was an office in the other room connected to ours that had a desk and I could not believe the picture that hung over the fireplace.

"*Look Gary, at the picture*" as I pointed my finger at it.

"*Lisa, you know who that is don't you?*" Asking surprised.

"*Why yes Gary that is Col. Leone. And why would his picture be hanging here in China when he is an American? In a secret underground tunnel? That is next to the underground safe?*"

"*Good question Lisa, something is really fishy about this whole thing with Col. Leone.*"

"*Last I heard he was supposed to help capture Knuckles, and Starfish.*"

"*I wonder what ever happened. Headquarters said that he was in Fernley, at the underground Maglev station last that they saw him.*" Gary said

"*Hum*" I said, "*that is suspicious, don't you think Gary?*"

"*Why yes, Lisa and wish that I knew his ties to China.*"

"*Maybe we can ask Hua,*" I said to Gary

"*Just maybe he wants to use that air less vacuum-tube with a Maglev train inside and send it into space? I have heard that this Great*

Wall of China is over 5,500 miles long and cannot be seen from space. He could do a lot of dirty stuff up there in space and no one would be the wiser."

"*You know Gary; I am too tired to figure this all out tonight."*

"*Me too Lisa, let's get into bed and solve the world problems tomorrow."*

We both crawled into bed and kissed each other goodnight

CHAPTER 46

The night went faster than I wanted it to and before we knew it was morning. Two Chinese girls came in with a silver tray with two cups of tea for us and put on the coffee table. One of the girls opened the shutters for us to let the air circle through then came over to the bed and help me get my robe on and the other girl went over to help Gary, get his on.

I said to Gary, *"I could get use to this."*

"Yes me too Lisa."

A few hours later Hua sent for us. We followed the guards to the Sanctuary. *"Shu Ren" (My Friends) h*e said *"I hope that you rested well"*

"Yes Hua, thank you for your hospitality and a great night's sleep. Hua, may I speak freely to you?"

"Yes, Shu Ren" (Friend)

"We could not help but notice Col. Leone's picture in our room. What is his connection here with your Country?"

"Well," Hua says to us, *"It's an old Chinese proverb that says, (**A rat who gnaws at a cat's tail invites destruction.**) He is our Dui Tou (enemy) and we want our people to know to stay away from this white Xun Lian (Train) his nick name. We have his picture everywhere so our people will recognize him. He is a very dangerous man, but he has many friends in the surrounding cities and we believe that he wants to be the ruler of China."*

"Wow! Hua, and our people think that he is helping us find the missing key and he is supposed to be helping our government get our

patents back from the underground safe. I think Hua that the secret safe is here under the Great Wall."

"I have not heard that before Gary," replied Hua.

"I just know that Col. Leone taught me all I know about Maglev trains, and trained me in boot camp with the FBI before I became a CIA agent. It sure is hard to believe that Col. Leone could be so dangerous." Gary said to Hua.

"Yes Shu Ren," (my friend)

"Now tell me something else Hua, why did you really go down in the dumpster to the secret tunnel?" Gary asked.

"There was no one else that I could trust." Hua said, *"And I knew that I needed to know if all the orders I was giving out were being fulfilled."*

"So it was true that I got in the dumpster and got locked in and could not find the passage from this side to get out.

It was only when you came and rescued me and then the Chinese gang grabbed me and then recognized who I was and brought me back home knowing that I was the Emperor of Shanhigua

CHAPTER 47

"That answers a lot of my questions Hua, but what is going on inside of the train station? We saw many hundreds of men, women and children just staring straight ahead and walking like they were in a trance. Where are they going and what is wrong with them?"

Just when I said that Hua got very upset and started speaking Chinese to me and said *"Ta Men Yuan Zhu, we want to help Jie Yue them from Dui Tou."* Then Hua said *"Sorry, I hurt so badly when I think about my people that I cannot help what I said to you in my native language. What I said was, they need help and we want to save them from their enemy. It is the great white Dui Tou (enemy) named Col. Leone, Ju Xun Lian (Fast Train) is responsible. He is working with the Mongol Nomads who are ruining and killing my people. Things are changing fast in China now. A company called Chinacare is taking over is healthcare and they did an experiment on them. That is making them ride the Maglev trains non-stop. Some of my people fell into the trap. They promised them riches, and new homes and temples and in return all they had to do was ride the Maglev train and be a test subject."*

"But things backfired on my people when they were not allowed to think for themselves and when they did they were giving a type of gas that made them go in a trance. They would fill the whole train through the gas filter and then with it they had full control over my people."

"You know Hua," Gary said, *"this all might be tied into together."*

"What do you mean Gary?"

"It's like this Hua. Since we know that Col. Leone is the leader in this, it would not surprise me if this all ties into the secret where the key is for the underground safe and all the patents for the Maglev trains. It

could also mean that there is more than just the patents on the Maglev train that is involved here."

"I never once thought that it could be a possibility, but Gary, you could be right." Hua said.

"We will get them released from their slavery if it takes the Army to come over here and do it."

"Many xiexiexie xie (thank you's)" says Hua

"Don't thank me yet Hua," Gary said

"I will say (Dao) prayers for you my friend. Gary, I just remember something?"

"And what is that Hua?"

"There is a ghost key logger here. He made the first prototype in 1947 but is well known in his key making and I feel that he may be able to help you. He may know where the old one could be hidden. He is well known with the rulers of our Country but kept secret of his whereabouts. I do know that I can find him without too much trouble." Hua says to Gary.

"That would be very helpful Hua, I thank you so much. In the meantime let's get back to your people, I may have a plan," Gary said to Hua, *"To get your people out, but I need to know a few things, like how many trains a day and how often that they come through the Shanghai train station?"*

CHAPTER 48

"There are about four trains a day and just two of them make the stop here at Shanghai train station," Hua said.

"And what about the other two trains?" Gary, asked

"They are always for the officials that travel around doing check points." Hua replied.

"Okay Hua, but if your people are always on the train, who are the ones walking around in a trance?"

"They are the ones that will be taken into space in the airless vacuum tube that shoots like a cannon in the sky and they were hand picked out of all my people. They were the stronger ones of all that could survive a ride into space but like I said before, Col. Leone as no reason to return my people to earth."

"You know Hua, we were on the Maglev train and before we knew it we were in a vacuum tube and traveling at super high speeds and on are way to Shanghai, China. I saw the map on the wall of the Maglev."

"Then it is true, my Shu Ren (Friends)," Hua said, *"and I never really doubted it so much. When the Chinese gang brought me back here after they captured us, they put me to sleep and when I woke up I was outside my Sanctuary."*

"But Hua, how did you get to be inside of the underground sanctuary?"

"Gary, my father did all he could to get us this safe house sanctuary sealed off before any one was any wiser when he realize what Col. Leone was doing to our people. We tried to warn our people but Col. Leone, promised them riches and no more poverty."

"We were able to seize it before the Mongol Nomads arrived to fight my people and only the code could get you inside here with the Maglev train.

"We heard that the Chinese communism had the Chinese gang steal the key from the American scientists and we believed that they might of hid it in our sanctuary before we sealed it off."

"Col. Leone, is also looking to launch 300,000 tons of payload into orbit. He had a dream that the cargo—only version did not need rockets nor propellant to launch payload into space. He figured that it was like a Mass driver. It's all about the acceleration Gary, that can launch these mass vehicles into space or around the world or even underground."

"But Hua," Gary asked, *"why did the code end up being engraved in a plastic bulb that shows up at Lisa's house?"*

"It's a long story Gary, my father made a trip to Washington D.C and that is where he met Col. Leone, and they became great friends."

"Col. Leone, told my father at one time that he could help our people, through building this under-ground tunnel. My people worked for years on it until one day, while my father was headed to Fernley to catch the train back to China. On his second trip he had a bad feeling that something was not right but never made it back."

"What happen was his private servant was given orders to deliver the code through someone that they could trust from Washington. It must have been you Gary that my dad choose and his servant found and picked out who would be smart enough to make you wise to Col. Leone, and to make sure that someone besides me could rescue our people and get you the code."

"My father thought that the key was hidden here somewhere that is why we think Col. Leone harmed my Dad. He would not tell them where it was."

"Do you know where it is?" Gary asked

"I just know that it could be here somewhere. He had found out that Col. Leone, was not the man he thought he was, but it is believed that Col. Leone had him killed, however the servant and messenger got away. It is believed that the servant is still alive."

"Wow! Hua that is almost unbelievable." Gary said

"*Now follow me to my temple Gary, I have something that is written on the wall that I want you to read.*"

"*Okay Hua, I'm right behind you.*"

There on the wall was written, "***Don't go through life so fast that someone has to throw a brick at you to get your attention. God whispers in our souls and speaks to our hearts. Sometimes when we don't listen, he has to throw a brick at us. It's our choice to listen or not.***"

Now Hua says to Gary, "*Listen to these last words carefully.*"

He went on to read, "***He sends us a Sunrise, he sends us flowers.***"

CHAPTER 49

"Now what is that on the bottom of the wall, Hua?"

"It looks like it says Mian Mu (Look) to the Ri Chu (Sunrise)"

"See the Hua" (Flowers) "Remove the Zhuan"(Brick)

"Find the Guan Jian" (Key) "Would you believe this Hua, it's telling us where the key is."

"Yes Gary, it sounds like we are looking at the key and its right in front of us."

"Gary, come over here and help me remove this brick that the flowers are near and the artificial sunrise is upon it." "Wow Gary, Look at this one brick, it is kind of shape like a key that's made from the brick. Of all things Gary, it has a picture carved into it of a gas can!"

"That's it, that's it!" yelled Gary, *"Lisa, Lisa, come in here quick!"*

"What is it Gary?" I cried. *"Lisa, we have found the key!"*

"Now settle down Gary, it has been here all these years." says Hua.

"Okay," we are all here in the temple and the two Chinese girls watch on.

"Lisa, while Hua and I push on the brick, I want you to touch the spot where the red gas can is."

"On the count of three then," Gary says, as him and Hua remove the brick, and stare in the hole. Low and behold, here hides a golden key. It must have been 5in high and pure gold as Gary and Hua pulled it out in amazement. Gary picks the key up and falls to the ground and kisses it over and over.

Hua is yelling, *"Dao, Dao,"* **Prayers to God**

"God Bless America." I said to Gary.

CHAPTER 50

"Gary, you can let go of the key now," I said

"Lisa, we worked too hard to find this key and now we need to get to the indoor safe and unlock it. Then and only then will I put down the key".

Hua said, "You have the key now Gary but I think that the safe you want is back in Fernley, Nevada my father did mention something about an old abandon rail road station to his servant."

"Yes Hua that is what I was afraid of but why did you not tell me this before?"

"Would you of listened to me Gary?" Hua said, "And besides you didn't have the key."

"Now I see." Gary said, "And I probably would have not listened anyway."

"My friend, my father knew that this was not a safe operation. His private servant told me after my father's disappearance that he is the one that send Lisa, the 2nd set of flowers."

"He only sent the last dozen roses with a plastic bulb with the secret code engraved to use in the Maglev trains console and it would open our sanctuary here and lead you to me and my people and maybe you would find the hidden gold key that was here before we enclosed the sanctuary."

"Right" Gary said "and my partner Felix sent one set of roses to Lisa. Your fathers' servant heard about it but then it was too late."

"Yes Gary that is what I suspected and that is when the second set was sent to her."

Gary said to Hua, "So you knew more about this than I gave you credit for, right Hua?"

CHAPTER 51

"Yes Gary, I knew much more information about your project. You see my father sent me his messenger. So that I could prepare our people for the coming events our messenger was friends with one of your secret service man, who also disliked Col. Leone so news travels well to me."

"When I ran into you and Lisa, I knew that things would get better. I had to be sure about you and your motives first so I never acted like I knew anything. I believed that you and Lisa were a sign from my father."

"Well maybe so Hua, I know that you saved me and Lisa, from the Chinese gang too. We are so forever grateful."

"No problem, my Dua." (Friend)

"I hate to eat and run Hua, after all you have done for me and Lisa, but I must get back to the States and open up the safe. I have everything I need now. I promise that I will be back here when I wrap things up in Nevada and we will get your people free from Col. Leone and his bunch." said Gary.

"Okay," Hua said, *"my guards will make sure you get on the right Maglev that goes away from the Bohai Sea to head home, but you must wait till dusk when the last two Maglevs come through that carry the Mongol Nomads, they are so dangerous and well equipped with guns. You must always watch out for the great white Dui Tou famously known as (**Ju Xun Lian**) Col. Leone."*

"Yes Hua, we agree with you" said Gary, *"though I think that Col. Leone still thinks that he and I are friends."*

"Gary," I said, *"I will go and pack up and get your things in order also."*

"*Great Lisa, and don't forget to cover the gold key and put it in the brief case, it is big and strong enough to be used for that.*"

"*Consider it done Gary.*" Evening came real early that night and Gary and I met his guards at the entrance. It was not long before the Maglev came and Gary and I were on are way. It was almost too easy the way we boarded the train and not a soul around. We were the only passengers. Not even a train operator. Gary came over by me and squeezed me so tight I thought that he would take my breath away. "*Lisa, I love you so much.*" Gary said.

"*Gary I love you also,*" I answered him as we put our arms around each other and kissed passionately. "*Let's go to the room that has a lounge upstairs where we might even have some privacy.*"

As Gary helped me up the stairs he said. "*Look Lisa, here is a couch.*"

I replied to Gary, "*It looks like someone was in this room recently.*"

"*Well, they aren't now,*" as we snuggled on the couch.

With his arms around me I fell asleep.

CHAPTER 52

We must of been hours on the Maglev train and I do remember going back through that vacuum tube but all I did was open my eyes, and realized that we were in the tube by its darkness. I just snuggled up more to Gary, and closed my eyes again then the next time I open my eyes I heard,

"Lisa, we are here back in Fernley, Nevada"

"Thank God Gary; it is great to be closer to home."

We grabbed our things and headed down the short stair way. The train stopped and a few minutes later the doors opened. *Let's hurry Lisa and get out of this train station. We need to find the old railroad station, and find out where it was moved too.*

"Did you say Lisa that you grew up here in Fernley?"

"That is right Gary" I replied.

As we hurried to the mural on the wall so we could get out. Gary pushed on the wall while I pushed on the red dot. The wall then opened to the inside of the casino. A minute later, we were standing inside.

"Well" Gary said, *"Nothing looks different or out of the way here so now let's get going."*

"Your right Gary, I'm right behind you. Hey look Gary, it is still there as we both held on to the brief case that held the gold key and ran towards the truck."

"Now Lisa, where is this Old Railroad station that the City bought?"

"Well Gary, they moved it behind a street that was called Treecut Ct. There were acres of bare land that stood behind these homes. The

subdivision is called Treecut Estates. I was reading the article in the Reno Gazette. From what I read they had a heated discussion at the town hall meeting to remove the old railroad station that was moved to their subdivision. The new owner stopped it all and threatened the neighbors in taking all their homes by Eminent Domain and build a freeway through the Estates since the owner worked for the State, or some kind of public office or official."

"*Supposedly the buyer was going to use the station for working on mini trains like trains of the future, like the newspaper described the trains did not need to use tracks. It was like the train floated above the ground just like a bird. So all the homeowners backed off and it's been quiet for some time now."*

"*Lisa, that sounds like the Maglev train don't you think?"*

"*Yes Gary, and if that is the case. We are hot on their trail."*

It did not take long before we were driving through the Treecut Estates. The homes were a modest build and just a few looked different in the front. They had sidewalks and a light pole every few hundred feet. The homes were about 15 years old. Some painted a pale color and then some were bright.

We drove around in the Estates for about 15 minutes before we spotted some railroad tracks in the front yard of a home. It was freshly painted a pale yellow with brown trim, I must admit it looked pretty nice one thing Gary said *"What goes around comes around, I bet anything Lisa, that in the back yard will be the continuation of the tracks."* as we got more excited.

"*We will park here Lisa, behind this roll of mailboxes so not to be obvious."*

We jumped out of the truck quickly and got closer to the yard. *Gary* I said, "*It looks like a miniature train and railroad station. It even has a yellow lookout tower in his yard."*

"*Let's get closer Lisa, and get to the back of the yard."* We sure were in for a surprise when we look at his back yard. A large 6ft. fence was there but the gates had been left wide opened and we sure got an eye full. We could see some small train cars that you could ride on and a small make believe mountain that was gray and about 7 feet high and had some toy soldiers with guns guarding the outside of it and a tunnel with a box car in it. On the outside were small trains running around this small mountain. On the other side of the yard was an engine house guess that is where they work on the trains.

"Maybe Lisa, the hidden safe is in his tunnel."

"But Gary, who in their right mind would move something like a train station to his own home and yard and add all these extra buildings and tunnels and tracks?"

"Well Lisa, it could only mean one thing."

"And what is that Gary?"

"This man must be nuts! Or maybe that is what he wants everyone to think, if he is holding what I think it is. Just maybe."

"Say no more Gary."

"Who owns this property Lisa?"

"I have no idea Gary, but we can go down to the assessor office and find out. It's all a matter of public record."

"Let's get down there now Lisa, and then we will come back here when we have more information."

CHAPTER 53

It wasn't long before we were down at the Assessor's office. *"Look Gary, over there is one of those things that they call a computer."*

"Do you know how to work them Lisa?"

"Not really Gary, but we can have fun trying."

"But Lisa, don't we have to go through the clerk." Gary Said

"Not anymore Gary, they want to let your fingers do the walking." I said as I laughed.

He chuckled, *"Come on girlfriend."* Gary said to me. We both sat down at the computer and a clerk came over to us and said, *"Now if you need any help just call me over."*

"Thanks," we said to her as we sat down at the desk.

"We can look it up by the address Gary," I told Gary.

"Okay, Lisa, I remember that it was 707 Treecut ct. I remember because the owner had a sign from the back of the house with the numbers on it and I thought that was strange." Gary said.

"Okay, here goes." I said to Gary, it did not take but a few seconds before the owners name came up. We both just dropped are mouths so wide open and both yelled, ***"No way,"*** as we read the name of the owner.

Well we must of look like we just saw a ghost and made enough noise for the clerk came back over to us and said, *"Are you guys alright? You look like you just saw a ghost?"*

Well, we both just started laughing and said, *"Just a ghost from our past, that's all."*

"Okay, but please be more quiet" the clerk said as she walked away.

I started whispering, *"I cannot believe this Gary,"*

"Neither can I Lisa," as we both stared at the recording of the owner.

Gary *"Who would of thought that this older track home belong to Col. Leone? That was odd"* Gary said, *"Col. Leone owns the whole state of Texas almost and is working on California very interesting I must say."*

"Come on Lisa, I want to call Headquarters and see if Col. Leone is back from his assignment."

"If he is out of town we will go back with flashlights and do a search."

"What are you waiting for Gary?" I said. *"Let's go!"*

Gary and I rushed to his phone that was out in his truck. Car phones back in the 80's were pretty big. Gary, picks up his car phone.

"Hello Captain," Gary says, *"I need to know if you have seen Col. Leone lately?"*

"What, When?"

"Okay" Gary said and hangs up the phone.

"Well, Gary what did they say?"

"We are in luck Lisa," they said that Col. Leone was out of state working on a mission.

We arrived back at the house in minutes, hid the truck behind the old railroad station and made our way towards the fake tunnel in the back-yard of no other than belonging to Col. Leone as we walked closer to the tunnel I said Gary, *"Look, those toy soldiers guarding this tunnel looks like they are watching us."*

"Come on Lisa, you have seen too many movies," as we made it to the inside of the tunnel, but all we could see was the mini train tracks and an old abandon miniature box car.

"Lisa, help me push this box car out of the way towards the light of the tunnel."

"Okay," Gary, as I reach down to help him push the small box car in that direction. Gary, got on his hands and knees, and was feeling the train tracks. *"Hey Lisa, this section of this track is loose. Lisa, you hold one end and I will hold the other so we can pull this apart."*

Within minutes we got the tracks apart and Gary yells, *"Lisa, look at this. Another key only a lot smaller than the gold key that you and I found in China."*

"Two keys?" I asked Gary and looked puzzled.

"Lisa, this must go to something really important, why else would it be hid inside a set of train tracks?"

"Good question Gary," I said.

"Come on Lisa, let's get into this other miniature building that looks like a look out station and is two stories. I will take this key with us."

Gary opens the door for me and we walked inside.

"Wow, Gary it looks so real and look there is a high window there."

"Yes Lisa, something is not right here. I smell a skunk." Gary said to me.

CHAPTER 54

"A skunk?" I asked Gary.

"Yes, now Lisa, look around this room and look at this wood platform, it is on top of this dirt."

"It does not look that heavy" I said as I leaned over to help Gary, lift it up and place it against the wall.

"Hey, Lisa there is something here, it's like a round old bomb shelter cover and look, it as a key hole in it!" Gary says, as he puts the key in the lid and turns it.

We were not ready for what we were about to see as Gary yells, *"Help me Lisa to lift this lid off!"* I got close and we were lifting it off, and oh my! There sat an older Chinese man staring at us in a corner. There were a few stairs to go down as I followed Gary inside this bomb shelter or should I say tomb.

"We are your friends." Gary said to him.

"Lisa, go find some water for him."

"Okay," as I rushed up the short stairs and outside the tunnel I found an old plastic cup and also a water faucet I filled it up and ran back to Gary,

A few minutes later Gary, is holding the man up enough to drink his water. Gary says, *"What is your name old man? (Gu Fu)"* in Chinese, (something that Gary, must of picked up in China) Then Gary said, *"We are your friends, we come to rescue you."*

"My name is Yao, I am from the Royal family of Kuang, I am the Emperor of Shanghai."

"Do you have a son, called Hua?" Gary asked

"*Yes, that is my son,*" said the pale weak man. "*Is he held Zhi (hostage) also?*" asked the old man?

"*No Yao, your son is safe. He is in China in your Sanctuary. He is a very brave boy.*" Gary said to Yao

"*Listen then my friend,*" said Yao, "*there is another floor beneath me that holds much Americans.*"

"*How many?*" Gary asked

"*Maybe ten please help them.*"

"*Okay, Yao, I will*" said Gary, "*but how do I get into the other underground room?*"

"*Follow me my friend, and I will show you.*" said the very weak Yao.

CHAPTER 55

Gary tries to hold up Yao, he is weak but wants to take us to the other tunnel.

"*Where does this lead to?*" Gary asked.

"*I don't know.*" says Yao, "*I have never venture here before, for big white Col. Leone threaten me not to leave my room that he put me in.*"

"*You know this is not underneath you this is a side tunnel. You must be confused for being in here for so long Yao.*" Gary said

"*But I heard noise's coming from below,*" Yao said

"*I think what you heard was a vibrations of some kind.*"

"*Qu Gu Zhi Liad (I old man held hostage)*" he cried.

"*It's okay Yao, please do not get frustrated we will have you home soon.*"

"*Lisa, stay close behind us, we don't need to lose you my dear.*"

"*I am right here*" I said.

"*Hey look.*" Gary said "*We must be below the engine house and here is another rock wall that the train tracks are going into.*"

"*Gary they just lead into this rock wall.*" I said

"*Exactly Lisa, now lets see if the tracks are loose.*" Gary bends over and yelled, "*They are loose and yes Col. Leone is just like a dog in the way that he buries his bones or should I say his keys. Sure enough there is a key inside of this track.*"

"*That is sure a strange looking key Gary,*" I said as Gary pulls it out.

"*No Lisa, this is a train key it will get us inside this secret tunnel under the engine room. I will go back and get that box car that you and I moved out of the way. I really think that this key will work that train.*"

"*Hurry back Gary,*" I said.

148

"*It's not that far Lisa, take care of Yao, for me.*"

"*He is in good hands Gary,*" I said as he disappeared around the corner.

It was only a few minutes that we heard the vibration that Yao, was talking about.

"*Yao it's Gary in the train, the key started the train.*"

Yao said, "*That is the noise I always heard from my room.*"

Gary shouts at us as he approaches "*Get in the box car guys we are headed inside the wall.*" Yao and I climbed in the box car. As our train got closer to the rock wall the wall started moving and what we saw next was the best sight that we could dream of.

Here were all the Guidewinds people that Gary used to work with sitting on the cold dirt floor looking at us like they were in a dream.

"*I'll be a son-of-a-gun*" Gary said to one of the men.

He answered Gary and said, "*It took you long enough to find us Gary.*"

"*Well, Josh, you being the president of the company, and disappearing was suspicious to everyone. Are you all accounted for?*" Gary asked

"*Let's see, I see Mary, the Vice President, are you alright.*" Gary said to her.

"*Well,*" she said "*with you being here I feel a lot better and to know that we will be getting out of here.*"

"*And there is Nate, Sr. Vice President and how are you?*" Gary said to him?

He did not answer Gary. Josh, hollered and said "*Nate does not say much anymore.*"

"*This is the first time that you were lost for words.*" Gary said to him . . . And all Nate could do was nod his head.

CHAPTER 56

"Okay Josh how in the heck did you all manage to get captured by Col. Leone?"

"Well Gary, it was like this" Josh says, *"little did we know that he was the enemy. He asked all of us in my company to meet with him in Fernley, Nevada at the old truck stop on Hwy 80 and exit 48. He wanted to buy us all lunch and show us his home in Fernley, and said that he had bought an old train station and had it moved to his home, that is how we got here. When he was showing us this hidden room, he pushed Mary, into us and locked the door and we have been here ever since. He heard about our highly classified project and he thought that we were a threat to him. He then wanted us to merge his private company with ours."* We told him no.

"He told us that he had all his money invested in the high speed rail, and that the United States would never see a national Maglev route because he was planning on putting in the high speed rail all around the 1-80 corridor. He knew that the Maglev went faster than the rail so he switches paths so to speak after also seeing how advance that China was underground. Now he wants all the patents and master plans for the tubeless vacuum tube."

"Remember Gary, when you went to work for us, and the race was on for high speed rail or Maglev trains?"

"Yes, I remember Josh."

"The government hired Col. Leone to find the patents and master plans for the tubeless vacuum tube that goes to space. Well, little did our government know that Col. Leone was about to double cross them and the Chinese. You see Gary, since we have been held hostage here we

150

found out that Col. Leone, is the sole owner in the high speed rail. All his money is invested in it."

"The United States had nothing but the patents hid until they got stolen from the scientists and China got the patents. They were once hiding in the secret safe. Col. Leone is also responsible for bribing and lying to the Shanghai, Chinese about riches by forcing them in riding the Maglev trains."

"We know all about that Josh."

"Well Gary, a new drug is also being introduced. It all started with the big pharmaceutical companies wanting to test their new drug for travel sickness. During travel the motion your vestibular system senses doesn't match what you see, it's a conflict between the senses caused by travel."

"So you see Gary, they made something like Hyoscine Hydro-bromide to block the nerve signals by confusing them. It is better than any drug on the market today. It can also control the brain to do what it is told. If ever needed they would have access to a proven drug for mind control."

"The U.S. mainly wants it for terrorist's control, then they could send the bad boys back, so to speak and tell them what to do in other words it's a double whammy. We can then control the enemy."

"Now if Col. Leone can prove that their medicine works and has been tested on all this new technology with the Maglev trains, well then?"

"Why Yes Josh. I understand now." Gary said

"Col. Leone would be very rich again, maybe the richest in the country and be able to get the money needed to finish his high speed rail around the United States corridor or change directions again and go for the Maglev trains and he would rule the world. We also figured out that there is more to this."

"And what is that Gary?"

"Well Col. Leone is using their people to also test the ship into space and he plans to make it a one way trip for them."

"Oh no!" said Yao,

"No worries Yao," said Gary, "your son Hua and I are working together on this."

"You are the right chosen one that I had picked, Gary."

151

"*Why thank you Yao, we will all get out of this mess sooner or later*" Gary replied.

"*Boy Gary, Col. Leone sure has his hands in all the different pots*" said Josh.

"*Yes that is for sure. And did you know Josh, that there are underground tunnels from here to China? They have 4 Maglev trains running in them plus a high speed rail.*"

"*Yes, we have all heard Col. Leone talking about*" this Josh, said

"*Well speaking of Col. Leone we better get out of here before he returns.*"

CHAPTER 57

"Everyone line up and I will take you out, but this box car only holds three at a time. Lisa, you and Mary come with me first."

"Okay Gary," I said as I helped Mary get in the box car, she was pretty weak from not eating much.

It was about 20 minutes later and Gary had everyone out and huddled in the engine house together. All the Guidewinds people were so happy to be rescued from Col. Leone and his horrible dungeon. The lights were bothering their eyes so Gary said, *"Just close your eyes and hold hands as we make it to the truck. It's a good thing that I have the canopy on the pick up so you can all crawl in the back of it when we get to it. We have plenty of blankets."*

We made it to the truck and just got the last person in the back of the pickup and put Yao in the front of the cab with us. We covered him in a blanket and about that time Gary said, *"Lisa, both of you duck down, I see a car coming down the street and it isn't the Calvary coming, I think that it is Col. Leone getting back."* The sun was just low enough he did not recognize our truck as Gary passed his car.

"Gary," I asked, *"how close was that?"*

"Yes Lisa, God was with us that is for sure."

With a big sigh of relief I said to Gary, *"He sure will be surprise when he goes down to his hidden rooms and no hostages."*

"Yea, Lisa I sure would like to see the look on his face."

"Where are we taking everyone Gary?"

"Well Lisa we will stop at the hotel and drop the boys off and then we need to stop at the hospital in Reno, for Yao and for poor Mary, they both are in a poor condition."

153

CHAPTER 58

Gary had called Headquarters for a room at the hotel for all the hostages and also told them not to tell Col. Leone about the findings of the Guidewinds people and Yau. We pulled up in front of the hotel and told Josh, *"Don't leave your room or let anyone out of here till I get back from the hospital."*

"I have rooms booked under the name Mayfield's and clean clothing will be there for all of you and food will be delivered also. All you have to do is get the key from the front desk."

"You got it Bro," Josh said to Gary.

We arrived at the hospital and after checking in Yao and Mary. The doctors wanted to keep them both for a few nights for observation.

It was late by the time we got back to the hotel. Gary and I had adjoining rooms with the boys. After going to our room and taking showers and also getting in clean clothes we then knocked on the door between the rooms and went inside to check on the boys.

What a difference it made with them having showers and eating.

"Gary! Gary!" Josh said, *"How can we ever thank you my friend?"* As he comes over and hugs us and about that time they all got up and made a circle around us and started singing. "Onward Christian Soldiers" we all started marching around the room. There was joy of laughter and tears and praise to God. It was such a wonderful evening to share with them.

The next morning we had breakfast delivered to their room and went over to join them. We were all sitting around the table and

154

the conversation got real intense when Gary was telling them more about the underground tunnel with the Maglev trains and how a high speed rail was also underground.

"Gary, Tell me something?" Josh asked

"And what is that Josh?"

"If all the tunnels and train stations are built underground how did they do it so fast?"

"Okay, Josh I will tell you what I know, The tunnels were built using a (TBM) machine also known as a "mole" they use it to excavate tunnels with a circular cross section and that can go through a variety of soil and rocks.

"These were first used on a project called the **Niagara Tunnel Project** *the machines were used to bore a hydroelectric tunnel beneath Niagara Falls. They named it* **Big Becky** *it's a reference to the developer Sir Adam Beck."*

"It can also bore giant holes in the ground and that may be how Col. Leone dug the pit that you and your friends were in. They can also use these machines for nuclear waste. All these machines are better than in the old days when they had to use alternative drilling and blasting."

"Now that's a little history class that you gave us Gary." said Josh

"Well Josh, I hope that you understand some of this madness about the Maglev trains, but as far as I know they do not have the patents yet for they are hidden somewhere."

"That is why we were at Col. Leone's place, we found it by accident we wanted to know where they moved the old train station to and had an idea some of this was related, just did not know how. We were looking for the safe that held the patents and noticed that this house had mini trains and tracks that went nowhere."

"That is how we found you and your group and also Yao. Lisa, and I had to see what this was all about, then we went to the Assessor's office to find out who this home belonged to and when we found out that Col. Leone owned it, that is when Lisa and I came back, although we did not expect to find any hostages."

"Thank God you guys did," Josh said and all in the guys in the room agreed.

CHAPTER 59

"Now Josh, I have been in contact with Headquarters. They want you all out of sight until they can investigate Col. Leone for kidnapping, murder, espionage and the list goes on. They need you all for witnesses."

"We will be keeping you all in the secret witness program until they get the goods on Col. Leone. Headquarters will have an agent pick you all up by noon today."

"I wish you all luck and until we meet again."

"Okay" Josh says, "we will do whatever it takes to bring Col. Leone to justice."

"That's the spirit," Gary said to them.

"Thanks again Lisa and Gary," the boys said to us as we were leaving the hotel room.

"We need to find the safe that this golden key fits in and I was thinking Lisa, we have been misled some. We have been looking in all the wrong places. Let's face it someone had to have planned this whole thing. Now think about it, we have been on a run and have been chased by the worlds most wanted; we have been to China and back. We have been so close to figuring where the safe is that contains the patents and the master plan. We hold the golden key in our hands."

"Well Gary, what are you saying then?"

"It's like this Lisa, for an example the entrance to the tunnel in New York City can be reached through an abandoned elevator shaft that few know about. Then there is the Liyobaa cave in the province of Zapoteca, it was sealed off by catholic priests who believe it to be an entrance to **Hell**, it's called the village of Liyobaa or better yet **The cavern of death.**

156

"Oh my gosh, Gary that is terribly sad."

"I know Lisa, but the list goes on like the Maltese Cave located on the Island of Malta near the small village of Casal Paula. It started out with a homeowner digging a well. They ended up in finding some caves underground. They are now sealed off because 30 students and their instructor disappeared after going into the caves, search parties never were able to locate any trace of them."

"That is all too strange," I said to Gary, *"but what does this have to do with us and finding the safe?"*

"Well Lisa, it got me thinking. The safe that we thought was at Col. Leones place could have been a decoy. I remember that he was working on a project that involved the Twin Bored Tunnels near San Francisco. The tunneling went from 1-80 to North Beach using two tunnel boring machines, and it was approximately 7 miles long."

"And Gary, you think that is where he hid the safe?"

"Well Lisa what I know is that the (TBM) machine never made it out of the underground because of its size. There is a good possibility that the safe is hidden in this TBM machine and we have the golden key for it."

"We must get to San Francisco, Lisa."

CHAPTER 60

It was only hours before Gary and I was driving towards San Francisco, California.

"Lisa, there is so much that you do not understand yet. I have a friend that is a special agent inside of the FBI. We will stop and see him on our way to San Francisco. He lives in Santa Rosa, California and he could be quite helpful for us. He has all the latest information about the Boring machine and more."

"Well Gary, I said I might as well learn all I can for I will be so glad when all this is over with."

"I promise Lisa, we have almost completed this operation."

"Sounds good to me Gary."

"A few more hours Lisa and we will be in Santa Rosa.

"Lisa, I will let you in on a little bit about what my friend David."

"Okay Gary, go ahead."

"Well it's like this Lisa, The US Military Traffic management command which is short for (MTMC) and the supply depots, and special agents, and members of the joint terrorism task force; some were recruited for a special operation."

"And what was that operation Gary?"

"It was all top secret Lisa, not everyone knew at the headquarters about this. They had to be specially recruited and sworn to secrecy."

"They have found underground bases and tunnels across America, if not world wide. The underground Maglev is nothing compared to what I'm about to tell you Lisa."

"The special recruiters including truck drivers, and military people in charge of government shipments had to be convinced to take part

*in this infiltration operations. It was discovered that they have a new boring machine that is called the **Subterrene** from Los Alamos and it looks like a giant mole."*

"Wow! Gary, go on."

"Okay Lisa, Well it can burrow through rocks hundreds of feet under the surface and it heats whatever stone that encounters into like molten rock or magma, which coils after the Subterrene has moved on."

"Okay Gary, but what has this to do with the boring machine that we are looking for?"

"Well Lisa, that convinces me more than ever that they left the TBM machine buried underground because it does not lift a candle to this new machine called the Subterrene."

"Col Leone knew that it was outdated and he probably felt it was a good place to hide the patents, but all he needs is the golden key that we have and he never thought that we would find it in China."

CHAPTER 61

"Your right Gary," I said as we were getting closer to Santa Rosa, and I was about to meet David, the special FBI agent.

"He lives near the Napa vineyards west of Santa Rosa. In fact Lisa, last I heard he had bought 70 acres of beautiful land and had built his own winery. He started out as a mom and pop winery and built it into a large company with huge corporate holdings."

"Wow! Gary, I can remember when nanny and I used to use a fermentation process which is an all-natural process that only happens through the use of yeast as well as fungi, bacteria, and molds. The yeast uses the sugar as food."

"Nanny was a bootlegger? You never told me that before Lisa."

"Well Gary, we don't have a lot of time to chit-chat."

"Look over there at the rolling vineyards of thousands of grapes."

"I see it Gary, It is so pretty." I said *"I wonder if David will have my favorite wine?"*

"And what might that be Lisa?"

"Well Gary, I am not so picky. I would settle for any kind of Zinfandel's, maybe a little Chardonnay, and some crackers and Salami would really top it off." I said.

"We will put your order in Lisa, real soon."

It was only about 15 minutes later that we were going down a long private driveway that had white fencing on each side and covered with beautiful vineyards on each side of the drive way. Flowers and shrubs were decorated in the front of this beautiful ranch style estate.

When we got out of the car you could almost taste the wine. The smell of fresh grapes, and lemons on the lemon trees were close to the front of the house. They had a good scent that carried through the breeze which was blowing through the air.

Here comes David, rushing out of his home as we were approaching the front door.

"I'll be a snake's tail," he said to Gary *"Where in the world have been?"*

"Well David, I'll be the tails snake," Gary laughingly replied.

"David meet Lisa, she is like a secret agent for the FBI. I have her in training."

"Wow Gary, she is one beautiful gal. I could teach her a few things also."

"Now David, she is spoken for." said Gary.

"Ah," said David, *"I'm always day late. Come on in guys."*

Gary, held my hand as we walked inside to David's home. He had a warm fire going in the fireplace and sitting room as we walked by it and I had wished we could stop there but he took us out in the kitchen and said *"Have a seat. I am doing an experiment here."*

"You see Gary, I have invented these grow tubes, they are like mini greenhouses. They are especially made to work underground."

"So you know David about the underground Maglev's and cities being built?" asked Gary.

"Well Gary, it certainly is no secret and a lot of ruckus is going on inside the Department Headquarters," David said.

"Something about Col. Leone almost catching a guy called Knuckles, and his brother Starfish, it seems that he let them get away, but rumor has it that he put them in one of the underground prisons."

"Wow! David, I sure hope so, they have been chasing me and Lisa for months."

"That is right," I said to David. *"I hope that we never see them again."*

"Well, you two sure don't need any more trouble. From what I hear he set your house on fire."

"That is right David, and had Lisa not come along I would be dead now."

"Don't give me the credit Gary; it was the guy whose car was in the way when my car rolled down the hill at your place that called the fire department when he saw the flames."

"I know Lisa, but had you not been there and inside looking for me after the fire started, well let's not go there."

"Your right Gary, I am glad that it is behind us and only a few burns and scars to show for it." I said to him.

"Okay guys," David said to us, *"What brings you my way? I am just an old retired fart from the FBI."*

"What David? When did you retire?"

"Oh, about a year ago." he said.

"I had no idea David," Gary said

"Well, there are too many leaks in headquarters and I just got fed up with it one day and walked out and did not look back. I tried to keep informed because the department always calls me when they need something or for advice."

"Well, I can see why David, you were the top man in the department."

"Come on now Gary, enough flattery for one day."

"I have some wine that I want you and Lisa to try."

"Gee David, we would be glad." to Gary said, and I nodded my head in agreement. (*Oh yes, I said to myself*).

"Have a seat guys, I will show you my finest Pinot Noirs in the west," David said as he filled up are wine glasses.

"Tell me more about your Grow Tubes David," Gary asked as he sips on his glass of wine.

"Well Gary, it will provide distinct advantages without irrigation. It also provides moisture at the base from condensation."

"I hope that you will try and keep this private David for the underground world will steal it from you."

"They already tried that Gary!"

"What? are you kidding me David?"

"Now would I kid about something like that Gary?"

"Well what happen?" asked Gary.

"Well Gary if you must know it happened like this. Remember the project in San Francisco with the twin bored tunnels and we were using the boring machines?"

"Why yes David that is why we are here. I know that you know more than anyone about those machines."

"Yes Gary I had already invented this Grow Tube and I left it hid underground in the boring machine knowing full well that they were not going to take the machines out of the ground, but little did I know that our government was building some kind of a safe inside of the boring machine. They thought that I had the key to it."

"The Chinese took and hid from the United States, supposedly a gold key. This all happen after they locked up the safe and all that I know is nothing and I wished that I knew what was in the underground safe."

"Well, David I am glad that you are setting down, because there may be a good chance of what is in the safe are all the patents for the Maglev trains and also the master plan for the airless vacuum tube that goes to space, and all of that data is worth billions of dollars."

"Lisa and I found the gold key in China and brought it back to the States. I guess your right David, China did steal the gold key from us. We need to get to the underground boring machine at the twin city tunnels."

"Oh my," David said, *"I had no idea. I will drive us there tomorrow when the sun is down."*

CHAPTER 62

"Well Gary and Lisa, I have a guest cottage in the back and want you two to spend the night."

"That sounds great David, we do appreciate that," I said to David, *"It sure will beat another motel room."*

"Yes," Gary added, *"We would love that."*

"Then its settled" David says, *"follow me."*

David led us outside down a pathway it was almost like a yellow brick road. Beautiful flowers along the way set in rocks and small fish ponds and ferns. Everything was in its place when we went inside the cute guest cottage. *"Now you two enjoy yourselves. You will find linen in the hall closet and fresh towels in the bathroom"* said David as he was walking out the door like he was in a rush to get back to his place."

"See you tomorrow guys," David yelled as he was leaving.

"Thanks David," Gary said

"Gary, why did he leave so fast?" I asked.

"I guess because he knew that we might be tired? Or maybe knew that I wanted to be alone with you."

"That could be Gary, but I am always suspicious of anybody that I do not know and you should be too."

"But Lisa, I have known David for years and years. He is one of the best friends that I have."

"Okay Gary, I just get carried away sometimes and I let my instincts get ahead of myself"

"Lisa," Gary says as he held me tight in his arms, *"alone again just you and I. Safe for the night my love."*

"You know Gary, I will be glad when it is like this every night, just the two of us," I said as Gary whispers in my ear and tells me how much he loves me and gives me a kiss goodnight.

What a fast night I told myself as I woke up with the sun shining in the window and I sat up in bed and threw the sheets off of me and then I heard Gary moan, *"Lisa, don't get up yet. I just want to hold you for a while."*

"Yes Gary, I'm not getting up," I replied as I turned around and we snuggled up closer together as we held each other tight. It was not long before someone was knocking on the door

"I will get it Gary, you stay still," as I reached for a robe and headed towards the front door. It was one of the farm workers coming over to tell us that breakfast would be served soon. I thank him and he went on his way.

The day went by quick as we got a tour of the winery and the vineyards.

"You have a beautiful place here David." Gary said.

"Thank you Gary, I sure would not trade this life for any other one. I love what I do and so do my customers."

"I can see why." I said to David. *"It is so peaceful out here and who would want to be anywhere else?"*

"You got that Lil Lady." David said to me.

Evening was here before we knew it and David says, *"We will take my van and I will drive."*

"That will work." Gary said to David, as we climb into his car.

"How far is San Francisco from here David?" I asked?

"It's a little less than an hour before we will be in the big city Lisa," he answered, *"And North Beach is not too far and we will be very close to the tunnel. It is closed off to the public but I can get us in through the hidden passage."*

"Great," Gary says to David, *"You have not loss your touch I might say."*

*"Well you know me Gary I try and stay one step above everyone else. Like the old saying goes, **All big fish start out in smaller ponds, but the first catch of the day is from the biggest pond.**"*

"I remember that saying David, from the good old days." Gary says.

It was not long and we drove up towards a deserted beach. The water was not so blue like China, and had a colored glaze to it. *"Why is the water so dark?"* I asked David?

"Well Lisa it was left over from the oil spill and the environmentalist are holding up the clean-up because they don't agree on how to clean it up. They are now fighting it out in court. In the meantime it is killing a lot of our fish, and by the time the environmentalists are through fighting about it all the fish will be dead."

"Hey," said Gary, *"that reminds me of the snake story."*

"I have not heard that story in years." David said.

"Yes Gary," I said *"Tell us the snake story."*

"Ok guys this is how it goes," Gary starts, *"They were building the Park trains in Oakland, California. The workers had been working hard in laying the tracks for the fast commuter trains, when one day an environmentalist shows up on the job sight and saw a dead snake. He immediately went to his superiors and told them he found a dead snake. They immediately closed down the job and many workers lost their jobs for a few months but it was mandatory that they register for a snake school."*

"Upon completing the course they were awarded an emblem to put on their hard hat that had a picture of a snake on it, which proved that they completed the course. The environmentalist relocated all the snakes to a different area. The job site was reopened, well one day a worker found a dead snake on the premises, and not wanting the job site to close again, he carefully took his foot and moved the dead snake underneath the dirt and never said a word. It wasn't long before the environmentalist noticed that there were hundreds of dead snakes dying everywhere including the new location where they had moved them to."

"What happened to all the snakes?" I asked Gary.

"Well Lisa, the crazy environmentalist moved them to a toxic area that was contaminated."

"How dumb is that?" I asked Gary.

Gary answered, *"Yes very dumb Lisa and they always stand in the way of progress and we believe that they are doing this to break our economy just like the trains and not giving right-of ways when needed and most stop any good thing for this Country."*

"Well guys, enough of the story telling now we are here.

CHAPTER 63

"We will exit here at the intersection of St. Lair and West Side. Now to get to the entrance we can access any of the holes in the fence. Now get out of the van and follow me." said David.

"Okay we are right behind you." says Gary.

As we were walking towards the passage David says, *"Here is something you should know now and the construction information that I will tell you. Initially the tunnel was to be constructed using a 70-ton steam-driven boring machine designed to cut a groove around the circumference of the tunnel thirteen inches wide and twenty-four feet in diameter, by means of a set of revolving cutters."*

"Go on" Gary said to David.

"Well, when this groove had been cut to a proper depth the machine was to be run back and the center core blasted out by gunpowder or split off by means of wedges, they realized that the opening was not big enough and it failed. They then brought the (TBM) boring machine in and that is when they decided to name the tunnel **The Tunnel of Freedom.** *When the (TBM) boring machine was to slow digging they brought in the Subterrene boring machine and finally finished the job."* Only the (MTMC) came back and built the safe inside of the boring machine and along with it is my Grow Tubes that I had already hid in the machine. Now the opening can be seen from the East Portal.*

"Slow down." Gary said to David, *"So Lisa, and I will get a better understanding."*

"Okay I will," said David, *"Now this is something like the* **Chads Tunnel** *It will be like a dark dungeon as we climb down the rifts. Now*

we get to different and various chambers by using portals that are in each of the rooms, and one portal goes to the next chamber."

"Sorry, guys I do get carried away." David said.

"No problem." Gary says to David, *"We will be well educated by the time we get there."*

I was utterly speechless as we continued going underground and deeper and deeper into the underground.

"I will be so glad when this is over." I said to Gary.

"Yes, Lisa, I think the same thing."

"Come on you cry babies," David said to us, *"we are almost there."*

The next chamber put us in front of this huge boring machine. It looked like a big overgrown giant metal storage shed and had a door on it and pipes going up and down and into the ground.

"Now Gary, did you bring the gold key with you?" asks David.

"Well David, what do you think that I have been carrying in my brief case?"

"Okay" David said, *"This is it!"* as we all look in awe.

"Who would have thought that something so large would be buried under the ground Gary," I said

"I know Lisa, it is amazing" Gary says as he was opening his briefcase to get the key out of it.

"Gary," I said *"let me help you with it and I can put the key in the lock."*

Before Gary could answer me we heard David shout *"No Lisa!"* in a stern voice, which made Gary and I look at him.

Then he changed his tune and said, *"I want you to just relax Lisa, Gary and I can get this door open."*

"Okay," I said and through my hands up in the air in disappointment.

"Lisa, wait here while we go inside of this room to the safe," David said to me.

"Okay" I said *"but don't be too long."*

CHAPTER 64

It seemed like forever that I was left outside the Boring machine. All of a sudden the door swings open and Gary comes running out of the Boring machine safe with a hand full of papers and all bloody and said, "Come quick, David, turned on us and wants the Maglev patents for himself."

He no sooner said that and David opens the door all bloody with a knife in his hands. David saw me at the door and grabbed me from behind and put the knife to my neck.

"Drop the patents Gary, or your little girlfriend is dead."

"Just don't hurt her" Gary said, *"I will give you the papers."*

"Throw them in that can over there Gary, then you get inside of that safe."

"But what about Lisa, set her free, she can do you no harm."

"Do you think that I am nuts Gary?" David says *"She can go straight to the police and then it is all over for me."*

"Take that knife away from her neck and let her go or I will rip up these patents." Gary said.

"You would throw away billions of dollars just to save your girlfriends neck?" David said.

"Don't doubt that for a minute David." Gary said

"Tell me one thing David, why in a million years that you would want to steal the Maglev patents with the money that you have?"

*"Oh you think that you are so smart Gary! I worked my **you know what off** for years and what do I get? Just like the song goes, **A little bit older, and deeper in debt.***

"*Col. Leone knew that you and I were best friends and he had a hunch that you and Lisa might stop by for some help from me. Col. Leone made me an offer that I could not refuse. So now do you understand Gary?*"

"*No David,*" Gary said, "*I guess that I will never understand.*"

"*Now one more time Gary, throw the papers in that can!*"

Gary said, "*There you go.*" as he gave them a toss in the air.

David pointed the gun with his other hand and said, "*Now get inside this Boring machine, and I mean now.*" as he held the knife closer to my neck.

Gary went ahead and got inside, a minute later David pushes me in and quickly locks the door to the boring machine with us inside.

I fell into Gary's arms and started crying uncontrollable then Gary says "*Lisa no worries!*"

"*Gary how can you say that? We are buried alive and all you can say is **no worries.***

"*What happen when you two were inside here and opening the safe?*" I asked.

"*Well Lisa, I was bending over putting the gold key in the lock and David got behind me and stabbed me in the arm and put a gun to my head. I turned just enough to pull him off of me and gave him a neck twist and that was how I got away from him. Now Lisa, I think that I have a plan to get us out of here.*"

"*How could you figure that out so fast Gary?*" I asked.

"*I thought about it when David was acting funny about you coming in the safe with us. When we first walked in the room I notice his grow tubes, and thinking to myself if the unthinkable happens. I bet a person could escape through them.*"

"*They for sure were big enough after all they were called the **Twin Bored Tunnels**, which meant that there was another one which would be side by side. I believed that the grow tubes duct work connects to the other twin tunnel. All we have to do now is take out the inside lining and the screens and crawl through the duct work and we could be back in the twin chamber of the cave.*"

"*Well Gary, what are we waiting for?*"

"Your right Lisa, now hand me that flashlight over there to your left. Now look around for something that I could use for a wedge Lisa."

"Ah Gary, here is a piece of sheet metal on the floor." As I picked it up and gave it to him.

"Well Lisa, this may just work." as Gary was pushing the wedge into the screens to pop them out. A few minutes later the screens flew off. Gary then proceeds to take the lining out and also the grapevines that had already grown 4 feet long. A rush of condensation filled the air when he pulled the plants out.

"Wow! Lisa his grow tubes really work. David was so set in getting the Maglev patents that he forgot about his grow tubes."

"Boy Gary, lucky for us." I said

"Yes, Lisa we will be out of here in no time." as he pulled the last of the grapevines out of the grow tube.

"Okay, Lisa I will lift you up to the duct work tube and all you have to do is crawl to the end of it and you will be in the twin chamber then push off the screen at the other side."

"I'm ready Gary," as he help me get into the huge tube that was made out of the duct work. It was round and not very hard to make it through it although I did see the screen that Gary was talking about and I gave it one big push with my foot and off it came. *"Come on Gary."*

"Lisa, I am right behind you."

"We did it Gary." I said as we both landed on the outside of the boring machine.

"Yes Lisa and here we are in the twin cave chamber." Gary said. He then gave me a big hug and said *"Lisa, you are so brave and it makes me love you more every day."*

"Then Gary, let's get out of here." I said

"I will have you out in no time." Gary said to me. *"Now follow me."* as we went up these rifts in the tunnel. I could see old mine shafts abandoned, and walls of clay and rock praying that it would not cave it on us. It was like a ghost hall for you could almost hear the men talking and laughing as they worked.

"There sure is some hard rock and narrow walls." I said.

*"Well get on your hands and knees Lisa, in this next rift. It sort of reminds me of the **Nutty Putty Cave**."*

"What about it Gary?" I asked.

"Well Lisa, it had many rooms that were connected by small tunnels and narrow corridors."

"Where is that at Gary?

"It is in Utah somewhere and was sealed shut with a concrete plug."

"No, Gary how can you tell me that at a time like this?"

"So sorry Lisa that does not mean that this side is sealed like that."

"I sure am thirsty Gary. Do you feel that way also?" I asked.

"Yes Lisa but we are going to have to crawl through this traverse."

"What are you talking about Gary?"

"We are coming to this twenty inch crack in the granite Lisa." *"What does that mean Gary?"*

"It means that we will have to traverse sideways when inside of it and you cannot turn your head at all."

"What Gary? Are you crazy?"

"No Lisa, but it should only be 5 minutes from the exit."

"I don't think that I can do it Gary."

"Yes you can Lisa, you can do anything and besides you will be left here if you don't follow me."

"What? You would leave me here Gary?"

"No Lisa, but please do as I say. I will go first Lisa, now follow me and remember do not turn your head or you will get stuck."

"Okay Gary, let's get this show on the way." As we both started in the crevasse. I kept thinking of my nanny, while inside that narrow opening and I felt that she was with me and was saying, ***Lisa, you will be the snakes tail if you don't get a move on now honey, keep it going*** and I actually felt a push on my back side. *"Nanny is helping me."* I cried as we got closer to the light and it finally broke into a larger opening when were near the top. The closer that we got to the opening the more light that we could see.

"Look Lisa, I can see sunshine through that crack up there."

"Awesome Gary," I said, as I made my way towards it.

We both got more excited to know that we may be getting out of this tomb soon. "Boy wait till I get my hands on David, I will tear him apart."

"Well Gary," I said *"Stand in line for I will give him a piece of my mind also."*

"Okay Lisa, looks like they have this section of the cave blocked off."

"Oh no Gary, now what?" I cried.

"Now we take inventory of the situation Lisa" as we both stared at the wall of the cave.

"Help me Lisa, get some of these rocks out of the way." as we clawed at the walls where the light was coming from. Little by little we threw the rocks away from the wall of the tunnel until we found like a wooden box the size that would hold a washer or dryer inside of it.

Gary started tearing apart the box and saw more daylight. *"Look Lisa, we can crawl out of here it is an old exit. I think that this was left over by the work crew that had to dynamite an opening before the boring machines got here to do the work and they just forgot to seal it up and the brush grew up around it."*

"Thank goodness Gary, we are in luck."

"You got that right pretty lady." Gary said as we made our way through the wooden box door to the outside of the cave. It had all been covered by old brush and weeds and nobody probably knew about this exit from the outside and plus who in their right mind would have crawled through that crevasse like we did?

We made it outside of the cave and hitched a ride back to a local motel. We took our showers and we both fell asleep quickly.

CHAPTER 65

"Lisa wake up, we need to go." Gary said.

"Where are we going Gary?" I asked while I was trying to wake up enough to remember where I was at.

"First we go and hot wire a car and then we will go and find David. I believe that he is meeting up with Col. Leone."

"Where do you think they are meeting at Gary?" I asked

"Well, I am sure that Col. Leone will go to David's place first to make sure he got the patents from us.

"Hurry Lisa, and get dressed."

"Okay Gary, but it is not even daylight yet."

"I know" said Gary, *"and that is why we must get going."*

We made it outside and looked for something to borrow or maybe I should say steal.

"Here we go Lisa, a small bug" as we are looking at the parking lot in the grocery store next door to the motel.

"What Gary? What small bug?"

"You know Lisa, a Volkswagen Beetle."

"You should have better class than that Gary." I teased.

"Your right Lisa that is why I have you."

"Come on Lisa, we don't have all day, Get in." as Gary leaned in under the steering wheel and 'hotwired' the car.

A few minutes later and we were headed to Santa Rosa again.

"Slow down Gary, we might get a ticket."

"Okay, Lisa your right. We are less than an hour away now." And Gary slowed down to the speed limit.

"You know Gary; I could not help but notice all those box cars when we were leaving the tunnel. What are they all for?"

"Well, Lisa I did not want to scare you but they are called prisoner box cars. They are propositioned everywhere in our Country.

"Gary, don't joke with me."

"Lisa, this is not a joke."

"There is a small possibility that we will be turning into a Police State someday in the near future."

"What Gary?"

"It's like this Lisa; our Country may be headed towards a revolution."

"Say again Gary?" I said

"Once the wrong people get the patents and the master plan for the tubeless vacuum tube I believe that there will be Marshal Law. Then they could do what they want at night and no one will see them working, In other words there would be no one to slow down the program."

"What would happen then Gary?"

"Well Lisa they have built many military detention camps around the Country."

"Get in there way and 'adios'"

"Gary, this sounds like science fiction."

"It may well sound like that Lisa, but I am afraid if we don't get those patents back, our Country is in real trouble."

CHAPTER 66

"Lisa, in Chinese culture every year has an animal mascot. This is the year of consciousness, or conscious awakening in a sense."

"Does this mean we're going to abandon the mundane daily news of planet earth Gary? Where we start chanting mantras and worshiping self-proclaimed enlightened gurus?"

"Hardly Lisa, in fact this is what I call grounded consciousness or **holistic consciousness.***"*

"And why Gary?"

"Because Lisa, it is the lack of consciousness that's behind every corporate crime, government conspiracy, political corruption, big pharmaceutical schemes and environmental crimes that takes place on our planet. Those who lack consciousness engage in **you versus me** *crimes of selfishness—stealing, exploiting, destroying, deceiving—yet such behaviors come from a place of ignorance about consciousness and the universe around us."*

"Like Col. Leone, and David?" I asked Gary.

"Yes Lisa, this is from popular culture."

"Yoda taught Luke Skywalker that all things are connected. **The Force** *he explained flowed through all living things and binds them together."*

"You can call it grounded consciousness or better yet, **Holistic Consciousness.***"*

"You mean like a kind of mystical universal energy?" I asked Gary?

"Well Lisa yes, it relies on the force and ally in the protection of life."

"This is some heavy stuff Gary." I said.

"I know it is Lisa, but hey we are almost to David's house.

"I will hide the car outside the gates and walk in."

"I'm right with you Gary." I said

"No Lisa, I want you to stay in the car where you will be safe."

"Okay Gary, I will not argue with you this time."

"Keep the doors lock okay Lisa?"

"Yes Gary." I said as he was getting out of the car and I locked both doors.

When Gary got up to the front of the house he could see David and Col. Leone talking. The window was open just enough he could hear them say, *"You are sure that Lisa and Gary are dead? Col. Leone asked David."*

"By now they are out of air in the boring machine and I know there was only enough air in there to last 15 minutes at the most." David said to Col. Leone.

"Ha ha! We finally fixed Gary" said Col. Leone, *"but you know I will be missing that guy, for he was one of my best students that I ever had. He was a fast learner and I think that I taught him too much for his own good."*

"Well Col. Leone, he was a good friend of mine, but not so good that I didn't trade him for more money." David said.

At that point Col. Leone pulls out his gun and points it at David and says, *"Just like I am trading you in for more money David. Why should I give you a dime? Besides, you may get drunk and squeal on are project."*

"Please don't shoot Col. Leone. I did all we agreed upon. Forget the money just give me my life." David said.

"Okay, David I will give you an eternal life." as Col. Leone pulls the trigger and shoots David between the eyes.

CHAPTER 67

Gary, made his way back to the car.

"Lisa stay still. Col. Leone just shot and killed David."

"Oh my, you got to be kidding?" I said

"No Lisa, but look he is driving away. We need to follow him."

"I just found a stun gun on David's porch" Gary said *"Now Lisa, you hang on to it."*

We were catching up to Col. Leone. We must have been following him for over an hour. *"Where is he going?"* I asked Gary.

"Good question Lisa."

"But it sure looks like he's headed back to Fernley, Nevada probably to his house."

"He is planning I bet on hiding the patents and the master plan there that he took from David after he killed him and he thinks that you and I are dead. He also knows that Yao is back in China and figures that the Guide Winds people will not go near his place again for fear of not wanting to be buried alive again. He feels safe enough to go home to his mini train station."

"I then wonder Gary he must have more hiding places there." I said.

"Yes Lisa it's like a maze you remember don't you?"

"Yes, Gary how could I forget, when we barely made it out in time before he came home."

"Maybe it has something to do with the toy soldiers guarding that mini mountain that he had built in his yard." Gary said. *"Leave it to the mountain Lisa, I bet that is another room."*

The hours seem to go slow as we followed Col. Leone down the 1-80 to Fernley.

"You were right again Gary, he is almost to his house. We will park down here Lisa, so he won't see our truck."

"Yes, Gary good idea." I said.

We walked down Treecut Ct. for about one block and stopped short of Col. Leone's house.

"Come on Lisa, stay close to me." as we sneaked in the back fence.

"Look Gary," I whispered, *"he is turning on a switch on the mountain there and all the toy soldiers are raising their weapons and turning towards the mini mountain."*

"Lisa, looks like those mini toy soldiers have stun guns."

"They must be for protection when Col. Leone is here." I replied

"Lisa, do you have that stun gun that I gave you in Santa Rosa?"

"Yes I do Gary, it's in the truck."

"Go back and get it Lisa, I have a feeling that we will need it."

"Okay," I said as I ran back to the truck. It was not long before I made it back to Gary, carrying the stun gun. *"Here Gary,"* I said when I handed him the gun.

"Thanks Lisa," he whispered to me. *"Now look at this Lisa, the soldiers are moving and they are getting all lined up."*

"Gary that is unbelievable. It looks like they are marching towards us." I said.

"Lisa, they are." Gary said we turned around and here are all these toy machine armored trucks with guns pointed at us and they started firing on us.

"Duck behind this big rock Lisa," as he sprayed the toy soldiers and the armored mini trucks with the stun gun. Sparks were flying everywhere and we were behind a rock trying to keep from getting hit. It wasn't long before the mini Maglev train was coming around the corner of the mini mountain and all the toy soldiers and armored trucks headed to the train and disappeared.

"What in the world was all that about Gary?"

"Well Lisa Col. Leone didn't stay around to see what happen with his toy soldiers. It looks like from what I could see is that when he pushed the button the mini mountain opened up and he went inside anxious to hide the patents and in the meantime he forgot to turn off the toy

soldiers that were guarding the mountain. Since all his tunnels and mountains are sound proof he had no idea what happen just now."

"Lucky for us Gary, but what kind of ammunition where they using on us?"

"It was more like B-B's, but they dissolved when they hit you Lisa, I have seen them in training when I was in boot camp."

CHAPTER 68

"Come on Lisa, I don't think that Col. Leone is going anywhere for a while."

"Where are we going Gary?"

"Let's go back to the truck and think about this."

"Okay," I said, as he put his arms around me and we went back to the truck.

"Explain to me Gary, how did he get those toy soldiers to do what they did? And get inside of the train?"

"Well Lisa, I will try and explain it to you. You see he used powerful electromagnetic suspension that attracts metal objects but the magnetic pull is only temporary."

"When the toy soldiers march towards the mini Maglev train they were going straight to the metal coils in linings of the guide ways and probably larger guidance magnets attached to the underside of the train. Now with the magnets on the toy soldiers, they would connect . . ."

"That is enough Gary, I am not a rocket scientist but I think that I understand more now."

"Good Lisa, our headquarters may be interested in you and may offer you a job."

"Lisa, this operation is about over with. Think about it. We all know now that Col. Leone is responsible for the stealing of the patents, and the murders of many agents including David. He is responsible also for the slavery of Hua's people forcing and drugging them on the testing of the underground Maglev trains in China. He has been behind all these horrific crimes."

"Okay Gary, I agree. It just gets old all the time and I just want you and me together and forever."

"Yes Lisa that is our goal. Now we need to get back to Col. Leone's place in case he does a fast one on us."

"Okay Gary," I replied *"let's get moving."*

We went ahead and walked back to Col. Leones place it was very dark, and just the street lights and the moon helped us.

"Gary, Col. Leone's car is gone!"

"Oh shucks, I never thought that he would leave." Gary said, hey this will give us a chance to look for the patents. Come on Lisa let's get inside of that mini mountain.

We went over and Gary got the key out of the guide way tracks and then put it in the slot and pushed in on the switch.

"We are in Lisa," Gary said as this mini mountain passage door opened up for us. We got inside and there is a table and two chairs and a big picture of Col. Leone and not much else.

"Okay Gary, nothing is here besides this table, and why the buckets and containers?"

"Just a minute Lisa." said Gary as he looks inside of a bucket.

"What is it Gary?" I said

*"Well Lisa, he is working on what is called the **Blue Alternative***

"And what is that Gary?" I ask.

"It's an alternative to transform deserts into green land by collecting rain water in the ground. Usually they terrace the land with small water catchments, like holes, ditches, weirs, and allow it to soak in the ground. Living in the desert like this it could also be worth more than money itself."

"So Lisa, one of these containers must be a private safe build inside of the bucket, it would throw anyone off that was trying to rob Col. Leone How much do you want to bet?"

"All bets are on Gary," I said.

Gary started taking apart the different water buckets, by the time he got to the forth one he found one that was all concrete with a hole in the top for a key.

"Lisa, here it is." he said, *"All we need now is the key."*

"But wait Gary," I said, *"try the key that is hid in the guide ways that starts the train that we found last time. It's just a hunch."*

"Oh Lisa, sweetheart you are so smart as he went over to the guide ways and loosen the tracks. Here is the key," said Gary all excited and happy.

Gary comes back to the bucket safe and puts the key in and turns the lock and it works.

"Holy, Mulley molly!" he yells as I got closer to what he was pulling out of the safe. *"It's all the patents and the master plans for the airless vacuum tube plans for space."*

"Come quick Lisa, we must get out of here before the Col. Leone returns.

CHAPTER 69

Gary and I tried to made a very quick get-away as we grabbed the patents from the safe and took off through the yard, the only strange thing that happen was that the little toy soldiers were following us out of the yard.

"*Gary,*" I said "*do something these soldiers want to come with us.*"

"*Hang on Lisa I will disconnect the electrical power source, that should stop them.*"

Sure enough when Gary disconnected their power source they just stopped cold in their tracks.

"*These toy soldiers may come in handy someday Lisa, for you and me.*"

"*Come on Gary, get serious now let's get out of here and quit being funny.*"

"*Okay, Lisa you got it.*"

"*What are we going to do with these patents and the Master Plan Gary?*" I asked.

"*Lisa I don't have an answer to that very good question. We need to hide them until Col. Leone is put away.*"

"*I need to get back to China to help Hua and his father Yao, in rescuing their people. I also think that Col. Leone is about to figure out that you and I are alive. Now where is the last place that someone would look for the patents, Lisa?*"

"*Well Gary that is too easy to answer.*"

"*Yes Lisa, I am waiting!*"

"*In a locker at the high speed bus station,*" I said

"Lisa, you are a genius they would never look there. They might think to look at a transit train station but never a high speed bus station. Let's head there now. It will free us up for me to get to China."

"Gary this may sound stupid but I want to go with you and help rescue Hua's people."

"Well Lisa, you know how dangerous that this could be, right?"

"Well Gary, it would not put me in any more danger than I have already been in."

"Lisa, you are something else and I want to keep you."

"Please Gary, let me go with you?

"Okay Lisa, but first let's get a locker for these papers."

We made it to the high speed bus station in Reno, Nevada they had one that had the lockers in it.

"Gary, are you sure this will be safe here?"

"Of course Lisa, you figured this out from the beginning as he shoved the papers inside the locker."

"Now it's off to China, Lisa"

"Yes, Gary, I am ready."

CHAPTER 70

"Lisa, there is something that I want to tell you since we have so much time in traveling to China."

"And what is that Gary?"

"Have you ever heard of the Operation paperclip?"

"Well Gary, matter of fact I have.

"Isn't it about when WWII ended in and victorious American intelligence teams began a hunt throughout occupied Germany for military and Rocket Scientists?"

"Yes Lisa go on." Gary said

"Well they were looking for things like new rocket and aircraft designs, medicines, and electronics."

"And did you know Lisa that they were also hunting down the most prized scientists whose work had nearly won the war for Germany, the engineers and intelligence officers of the Nazi War Machine and the race into space."

"I thought it went something like that Gary."

"Right Lisa, but following the discovery of flying discs, the War Department decided that NASA and the CIA must control this technology."

"But what does that have to do with us and getting the Chinese out of the trance that Col. Leone has them in? And the airless vacuum tube for space?"

"You will see Lisa, it will all tie together."

"Where do we start Gary, to find the old timers that are the rocket scientist?"

"It's this way Lisa, it was rumored that when the States and the Soviet Union were fighting over the scientists from operation paperclip that little did they know that there were two brothers that design the aircraft that was designed like a flying saucer or a space ship plane. I know that our CIA kept the plans that were left behind. We could barter with the brothers and offer them their plans back if they help us."

"You are kidding right?" I said to Gary.

"No kidding aside. These two brothers worked as aerospace engineers, if they can tell us how to stop the mustard gas from the Maglev trains then we got a deal."

"Do you know their names Gary?"

"I do know that their last name is Joachim, last I heard Lisa, is that they were in Military intelligence who specializes in infrared and radar imagery, and they also do surveillance."

"We need to talk to the German Consulate General, under the freedom and information act." said Gary.

"Sounds like our men Gary. That is some hot stuff," I said. "Tell me what does that have to do with us?"

"Everything Lisa."

"Okay, Gary but I heard that they are still looking for some of the rocket scientist."

"Yes Lisa, they are."

"But Gary that was in the aftermath of World War II, they could be dead by now."

"I know that it is a possibility, but I believe strongly that they may still be alive."

"I also believe that they can make an antidote for the gas that Col. Leone is using on the Chinese while he forces them to ride the Maglev trains that they have underground."

"Col. Leone could also be using the gas that was related to a type of the **Mustard Gas** that was used in the war against Iran, but until we find the scientists we will never be able to stop the gases from the trains."

"Now if it is the new gas, it destroys the immune systems and the brain waves, used in mind controlling and that could be what Col. Leone initially wanted."

CHAPTER 71

"We should be in China within hours riding in this Maglev train after it goes into the airless vacuum tube." Gary said.

"Hey Gary, it's not so bad when you get used to it. I kind of like it. We can pretend that we are going into space."

"Right Lisa, but you would be in a seat belt looking straight up at the skies if that were so."

"I so will be glad to get this mission over with Gary."

"We will soon, we will go to the ambassador and have him set us up with his military intelligence. They can be very helpful to us Lisa."

"Gary, when did all this chemical weapons come in to effect?"

"I believe that it was the German Army that used the first gas, but it was initially started by the French."

"Really Gary?"

"Yes Lisa, but the first gas they used was chlorine gas and within seconds of inhaling it the vapors from it destroyed the victim's respiratory organs and they called it the choking attacks. Bad stuff Lisa."

"I know Gary, and so sad for our Nation."

"Is that something like Col. Leone did to Hua's people?"

"Yes, it was Lisa we just have to find a way to reverse its effect."

"Well Lisa, we better get some shut eye before there is no time left for we only have about other hour."

"Let's go upstairs to the lounge and rest until we get to our destination."

"That is a great plan Gary," as we both went upstairs to the train coach.

"I feel so tired Gary."

"Yea Lisa, it is like jet lag after a while."

The next few hours went fast as we went through the airless vacuum tube and it seemed like minutes when we pulled up to our destination in China.

"I did leave a message for Hua Lisa and he is expecting us."

"That is good Gary."

"Here we are already Gary."

"Yes and here are Hua's guards to pick us up. Stay close to me Lisa, just in case."

"I am hanging on your backside Gary" I said.

It was not long before we were at Hua's sanctuary and I felt safer there.

Hua said to us, *"I have an appointment with our embassies and consulates like you asked for Gary."*

"Great Hua, what I need to do is find the two brothers from operation paperclip that the governments almost overlooked a decade ago. They can be very helpful for us in knowing how to reverse the gas effect on your people, and then we can rescue them from Col. Leone."

"Tomorrow my friend my people will take you there." Hua, said.

"Let my Tasha girls give you your baths for a good night's sleep." Hua said to us.

"That sounds good Hua, for we need a good night's sleep." said Gary.

All went well that evening and we had a wonderful time with Hua and his family we had lots of laughs and also got serious about the planning of the escape of all Hua's people. We all prayed that it would happen real soon. We were offered tea before we left and accepted it with thanks. We were anxious to get to the Ambassadors early the next day. When we arrived we were taking to the office of the Consulate of China.

Gary explained our dilemma that we needed to find the Joachim brothers and that they were from Germany but heard that they are in Military intelligence.

They had us wait for about an hour and called us back into their office.

"Good news my friend" the Consulate said, *"We found your boys."*

"You're not kidding right?" Gary said.

"No, actually your timing is the best. They are over here for a meeting with all the Ambassadors from different Countries."

"They are scheduled to leave for the States tomorrow. Knowing the urgency I have requested their presence here immediately."

"Thank you so much Consulate General we are extremely grateful for your understanding."

"It's like this Gary, you will save many more lives by getting this problem resolved and if my department can help so be it."

"Now then please go to the parliament room and wait, my guards will bring them in soon."

"I cannot believe Gary that we found them this quick."

"Yes Lisa, it's a miracle!"

About an hour passed and we waited patiently and in walks two older men dressed in black slacks and a white shirts and a red ties. They looked tired and worn. One had a beard and grey hair. The other brother was bald and clean shaven.

Gary, explained to them that he knew their previous activities and all we wanted to do was get some help to detoxify the gas effects on Hua's people taken hostage.

"This is what I know." said Low the bald brother. *"After you explained what type of gas it was and you think that it was like a mustard gas, then first what we need is some Sanoviv that will help eliminate stored mercury in their bodies."*

"Once we have that then we would put them both in a pill form with (EDTA) which is called Ethylene Diamine Tetra Acutic Acid and then resume Chelating therapy. That would remove all toxins and metabolic waste and metals and reverse the effect of the poisonings gases in their bodies."

"Now does that mean Low that they would be back to normal."

"Yes Gary, maybe more than you and me."

"My brother and I could make some pills that would work just as well as an injection and would be much easier for you to give them."

"That would be wonderful Low, but tell me what you need first?"

"Get me the Sanoviv and the (EDTA) we will have you a pill in no time that you could give them."

"Yes" Gary said, *"and we will get back your old blueprints and copies of your space planes that you drew that should never been stolen from you or your brother."*

"That is a good deal my friend." they replied.

"I know." said Gary, *"We will have your drugs by morning, but can you stay somewhat longer to get this made for us?"*

"Yes," Low said *"This is very important"* And we parted ways.

CHAPTER 72

"Gary, what was Low's brother's name? Did he ever say?"

"He did mention once Mos, we can do this."

"Yes, that is it Gary. You know all of this seems like more of a conspiracy all the time."

"What do you mean Lisa?"

"Well Gary think about it. We find out that your best friend David, double crosses you, and then Col. Leones involved with the communist and heaven knows what else. How could anyone build a secret worldwide underground tunnel system with a Maglev train on it and a high speed rail and not a person be told? Or even knows about it. Gary, this is big!" I said

*"Well Lisa, it's sort of like **Project Blue Book.**"* Gary said.

"What do you mean Gary? And what is Project Blue Book?"

"It's like this Lisa," Gary said, *"I believe that it was in the '50's when a wave of reports came in to the Air Force everyday about a unidentified flying objects and they had over 100 sightings in one day. One such particular morning in Los Angeles an aircraft company, called Hughes Aircraft Company was conducting a test of some new experimental radar. It worked well all morning tracking aircraft in the Los Angeles area, then near the end of their testing the radar picked up what they assumed to be a DC-3 coming across the San Gabriel Mountains north of Los Angeles."*

"Go on Gary" I said

"As the scientist monitored it they thought it might be the last good airline target for the morning."

"And did it Gary?"

"Well it did prove to be one of the last radar targets that day and no other aircraft performed the way this would-be DC-3 did. Some instruments tracked it in a 35,000 feet per minute and climbing, it then dove until it leveled out, heading southeast near Riverside, California. Then after checking with local Air Force officials, the technicians confirmed that no high performance aircraft had been in the area."

"Wow," I said to Gary, *"Are you kidding me?"*

"No Lisa, the radar set was rechecked, yet Hughes engineers felt confident that the radar recorded the information accurately."

"Could this have been the start of the airless vacuum tube Gary?"

"I don't know Lisa, but at that time they called this unexplained flying objects, better known as **Project Blue Book.**

"Well, Lisa my theory is that Low and Mos knew something about what was in our skies back in the early '50's even though they had only been here for a few years. That is why the CIA and NASA went on the look for the rocket scientists after the war ended and needed their help."

"They thought that the brothers were responsible for making these flying saucers so they offered them a job in military intelligence and infrared and radar imagery."

"Don't they do surveillance activities Gary?" I asked.

"Yes, Lisa that is there job."

"Now Gary, it's all starting to make sense."

"Well Lisa, we will see how smart they are in a few days when they come up with the antidote for the mustard agent."

"And they do know that it could be contaminated with mercury?" I said

"Yes Lisa, but they use Mercury in all the shots that they give the American people."

"Why do they do that Gary, when they know that Mercury is bad for our health? I was just reading about it."

"Lisa, don't make me answer that question about our government."

"Now it's morning and we need to call Low, and see if he got the ingredients to make the antidote" Gary, said

CHAPTER 73

"Lisa, Dial Low's number now and see if he got the antidote for the poisonous gas."

"It's already done Gary, I just called them and they are waiting for some Atropine and if that cannot get that they said that they could substitute Biperiden for it."

"Great Lisa, but I would feel better if we stay on top of this and hang out while they get it ready."

"Okay Gary, let me grab my coat."

"We will take a few minutes and stop by Javabucks and get some coffee."

"Sounds good to me Gary." As I rush behind him grabbing my purse.

We proceeded to drive down to Javabucks and get our coffee and headed towards the Embassy to meet with Low and his brother Mos. Within an hour we drove up to the front of the building and as we arrived saw a security guard carrying an ice chest.

"Lisa I bet that is the antidote."

"Yes Gary, it must be."

We headed upstairs to the pharmaceutical area of the building. We opened the door and here was the security guard handing Low, the ice chest. Low, turned and looked at us and said, *"Oh Gary, so glad that you are here. We need to go over a few things."*

"Great Low." Gary said.

"Go in the other room and have a seat and I will be there shortly."

"Thank you." Gary said to Low as we went into the conference room. It was just 10 minutes before Low and Mos walked in the room with their white coats on.

"Gary, it looks like we have the best of the best. They found us some Biperiden, which is much better than the Atropine. I want to mix this and load it into an auto injector that was used in the field of military personnel. I am also working on a pill. It's a psychoactive drug whose core chemical, normally called a (Benzo) will enhance the effect of the neurotransmitter in the antidote."

"And this will work Low?"

"Yes Gary, they will be given a pill of Benzo, or better named Benzodiazepine which will result in a mild sedative and put them in a hypnotic sleep. They will do exactly what you command them. When you get them safe and away from the train, you then will give them all a shot of Biperiden that will be already loaded in the auto injector. This will bring them out of the hypnotic sleep. They will remember nothing from the sedatives because it has an amnesic effect."

"That sounds too good to be true Low and Mos, when will it all be ready?" Gary asked.

"Give us a few days and you will have all you need to rescue all of the Chinese hostages."

CHAPTER 74

"Gary, how exciting for us all to know that in a few days we will have rescued all the Chinese hostages from Col. Leone."

"He must at this point be furious that his patents and master plans have been stolen from him plus we released all his previous hostages from his home and by now he must know that you and I are alive."

"Oh yes Lisa, I bet that he is fuming and is looking for us. Well hopefully we can pull off this operation and get the pills in the hostages before he finds out."

"But Gary, how do we give hundreds of people the pill all at once?"

"It's easy Lisa," said Low who was listening to us talk.

"I am making a special **Grand Finale** *antidote for Col. Leone that we developed in Germany many years ago during the war. It is a nerve agent and better yet came from the G-Agent, it is the most volatile nerve agent around. It's odorless and highly toxic and will be fatal within minutes depending how many compounds that we put in it."*

"Well Low, how will we give it to him without him knowing?"

"Like I said it is odorless. It can be put in his drinking water before your operation rescue is completed."

"This is such amazing work that you and Mos are doing for China and probably the world," Gary said, *"and also to get Col. Leone out of the way."*

"Well Gary, I have more to tell you and Lisa."

"And what more can you possibly tell us?" Gary and I asked at the same time.

"Killing Col. Leone is not enough punishment in our books. We want to make just enough (GA) agent known as (Sarin) to put him out.

We think that after he takes the GB agent and passes out you should put him in the Airless Vacuum tube, the one that is ready for space. It will be a one way trip for Col. Leone into space and when he wakes up he will not only be miserable with chest tightness, shortness of breath, pinpointed pupils, and the list goes on," said Low, *"but he will be in space all alone and never to bother anyone again."*

"Wow! Low, that is extreme!" Gary said.

"Is that called a war crime Gary?" I asked?

"Well, he sure deserves to die like that." Gary said

"Yes, it is a slow, slow death." Mos said,

"We will be more than happy to give back your space plane blue prints to you and Low after we pull all this off."

"We will be so grateful Gary." Low said.

"Not as grateful as Lisa, I and the Chinese government to get rid of Col. Leone and rescue all the Chinese hostages."

CHAPTER 75

After yesterday and all the news that Low and his brother Mos had for us we really got excited.

"Lisa, we need to meet up with Hua and Yao have them get us a small army to go to the Maglev station to give out those pills so that everyone of their people can be rescued."

"Great idea Gary, and won't they be surprised that we have such a great plan?"

"Yes they will Lisa, and also as we were leaving yesterday Low was telling me that they will make the pills where they dissolve under the tongue, which will make them fast acting."

"They are also planning to use some Sanoviv that will help them eliminate stored mercury that is in their bodies. It is all so perfect Lisa, and I hope that it goes well."

*"The whole **Operation Rescue**, which we have named it now will go a lot faster. Let's get on over to the Sanctuary, so we can make plans with Hua and his people.*

"I'm right with you Gary," I said as we proceeded to the car. "Time is a wasting."

It was about one hour later and we were at Hua's place. We were welcomed with open arms and led to the throne. There sat Hua on one side and Yao on the other.

"Welcome my friends. Thank you, thank you my friends." said Hua, and then he and Yao bow down to us. *"I was so surprised when I found out that my father was not dead"* said Hua as Yao nodded in agreement.

"Thank you again for saving me from being a (Zhi) hostage." Yao said to us. *"I was (Liao) taken from my people and thanks to you and Lisa, we are free."*

"Yes," Gary said, *"but now we want to set your people free from Col. Leone and we have a plan that is in the works."*

"Tell me (Fu) man Gary, what is your plan?"

"Well it starts like this Hua and Yao," as Gary proceeded to tell them about the pills, *"and then when we have them safe they will get a shot with an auto injector that will bring them out of their hypnotic state of sleep. All memories of their ordeal will be erased from their memory because of the amnesic action."*

"Gary, that is just wonderful news, but what can we do to help?" asked Yao.

"We need a small Army of your people to help put the pills under their tongues."

"What about Col. Leone?" Hua asked.

"No worries my friends." Gary answered, *"He will be taken care of before we give your people the pills. "Now in a few days we will have all the antidotes and be ready to move on this."* Gary said.

"The sooner the better when our people can be home with us." Yao says.

CHAPTER 76

Well the two days seemed like almost a lifetime when we got the call from Low.

"Gary we got the Biperiden ready for the auto injector and the (Benzo) in pill form ready to give to the hostages and the Grand Finale of antidote of poison for Col. Leone was in the works" said Low."

"When should we come and get the Grand Finale for Col. Leone for we need that and also a few pills of the (Benzo) to start out with Low?" asked Gary.

*"Well Gary, by the time that you and Lisa get here we will have Col. Leones future trip to space ready for you. One small drop of this chemical of Nerve gas in his water will put him in **La La** land until he arrives in space."*

"You're a Saint, Low. We are on are way."

"Okay Lisa get your hat."

"Right behind you my love." I said.

Within hours we made it to the Embassy and picked up the vile that contained the poison for Col. Leone and we were on our way. We arrived at the train station and two of Hua's security guards were hidden in the station to give us our disguise.

"Lisa I forgot to tell you that we will be dress like the Chinese here so that we blend in with the hostages."

"Okay Gary that would probably be a good idea."

"Yes Lisa, I knew that you would agree." as we met with the guards and changed into our disguise.

"Wow Lisa!" Gary said, *"You look so beautiful in that red silk gown with all the colored fans on the material and a figure that goes with it."*

"And Gary, you look handsome in your black robe that has all the oriental drawings on it."

"Okay enough of that you guys." said the guards, *"We have to get out of here before they catch us."*

"Many thanks." we said as they disappeared as fast as they showed up.

"Now Gary how are we going to put the poison in the drinking water, and know that he is the only one that drinks it?"

"I have a plan Lisa, Col. Leone has what he calls a Terrorist Patrol Sand Car, he uses it for running up and down the Maglev station to keep an eye on the hostages, and his crew."

"He always keeps a container of a water bottle with him in the vehicle, all we have to do his put the contents of the vile into his water, and he is out of our way. I also know that he does not share anything and I assume it means his water bottle and I'm counting on his stingy reputation."

"Okay, let's get over here and mingle with the crowd Lisa."

CHAPTER 77

"Now remember to stare straight ahead Lisa, we cannot show any emotions, we must blend in with the crowd."

"Like this? Gary" I asked, as I walked straight ahead with my head held high.

"No Lisa, your too dang beautiful, hang your head down woman and walk hunch back, and quit drawing attention to yourself."

Now I told myself I must try harder. Just think of my grandma and how that poor women could not even stand straight. I was able to pull it off as one of Col. Leone's guards walked pass me, though he did a double take, I held my breath and then I heard someone call his name, then he lost interest in me. That was close I hope that he don't come back.

"Lisa," I heard Gary say, *"There is the terrorist patrol sand car that belongs to Col. Leone, slow down and go over to the corner of that red post. Now I need you to give me a signal if any of the guards come near here. I need to have enough time to find his water bottle and put the ingredients in it from the vile."*

"Okay," as I turned around like I was lost to make sure that the coast was clear. Gary went to the rear of the sand car and climbed inside and put his head down looking for the water bottle and to make sure he was not seen. I took a quick glance around the station and could see another sand car pulling up on the other side of the parking lot tunnel.

Oh shoot, it looks like Col. Leone, is getting out of the sand car. I started to whistle a tune, and Gary, could hear me, and knew that it meant danger but oh, it was too late. Col. Leone was headed towards his sand car that Gary, was in.

I moved forward some to try and shield Gary, but then I notice that he found a tarp and covered himself up and laid low in the car. I kept walking ahead hoping that he would not notice me. A minute later Col. Leone is jumping in the sand car. He then looks around in the glove compartment like he was looking for something, and then quickly jumped back out of the car.

Col. Leone was headed back towards the other car that was across the tracks. About 3 minutes later I could see Gary peak out from underneath the tarp. I motion him to get out of the car. Trying not to draw any attention I continued to keep walking with all the rest. A few moments later I could see that Gary made it out of the car and was being careful not to draw attention to him.

Gary caught up with me and said, *"Wow! That was close."*

"Yes it was Gary, and no one saw you get in or out of the car thank goodness for that."

We must have walked around in circles for over an hour before we saw a Maglev train carrying the rest of the hostages and stop in front of the station.

"What are they doing Gary?" I asked.

"I guess they are transferring them to the high speed rail but I don't think it's going anywhere soon Lisa, looks like it has not been operated for months, plus it travels slower than the Maglev train does. They may want to do some maintenance on the Maglev."

"That could be." I said

"Lisa do you see that bench over there in the corner and that young man is sitting on?"

"Yes, the man with the red robe?"

"That's him! Now walk over there and sit down by him. While you are sitting down I will come from the other side and sit down and I will quickly put the pill under his tongue. It will work immediately and then he will do whatever we say."

"That is good Gary, but what will you tell him to do?"

"Well, Lisa we want to cause a scene where he gets the guards attention in this direction and you and I will escape the other direction

and find Col. Leone. I will tell the man sitting to get all his people to follow him and they will all march in this direction, the guards will not understand what is happening and you and I are free to roam around."

"Great plan Gary!"

"Yes, now get over there on the bench."

"Yes Sir." I said.

It did not take long for the plan to work just like Gary had planned; once the man got the pill under his tongue he followed directions.

"Okay Yun, you get all your people to follow you to the East. I want you to keep walking until I tell you to stop."

With those instructions, Yun stood straight up and started motioning his people to follow him, some were turning around if they were going in the wrong direction but they all got in a line like an Army.

"Gary, how did you know his name was Yun?"

"Well Lisa, I took a lucky guess."

CHAPTER 78

"Yun had a name tag on behind his jacket and when he leaned forward I saw it."

"Oh, you are tricky Gary," I said as I teased him.

"Lisa, I need to explain the rest of this operation and there is not much time so listen my love. When a train comes, the cars are stopped, and this causes a gap in the traffic. When the train has passed, the stopped cars speed up until they catch up with the traffic in front of them. To the observer, the flow seems quite normal and there is no evidence that a train has crossed the intersection."

"What are you talking about Gary?" I asked as we were waiting for a chance to go in the other direction.

*"Lisa, I am talking about the Pentagon and how they invented a backed **time cloak** that stops the clock. We can use that to rescue the hostages."*

"What do you mean Gary?"

"Lisa it is like this, it makes an event undetectable, like making a flow of light in such a way that the merest fraction of a second an event cannot be seen."

"Do you want to explain that better to me Gary."

"Alright Lisa, but we don't have much time left."

"A beam of a green light passed down a fiber-optic cable then the beam goes through a two way lens that splits it into two frequencies of bluish lights which travel fast and the reddest lights travel slower, now after they go through other obstacles which this time speeds up the red and slows down the blue and reverses the lens that reconstitutes them as a single green light."

"*Okay, Gary that is enough. I think that I understand.*"

"*Well Lisa that is what we need to do in order to get them away from the guards. Trust me this will work.*"

"*I am at your command Gary*" I said.

CHAPTER 79

"We will be there soon Lisa," Gary said as we tried to walk slowly towards the storage cans and not to be noticed by the guards. *"Let's hope to find the fiber-optic cable and the two way lenses hid there. That is what we will use to accelerate light."*

"I sure hope Gary that Hua's troops get here for reinforcements before we head back."

Then Gary whispered to me and said, *"I had Low send the equipment down with Hua's guards before we got here and it should be in the first storage container that holds the cans that we pass here in the tunnel."* Gary said. *"Keep your distance from me Lisa, but I want you just to walk slower and with your head down as we walk pass those security guards."*

"Okay Gary" I said.

"Remember now Lisa that we will use the laser beam as a probe and pass the beam through a device called a time lens. It's just an illusion created by light rays and point it at the guards and they will temporary disappear after the guards disappear then we give out the pills." Gary whispers to me as he explains our plans.

"But Gary, what if Col. Leone appears before we are finished getting everyone out?"

"It's simple Lisa, we will point the beam at him and he will disappear temporarily and by the time it wears off he won't remember or realize what happened to him."

"Gary, when did you put the poison in the water bottle?"

"I did it Lisa, when I was hid underneath the tarp in Col. Leone's sand car."

"I'm glad that you had time Gary."

"Yes, just enough time to take the vile and fill most of it with the poison. It should be enough to work. After he drinks the water and passes out, we will put him in the space machine that is in the airless vacuum tube and adios."

"What a great place that this Country will be after Col. Leone is in space."

"We made it Lisa, and all the equipment seems to be here. Everything we need to zap the beam at them. Now you can carry the pills and hand them out to all the hostages after we shoot the beams at the guards."

"Hey look, here come the troops now to help us with this operation." One by one they marched in with their uniforms on. They looked like a Space Army with the main color a blood yellow, and then the shoulders are ultramarine red and trimmed in gold and have a dragon on the shoulder pads. It is some kind of symbol for a chapter that they belong to. Maybe like a foot soldiers symbol.

"I do know Lisa, that the space Army squads are quite robust and their weapons vary from soldier to soldier."

"Okay guys stay hid, but close by until I call you," Gary gave them the instructions.

"You got it my friend" said Hua who came from the back of the line.

"Hua, what are you doing here?" asked Gary.

"Gary I would not miss this for anything, besides who is going to translate Chinese for you and keep you out of harm's way?"

"Well it looks like you will Hua."

"Okay, we must hurry" Said Hua.

"Aha, look our first victim is coming towards us and he is one of Col. Leone's security guards" I said."

"Quick hold the cable and the lenses." Gary said as he shot the beam of light towards the security guard. A split second and he disappeared.

"Hey it works," I said

"Yes, like a charm" Gary said.

"Now spread out and distribute the pills, remember to put them under their tongues and command them to give others the pills and then march them to the sanctuary that is waiting for them. They will do anything that you say. Then we will give them the (Benzo) from the auto injector when they are all safely inside the sanctuary."

CHAPTER 80

Looking down the train station over by the platform are two sand cars and one of them was Col. Leone's Terrorist Patrol sand car. In front of it was a mechanic doing something underneath of it.

"Hey Hua, look at that man over there."

"Yes Gary, he is putting something under the car and it's not new brakes."

"Let's get a little closer to him." Gary said.

"Look Gary, he is putting on a mechanical clock."

"What do you mean Hua?" Gary asked.

"Well it's like a time piece turned into a weapon. It was used in the war with the Japanese. They used it for a high explosive incendiary bomb known to give aerial blast and better known as the 32-kg bomb."

"You mean that someone wants Col. Leone dead besides us?"

"Yes" Hua says, *"But if they have their way Col. Leone will have just a one way blast to hell. That is just like the assault with the blood angels, better known as perhaps the blood of the dragon"* Hua said.

"Yes." Gary said, *"In getting back to the mechanical clocks, they are found in the military manuals, I think that I have seen them before and these alarms are also known as weights and wheels time piece."*

"That is exactly right." Hua said, *"But who else would want him dead besides us?"*

"That is a good question." Gary answered, *"But we got better things to do now than worry about someone else trying to kill Col. Leone, besides that would save us lots of work."*

"Yes Gary, but you are forgetting one thing!"

"And what is that Hua?"

"If Col. Leone gets in that sand car and the timer goes off, we all will be going with him for all eternity, with that many explosives in it. It would blow up this underground tunnel and trains and put us all in space without the airless vacuum tube."

"Then we better hurry up and get everyone rescued."

"I see another guard coming around the corner, get ready and we will zap him."

He sees us and is pulling out his gun as Gary points the laser at him and a beam of lights take over. He disappears as his guns fall to the ground.

"Great job" Hua says to Gary.

"I want 50 of your troops Hua to start giving out the pills to all your people so we can get them out of here pronto. This place may go to kingdom come."

"It looks like Col. Leone just got off the Maglev train that just stopped and he is headed to his sand car. What do we do Gary?"

"Well Hua, I will zap him with the beam and put him out of his misery or at least we will make him disappear for now."

"Well," Lisa said, *"You better hurry for he just saw all of us and is looking for his gun."*

"Here goes!" as he shoots the beam at Col. Leone

CHAPTER 81

"I don't think that he is pulling the gun out for us, look he is pointing the gun the other way," Lisa said.

"Well too late now I have zapped him with the beam." Gary said.

"Now it looks like that strange man saw us," Hua says.

"Well bye, bye blackbird," Gary says as he zaps the stranger.

"We will find out who he is later. Hurry guys we need to finish up the rescue operation."

"Oh no, I see about twenty of Col. Leone's friends whom are called the 'Mongol Nomads' coming in this direction," Lisa said

"Okay," Gary said, *"everyone stay behind me."*

"Yes!" Hua, hollers, *"Fall back men, fall back!"*

Gary hits them all with a beam of light, *Boom, boom* and back and forth the beam travels as the red lite rays beams across the station at them and one by one they just disappeared.

"Now," Gary said as he shot a beam of light at another guard, *"we need to get down by the Maglev train station soon. I will need to get to the operators cab and get to the y-end which is where all the controls are."* Gary said. *"Then Lisa, you go to the x-end and push the button to disconnect all the cars and this will separate them from the lead train. If we have the train cars separated it will be easier to rescue all the hostages."*

"I want each group of your troops Hua to be assigned to a train car. Without all the Mongol Nomads in one spot, I can go along to each train car after I leave the y-end control booth and zap the Nomads that will be waiting at the station to check all the passengers inside the cars.

We will do the same with the high speed rail train that are still holding some of the Chinese hostages."

"Just make sure that your men hide from them until I get there with the beam of lights. After they disappear, your troops will go inside the individual trains and give all the hostages pills then start marching them to the sanctuary before everyone reappears."

"Here comes the Maglev now. Ah, here is the first of the Nomad guards, I will use the beam on him first so I can get inside the operators cab."

Zap, zap the beam of light is still working and making them disappear.

"Follow me Lisa, now you go to the back of the train car and do what you were taught to do."

"Yes Gary I will."

The project of going to each of the train cars and Gary zapping the guards one by one was almost too perfect of a plan until some of the earlier zapping's were starting to come back one by one. Gary had just got through zapping the last of the Nomad guards when the others started to come back from being zapped but by this time all Hua's space troop soldiers had all under control and the plan went very fast.

The good thing was that all the troops had giving out all the pills and every one of the hostages were headed back to the sanctuary. Mission was accomplished! Well almost.

CHAPTER 82

"Okay, Hua I need about one half dozen of your troops to come with me, we need to get back to the tunnel that we left Col. Leone in," Gary explained. *"I'm afraid that he probably has reappeared by now and if he starts his sand car it's all over for him and us."*

It only took about 15 minutes to get back to the other side of the tunnel where we left Col. Leone. We were in for a big surprise, for here was Col. Leone spread out on top of his hood with the water bottle in his hands.

"Look Lisa, the poison worked, Col. Leone and the Mongol Nomad drank it after they reappeared and passed out before they could turn on the engine to the sand car." Gary said. *"Now we need to get the troops to help us carry Col. Leone to the space ship. I also want somebody to get ahold of Low and Mos to help eliminate this time piece weapon before it goes off or blows up."*

"I will do that," said one of Hua's soldiers.

"Okay" Gary said, *"What is your name?"*

"My name is Chen, and I am the one of Hua's men that was in New York with him. I just happen to know Low."

"Okay, that will be your orders." said Gary.

He then went on his way in a hurry and we were dealing with Col. Leone as we packed him into the other sand car that was nearby.

As we were driving to the space center Gary says, *"I sure hope Col. Leone does not find a habitable zone in space."*

"What are you saying Gary?"

"There is a possibility that Col. Leone will wake up and find himself near the black hole. A black hole fires many gas bullets into space. It goes at least one-quarter the speed of light. If our Maglauncher accelerates the spacecraft in the first phase of the black hole, well then Lisa, it may just push Col. Leone into a habitable zone."

"What would that mean Gary?"

"Then the black naked gases that produce the bullets would push him to the outer limits zone. And Lisa, the chances are slim but Col. Leone might be able to sustain life on another planet."

"Boy Gary, this can be confusing."

"Not to worry Lisa, besides the naked black hole hearts live in the fifth dimensions. And naked singularities might exist in the extra dimension that is proposed by the string theory."

*"Like they say, Lisa, (**One small step for mankind**)"*

CHAPTER 83

Gary explains, *"We are here now and take a look at the Maglauncher where we will put Col. Leone which is inside of the airless vacuum tube. We will strap him away from the spacecraft control panel. If for some reason he wakes up and moves around the alien indicator light will come on and then the thruster will automatically accelerate. The speeds and restraints will be so fast that he will be unable to get out of his seat. This all means that he could never turn it around to come back to earth."*

One of Hua's space troopers named Cheng was helping prepare the launch and said to Gary, *"You know Gary if Col. Leone does survive the trip to space he will be living in microgravity. His muscles will stop working and his bones will become weak and brittle. When he sees his reflection his face will be fluffy and he will have what we call chicken legs."*

"I never knew that Cheng," I said.

"Yes Lisa it's all true," says Cheng, *"and there is a chance if he makes it that far that after a few days his body may recuperate some."*

"Gary replies, "Well we have no time to worry about his surviving up there if he does make it. We need to be more worried about getting him out of here before more Mongol Nomads get here. They could have us captured and put us into space."

"Okay," says Cheng as he helps carry Col. Leone and put him into the spacecraft. I could not look anymore, just to know the kind of destiny that he was going to have, I almost felt sorry for the old man. Within minutes they had Col. Leone strapped into the spacecraft and were getting ready to launch it.

Gary continues, *"I want everyone in the launch pad to take a seat. We will set the controls for his space trip. Usually the astronaut's control the spaceship and they use buttons and thrusters. This peculiar trip will all be controlled from the control room inside the launch pad."*

"We have it about ready," the space army troops told Gary.

"Great!"

And we all just stood there in disbelieve but glad that Col. Leone could not hurt anyone else as we watch the rocket take off and shoot out from the inside of the vacuum tube. Gary said, *"Let's go check on the troops and make sure all the hostages are safe and that all the Nomads guards have been arrested by the Chinese troops."*

When we got back to the train station there was hardly a soul around just a peace and quiet. Hua's troops had dismantled the time piece mechanical bomb and were just leaving.

"That was sure a relief." I said to Gary.

"Your right about that Lisa." says Gary, as he and I held hands while walking down the long tunnel checking things out.

"Just today we have rescued hundreds of Hua's people, captured Col. Leone and sent him off to space, and with the antidote thousands more lives will be saved. We hold all the patents and master plans to the Maglev airless vacuum tube and that are worth billions of dollars, even after we give back Low and Mos their master plan for their space airplane that they lost many years ago." says Gary.

"It was a promise we made for the antidotes."

"I just got word from Hua's people that all the hostages got their shots from the auto injections that had the Biperiden in and it worked very well. They are all back to normal and never knew what happened. But one thing still bothers me Lisa."

"And what is that Gary?"

"Who was trying to kill Col. Leone? And why?"

CHAPTER 84

The next few days were filled with excitement has Hua's people celebrated their freedom. It was a beautiful celebration with music and wearing of mask on everyone's face and holding signs up that said Jie Yue (*Friends*) Jie Yue (*Saved us*) there also was a feast of foods everywhere.

We all were very happy until later that evening we were setting in the sanctuary with Hua and Yao and a messenger comes in and hands Hua a note that read, **White men escape from prison** *A Great Escape just happened when 50 convicts escaped during a countdown. Fifty of the prisoners that escaped were rounded up and shot by the guards while only 3 succeeded in reaching neutral territories. The escapee's names were Knuckles, Starfish and a third named Hugo.*

"*Hey, that is the man that was working on Col. Leones sand car yesterday and put the time bomb in it. Knuckles, wanted Col. Leone dead.*" Gary said,

"*But why? I cried*"

"*Well, remember the rumor that Col. Leone hid them away in a prison and was hoping someday to use them for his horrific crimes if he needed them. I heard that from the department a few months ago after they disappeared.*" Gary said

"*No worries,*" says Hua, "*we will be your Bao Hu Zhe (Protector)*"

"*We will help Jie Yue (save you).*" Yau said.

"*Thanks guys but Lisa and I will need to get back to the States soon. We still have some unfinished business to take care of.*"

"*Do you think Hua that we could leave tomorrow for the States?*" Gary asked.

"Whatever you She Ren (my friend) want"

"You should all be okay now." Gary said.

"Yes, we are okay, but we worry now about the big Piao Yang (wave)" Hua said

"What are you talking about Hua?"

"Well it is like this, the Da Hai (sea and ocean) are coming soon and a big Piao Yang (wave) Ju Ren (Giant) may take out our people and are land."

"Wow! Hua, if it isn't one thing it's something else."

"We will get prepared my friend, now that all my people are back they can help us be ready."

"Good Hua, we will help if needed." Gary said.

"When are you expecting this giant wave, Hua?"

"Soon," Hua said, *"we do not know the exact hour or day."*

"Come Lisa, we need to go get some rest for the trip tomorrow."

"Good night," (Shang Pin Wan) Hau and Yao said to us.

CHAPTER 85

The morning came too quickly. We were invited back to have breakfast with Hua and Yao.

"Come my Shu Ren (Friends)," Hua said when he saw us walking into the room

"Good Morning my friend Hua," Gary said.

"Let's all set down for breakfast." We knew by now that you sat on the floor with no shoes on and your legs crossed as we continued to follow his commands.

"I have something that we need to talk about." said Hua

"Go ahead." Gary said, as the Chinese girls filled our tea cups.

"I started to tell you this last night and I wanted to give you more detail of our new dilemma, it's like this my friends. Many many moons ago we were told by the great white Yan and a very close friend of our family that there would come someday, a big Da Hai (Sea Ice). It would expose the great Pio Yang (Wave). When the tide is just right and goes out it would expose the sea bed and that you had only one half hour before the tides came back in to go inside underneath the huge blocks of ice. There is only one place in the world that you can go underneath this Sea Ice and until this day we had no idea where. You would risk death under huge blocks of ice and if you cannot get out you die. It is frightening when you are under there. The tides are extreme and only minutes to get out. Then the sea flows back and leaves ice over your heads."

"Now what I am trying to say is that what sensors are telling us about sea ice which was updated this morning that there is activity going on and that the Sea Ice regulates exchanges of heat, moisture and

220

salinity in the polar oceans." Hua went on to say that, "*It insulates the relatively warm ocean water from the cold polar atmosphere except where cracks, or leads in the ice allow exchange of heat and water vapor from ocean to atmosphere in winter.*"

"*In other words Gary it is just not from Polar areas anymore for it has reached the Bohai Sea. It concerns me that if this happens while you are in the Maglev tubeless vacuum tube headed to the States, big glaciers could break apart and plugs the whole tunnel and everything that is in its way, causing mass destruction. The seasonal sea ice cycle affects both human activities and biological habitats. It is for your safety that you stay here Gary.*"

"*Gosh Hua, we need to find Knuckles and Starfish they could be as dangerous as Col. Leone was to us. Like they say, friends don't let friends rot in prison and Knuckles had many friends who helped him escape.*

"*I talked to headquarters this morning and they said that they sawed through bars of a recreational yard roof and then jumped to the ground, and scaled a fence topped with razor wire. There were four vans lined up outside the prison to pick them up, so you see Hua, Lisa and I have to take the chance and get back.*"

CHAPTER 86

"I might have another plan for you and Lisa to be safe on your journey if you want to hear it Gary?"

"Yes, of course Hua, what is it?"

"Do you know anything about the underground Railroad that was built through the United States including New York, Cincinnati and all through the south?"

"Yes some." Gary said, *"They used that underground railroad to help assist and free slaves.*

"Your right Gary, and it help them escape to the North and to Canada but did you know that they had many from China that help build the top secret underground tunnel that they built for the transcontinental railroad? Their plan was to give them the materials and train for the Maglev route to China and it's not in the same location like the Maglev underground tunnel, this one is very old."

"No Hua, you got to be kidding?"

"No kidding Gary, my people built it all underground and the tracks stop when it turns into the guide ways and picks ups all the way to China. John Little honored the Chinese community for laying the guide ways underground which was kept top secret."

"The underground guide ways came all the way to China and so the good news is that the location of it may be out of harm's way for the coming sea ice and big wave."

"Wow Hua, I never would of guessed, but how fast does the train go?"

*"I believe at least as fast like the Maglev only this is called **The Maglittle**, named after John Little,"* said Hua. *"Now this Maglittle*

is kept for my people as an escape whether its floods or wars. Please do not tell anyone or trust anyone with this information. Even the Chinese government does not know."

"*Mum's the word Hua,*" said Gary.

CHAPTER 87

Nothing was ever said again about what Hua told us. We decided to take our chances and take the regular Maglev to Washington D.C to the National Mall. We were taken down to the underground Maglev station and got on the train.

"*Lisa, don't worry now my dear, we will be alright.*"

"*Yes Gary, everything will be alright.*" Or will it? I thought to myself.

Within an hour of our trip we got very cold. "*Gary why is it so cold in here?*" And before he could say a word, there was a huge bang and the inevitable happened. The Maglev was losing all power from its magnetic source and the magnets were being drawn away. "*What is happening Gary?*" I asked.

"*Guess there must be strong electrical currents in close proximity to the magnets that may be causing this to happen.*" Gary said. "*Just stay close to me.*" He said as he put his arms around me and held me tight. "*It could be caused by possibly heat or Radiation.*"

"*Well Gary, we know that it's not the heat with all the ice cycles forming inside this club car. Do something Gary!*" I cried.

"*Lisa, we are having an effect on electrical conductors when the magnet and conductor are moving in relation to each other; you see Lisa, that they may very well have an effect on the path taken by electrically charged particles traveling in free space.*"

"*Tell me more Gary, but just keep talking and please talk in laymen's terms.*"

"*Okay Lisa I will. They can tract certain materials—such as iron, nickel, and certain steels. We do know that shock and vibration do not affect modern magnet materials, unless sufficient to physically damage the material so no worries about the bang that we heard. On the other hand Lisa, other magnets could be close in proximity to us and its slowing us down. Now maybe when we get pass this part of the tunnel the train will resume to normal."*

"We must pray Gary"

"Yes Lisa, let's take a moment of silence." That was about the longest moment of silence I ever had but soon the Maglev picked up to its normal speed. We were on are way again.

"Do you think that will happen again Gary?"

"No Lisa, don't worry your pretty head off about it." He said, as we snuggled closer together. A few peaceful hours passed and we were coming up to the National Mall. I recognized the underground train station.

"Now the first thing that we want to do Lisa is to go to the high speed rail station to pick up the patents and master plans from the locker there. We will get a motel room and get cleaned up with some showers and food and rest then we will go see Low and Mos, we will catch them in the morning, they should be back from China and back at work."

"That sounds so good to me Gary." I said as we were departing the underground Maglev station. It has been a very long journey for us and I was extremely tired. We made it to the high speed train station and picked up the papers then went to our hotel room. I thought that we would never arrive there but we did and all in one piece. Like always, the night was too short. We took a subway down to the building where Low and Mos worked.

"Good morning my dear friends." Low said when we walked in.

"Greetings!" Gary said in return. *"You and Mos sure did a great job in the antidote that you made."*

"I take it that it went well Gary?"

"Yes Low, it was great using the light ray beam and the drugs that you made were excellent. All of Hua's people are back to normal."

"That's all we want to hear." said Low.

"I have your master plan here for the space plane that you and Mos had made so many years ago. You two more than deserve these papers.

The only thing is no one can tell anyone how you got them back or what you have done for all of Hua's people."

"No problem." says Low, and Mos agrees as they reach their hand out to take their master plans back. *"Maybe we can do business again someday."* Mos said.

"Funny that you would say that Mos, for China is worried about the big wave coming they call it the Sea Ice."

"We have heard about that my friend." Low said.

"Well there is a possibility that it is stirring in the ocean for Lisa, and I had an experience with the Maglev train while we were riding it."

"Really?" Mos asked.

"Yes, it was very real and ice cycles formed on the inside of the Maglev box car."

"Could it have been that the train passed some other source of magnets?" Mos asked.

"Yes, that is possible. It also may have been an effect of an electrical conductor for when the magnets and conductors are moving in relationship to each other you know such as attractions and repulsions anything can happen." Gary said.

"True my friend." Mos said.

"Well Lisa, we need to get going."

"Okay Gary." I said as I took his hand.

"Again Low and Mos you went way above the call of duty, many thanks." Gary said as we left the room.

CHAPTER 88

"It was nice to see the great rocket scientists again." I said to Gary.

"They are quite intelligent to figure out that antidote and all that we needed in such a short time." Gary said

"You know Gary, is it not strange to you that they could give you an antidote so fast? I mean within 24 hours and they even had the name of the gas and the mix for it."

"Yes Lisa, but what would they have to gain by giving us this Lisa?"

"First thing Gary, the master plans that you gave them for their plane."

"But I did not barter until after they said yes, they would do it."

"I do have a theory." I said to Gary.

"What is your theory Lisa?"

"Well number one Gary, how did they being refugees from the war get such a good job in our country protecting our security? Being immigrants?"

"That is it Lisa, Col. Leone got them their job and knowing that they would be useful in his operation."

"Col. Leone probably promised them the same thing that we promise them."

"The master plans of their plane, plus maybe they were going to double cross Col. Leone and steal the patents from him after he found them."

"That would explain Gary, why they made the antidote for Hua's people and knowing that we would get rid of Col. Leone for them." They did encourage us to send Col. Leone off to space.

"*Oh great Lisa, that means that they will come after us for the patents. I think Lisa, that they might be responsible for the big escape at the prison. They needed Knuckles and Starfish out to help them with their double-crossing and after they knew that we would take care of Col. Leone, the brothers were to take care of us and steal the Patents back from us.*

CHAPTER 89

When we thought that things were almost back to normal we then believed that Low and Mos were up to no good and had hired Knuckles and Starfish to steal the patents from us and possibly do away with Gary and myself.

"*We need help and help fast.*"

"*Gary, what are we going to do now?*" I asked

"*No worries, my love I've already taking care of this.*"

"*What do you mean Gary?*" I asked.

"*I got a call into China last night and I talked to Hau, he is sending the best of his people over here to help us.*"

"*But Gary,*" I said "*what can they do?*"

"*Lisa, let me finish. I have a plan.*"

"*And what is that Gary?*"

"*It's very simple Lisa.*"

"*Hua and Yao are sending over the best of their space army. They will find and pick up Knuckles and Starfish. They also will be sending them back to China and once there, will get a ride on the one-way space ship, then they can visit Col. Leone. That is if they land on the same planet.*"

"*But how will they capture them Gary?*" I asked?

"*Easier said than done. All we have to do is spread the word and say that we are going back to China with the patents. They will follow us into a trap and Hua's space army will be at the underground Maglev train station and apprehend them both.*"

"*Boy Gary that sounds like it may just work. But what about Low and Mos, they are such a danger now to our Country.*"

"No Problem with them either. Headquarters will arrest them soon as they hear what I have to tell them. In fact Low and Mos might of been under suspicion for some time now for being involved in making a biological weapon to give to Iran so they can use it on our Country. They will never see day light again If this is true."

"When is all this supposed to happen Gary?" I asked?

"By the next sunrise Lisa."

"Well, that does not give us much time Gary."

"I know Lisa, but after this you and I will be free to start a new life."

"Gary, please hold me tight and tell me this will all work out."

"Lisa, God is my witness, we will be together always." He says as he put his arms around me and kissed me goodnight.

"I love you Gary, so much." I said.

"Lisa, love is our bond."

"Together forever." We both uttered as we fell asleep in each other's arms.

CHAPTER 90

The next morning was here before we knew it. *"Get up Lisa, we have a train to catch,"* I heard Gary say. As I rubbed my eyes and said *"Already its morning?"*

"Yes sunshine." Gary said. *"I got an early call from Hua this morning and he says that his army has the new XM25 rifle and it has twice the range as an AK47."*

"Come on Gary, what are you saying?"

"Lisa, this artillery is more accurate. I heard about it when I was stationed in Afghanistan when they were testing all XM25 rifles and they found out that it has less collateral damage than using mortals and other alternatives. All you have to do is find the target, aim it, and if the target moves the bullets will find it."

"They are only thinking of our safety Lisa, especially with us being in the underground tunnel and if they have to use the XM25 smart gun it won't blow the whole tunnel up including us."

"That sure is some heavy stuff." I said to Gary.

"It is Lisa, and it also has been used in all the Shadow Wars.

"What do you mean Gary?"

"Well it is a secret expansion of wars and all about our country winning the war on terror and it will start this morning on Knuckles and Starfish, if need be. Enough talk Lisa, get dressed for we have a very important appointment to keep."

"Aye, Aye Sir!" I said and winked at Gary. Within the hour Gary and I were headed to the underground National Mall Maglev train station, pretending to be going to China with all the patents.

"Follow me." Gary said as we arrived at the train station.

"Gary," I whispered *"I don't see the space army here yet."*

"Lisa trust me they are hidden. See that plant over there to your right?"

"Yes. Gary, hey it is moving."

"Shush Lisa, before someone hears you."

"Okay." I said.

"The Maglev will be here in a few minutes Lisa, now we need to board it".

"But Gary, I don't want to go back to China."

"I know Lisa, neither do I."

"Here comes the train Lisa."

"Well Gary, it's not the only thing that is coming towards us. I see Knuckles and Starfish right behind us."

"Quick Lisa, get on the train."

"But Gary, it is only 60 seconds before the door closes."

"Lisa, just get on and go to the x-end car and there will be an exit there and get back off."

"I can see now that all of Hua's men are hiding on the train, they will capture Knuckles and Starfish."

CHAPTER 91

Gary was right, I rushed to the X-end and found the exit door and made a fast exit and then when I got outside on the other side of the train the space army soldiers grabbed me and took me into a secret room that they had there to keep me safe. I could hear all kinds of firing and noises going on. I just clinched and hoped that Gary was alright. It was about 30 minutes later and I could feel a rolling motion and shaking of the ground. It was horrible with the walls of the tunnel swaying in all directions.

"*What is happening?*" I asked the soldier.

"*I don't know.*" he said, "*Now wait here.*"

"*Okay.*" *I said.* But I was not going to wait long. I went outside the secret room and could not believe what I saw. The Maglev train had left, but behind it was a mass of destruction. There were trains and guide ways collapsed everywhere in the underground tunnel. I also saw water leaking through the walls and some that already flowed in from the leakage from the waterways. I was not sure where it was coming from until I yelled to one of the soldier's

"*Somebody come here and tell me what is going on?*"

"*I believe that we just had a great earthquake.*" A trooper answered. "*And it was from Washington D.C. to China, and now we have water coming in through the new holes in the tunnels, it's the main body of water and is fed from some surrounding rivers like the Anacostia and Chesapeake that I know.*"

"*Please help me find Gary.*" I asked, "*He was on the Maglev train, in the middle of two criminals who were chasing him. Before I knew it he had me get off of the train and exit by the x-end and then that is when you grabbed me."*

A few minutes later another soldier comes running over and says *"Bing Tuan (Army) Fu Ji (Ambush) all troops held Fu Lu (Captive)"*

"Did I hear that right? So the space army never made it here to Washington DC and was held in China? But who are you people?" I said.

"We were sent by Hua and Yao yesterday to get ahead of the space army just in case there was any trouble."

"It sounds like Hua made the right decision," I said

"But what happen to Gary?"

"We will seek out now and look for him"

"Please, just hurry!" I pleaded *the water is coming in fast.* He proceeded to tell me that all the troops on the train were getting ready to capture Knuckles and Starfish and taking their position when we showed up.

"That means that whoever was on the Maglev train must be dead now with this earthquake and big wave coming and Knuckles and Starfish could have been on that train. I saw them when they were chasing Gary and me."

"Does that mean that the big wave of what Hua was worried about did happen?"

"Maybe," he said, *"and they are expecting the biggest Tsunami this world has ever seen. It just came over the airwaves."*

"Luckily they have another means of escape from the China." I said.

"What do you mean?" He asked me.

I remembered then, no one is supposed to know about the other Maglev train that was built on the other side of China with the help of John Little many years ago.

"Nothing," I said. *"I just got confused."* About that time a guard come running over and yelled! *"There is something beneath the steel rail we need help."*

We all went running over there and here underneath was a man deep in water up to his neck and the water was so quickly filling up around him and he was stuck between two things of steel rail.

"*Oh my gosh, it's Gary!*" I screamed.

"*Stand back lady and we will pull him out. Go fetch that bar over there that was leaning against some garbage cans.*" the soldier said to me.

I ran over and grabbed it and came running back. They quickly tried to pry the steel rail track off of Gary. "*It's alright, they are working fast as they can,*" I said to Gary trying to calm him down so he would relax enough that they could do their job.

The water was getting deeper around Gary's face and they were trying endlessly to pry it loose.

"*Here goes.*" says one of them, and all at once Gary was free from the track and they started slowly pulling him up out of the water to higher ground.

"*Gary are you alright?*" I asked as I helped hold him up.

"*Well Lisa,*" he said, "*I always told you that I prefer Maglev over steel rail.*"

"*How can you joke at a time like this Gary?*" We got Gary over to one of the trains that were still on the guideway and grab a blanket that we found and covered him up. He would go into shock if we could not get him warm.

"*I will be alright.*" he said to me.

"*Gary what happen back there on the train after you had me jump off?*"

"*Well Lisa, I was right behind you and then I got hit in the head and pushed over board.*" I could hear Knuckles yelling, at Starfish (You dumb fool, he was the one to search and had the patents and you pushed him overboard.)"

"*About that time Lisa, it was too late; the Maglev train took off with Knuckles and Starfish on it and they did not have time to stop it. Then I heard a large noise, must have been an earthquake or explosion of some kind that rocked the inside of this tunnel and that I believe is when I got wedge between the high speed steel rail tracks.*"

"*From now on Gary, we stick together.*"

"*Yes Mame,*" he said.

The friends of Hua came over and said "*We need to get out of this tunnel within the next few hours for the seismic waves will hit soon and the flooding is getting worse.*"

"*Okay but let's get Gary warm first and tell me, why do you call them seismic waves?*" I asked

"*It's like this; they are the most destructive type of waves. The energy that travels through the earth as a result of an earthquake or explosion makes them a Tsunami. Now my friends, your criminals that were on the Maglev train are probably dead by now no matter how far they got. The body waves that travel through the interior of the earth by varying density and stiffness of the earth's interior would force and totally destroy the Maglev train into the deep sea and break apart the airless vacuum tube in pieces.*"

"*Lisa, if that is true we are now rid of Knuckles and Starfish once and for all. We will now have Headquarters move in on Low and Mos. This operation is almost finished.*"

CHAPTER 92

Gary was getting back to normal with his temperature and Hua's men left but said that there would be a safe route out and follow the writing on the wall and that they would mark it in red.

The tunnel was starting to fill with water and I notice that these pipes on the wall were leaking and getting worse.

"Gary, look at these pipes? It looks like water is leaking out."

"Lisa, we call those sand pipes and they hold water. In case there is a fire in the tunnel and that is why we have the entire cross over's every thousand feet or so. If you're on the train and a fire starts you can go through the cross over into the other tunnel. In this case Lisa, no fire but flooding in both tunnels so we have nowhere to run unless we get out of here pronto."

"Follow me Lisa I see the red dots on the wall."

"Yes and this is a different direction to go than when we left this area the last trip."

"Just think Lisa the National Mall is above us."

"Do you think that it will be flooded also Gary?"

"I hope not Lisa; I think that this water is from the Potomac River. The tsunami is not here yet and if we are lucky it may not hit Washington DC so we may still have time."

"Gary, I hear something and its getting louder,

"So do I Lisa. Stay still for a minute."

"Okay," I said and about that time we saw hundreds of mice coming from the direction of the red dots. I started to scream as they got closer to us.

"Gary look mice and they are coming in our direction!" I yelled.

"*Lisa those are not mice, they are river rats and the water is running them out.*" I was almost speechless as they ran past us and some on the sides of our bodies.

"*Oh no Gary, what are those things coming from the holes in the pipes?*"

"*Lisa no problems, they are just little sea creatures.*"

"*What Gary? But we are not near the sea or ocean.*"

"*I know Lisa, but the earthquake made the sea turn into big waves and that is how they got here.*"

"*The red dots Gary are getting smaller.*"

"*Well Lisa, just follow me and hold my hand.*" Gary said as we were stepping in about 3 feet of water. We went about 500 yards more and Gary started shouting, "*Lisa look! A red gas can is painted on the wall.*"

"*That could only mean one thing Gary.*"

"*Yes Lisa and you can have the pleasure of pushing the red dot on the gas can and if it is like all the others we will be out of this water in no time.*"

Gary reached for my hand and put me in front of him while I pushed the painted gas can. Within seconds we were able to give a push on the wall which opened up.

"*Lisa, this is what they call a **Man cave** as we looked around this dark room.*"

"*What is a man cave Gary?*" I asked.

"*Well it's like where men gather to watch football and well . . .*"

"*Yes Gary and what else?*" As I looked around the room I saw a pole in the middle of it.

"*Gary, what is that pole for? It looks like a fireman's pole that they use to slide down to get in their fire trucks.*"

"*Lisa, this one looks like it was used for a female stripper pole.*"

"*You're kidding right, Gary?*"

"*No Lisa, I always heard that Col. Leone liked his women beautiful.*"

"*But how did he have time for all this Gary?*" I asked.

"*Lisa it's a man's thing.*"

"What Gary? Well it better not be a man's thing for you!" I said kidding him. (But I was serious).

"Lisa, look over here. I see some pictures and see a woman, and a man and a little Chinese girl."

"Who is that sweet young girl in this picture?" And look, the man *is very handsome, and he's very big."* The big man was all are dressed in white like a karate outfit and the beautiful young Chinese girl is wearing a pretty colorful Chinese robe. She is looking at the white women who also had a white coat on and she is smiling at the girl and the girl is smiling back at her. The look on their faces is a look of contentment and the big man seems pleased.

"There must be a big story behind this picture Gary," I said

"Yes Lisa, if only pictures could talk."

"Well Gary, it is true when they say, a picture is worth a thousand words."

CHAPTER 93

"Now Lisa, look at this writing on the wall. It reads **Bamuyita Jesu** *and look here it says* **A Talema** *what are they saying?"*

"Well Gary, during my earlier years in College I went to Uganda, and if I remember right it is saying (His name is Jesus) (Who never fails)."

"You know Lisa, *this room looks like it's been lived in, now look at the furniture and there is an old bedrail in the corner and a lamp on that old dusty corner table, and some old plates in the sink."*

"Yes Gary, I think that you are right. But who would want to live in this underground tunnel turned cave, unless, you had no choice."

"That's it Lisa, someone was held hostage here and it wasn't for overnight. Maybe Col. Leone had something to do with this also."

"Maybe so Gary, but we won't be able to ask him that question now that he made a one way trip to space."

"Look over here Lisa, another red dot for a gas can."

"No way Gary, another hidden room?"

"What are you waiting for Gary? Let's go in and see. Okay, here goes. "As we both pushed on the rock wall. It was dark, but just enough light to see something so surreal.

"Oh my God, Gary she's alive." At that point we were not ready to see what we did. Here sat in a rocking chair a Chinese lady that was rocking back and forth and never said a word, she just stared straight ahead and rocked and rocked in the chair. Her hair was uncombed, and must have not been washed in months. There were spider webs all around her and some of her teeth were missing as I got closer to look. Her clothes were all faded and torn and her feet

were black with dirt. Gary, and I slowly walked up to her and she made no motion at all that she even noticed us in the room with her. Tears weld up in my eyes as I looked at her and it was hard not to get emotional at this point. Gary and I both were for a minute speechless and just looked at each other. How could anyone treat someone like this?

Who did it? Was the question that is what was crossing my mind.

"Let me talk first Lisa, we don't want to scare her and second I don't think that she has had any food or water for quite some time. Look around for some drinking water Lisa."

"Okay." I said and I found some in an old bowl and gave it to Gary to give the poor lady. I saw a piece of paper rolled up on the floor.

"Hey Gary you need to see this."

"What is it Lisa?" asked Gary as he was telling the lady not to be scared that we were there to help her.

"It is an old newspaper article that reads," **Missing Chinese teen ambassador's daughter believed to of been kidnapped during the raid on the city of Nazi, Germany when her father and her visited the Consulate General.** *"Oh, do you think that she has been held prisoner since World War II?"* I asked. *"The date on the newspaper is 1963 and I know from reading that during the war that the Germans were looking for what they called* **Comfort women,** *some were kidnapped from Korea, China, Japan and the Philippines through some occupied territories."* *"Oh that is just so unbelievable and what a life for a poor young girl and to be held over 20 some years. I bet she is the little girl in the picture in the other room."*

"You guessed it Lisa."

"Here is other piece of a newspaper in the drawer over here with a picture Gary."

"What does it say Lisa?"

"It's a picture of two brothers, Low and Mos shaking hands with none other than Col. Leone for some kind of a reward."

"Lisa, the US planned to kidnap the Germans that were Atomic scientist in World War II and maybe Col. Leone offered them freedom

241

to work for him. Remember that picture in the other room and the big white man also had the same ring on well it's a Mason ring, at least it looks like the same one."

"Wait a minute, the picture of the big man with the karate clothes that was Col. Leone when he was younger."

"Yes, Lisa and it looks like he was a German. We always wondered that about him but never asked, but he did look German."

"Yes, Gary a lot younger and is better looking at that time."

"He's trying to get the young Chinese girl to marry him and it looks like that was his mother in the picture with them.

"Yes, I agree and when the girl would not marry him he kidnapped her and held her hostage all these years. I bet no one knows about her being here and now with Col. Leone's gone she would have starved to death if we did not find her."

"How convenient for Col. Leone, for his office at headquarters is upstairs in the National mall."

"Come on Lisa, we will throw this blanket over her and I will carry her and we need to hurry the water is getting deeper. Gary then gently picked her up and we made our way to the exit of the old room that was made into a cell.

CHAPTER 94

It was not long before we were going inside of the National Mall.
Not many people were there just a few running down the strip.
"Hurry Lisa we need to get her to the hospital." Said Gary as I
rush outside and flagged down a taxi. Gary gently lifted the Chinese
girl into the car. She was not aware of anything that was going on
around her and just laid her head in Gary's arms.
"What a sweet women she must be Gary."
"Yes, Lisa let's hope that we are not too late."
It was hard for the taxi driver to get down the street due to flooding
but luckily he knew the back way to the hospital. We notified the
police on what was going on and got her to the emergency room.
We told the nurse that we would be back later today.
Then Gary said *"We need to get to Headquarters and find out
what is happening with Low and Mos and if they were arrested yet."*
*"Lisa we are real close to wrapping up this operation. I heard that our
department wants to have a talk with you about employment into the CIA."*
"You are kidding Gary. Right?"
*"No I am not Lisa, they have seen how brave and smart you are and
want to enlist you."*
*"I do feel privileged, for them to consider me after all I was trained
by the best."* I said.
"I know that Lisa, why do you think that they want you?"
"Okay Gary, we will see." We made it to Headquarters, and it
was so different than I had expected. A large room with a few desks
and piles of papers on top of them and a few old fashion phones still
hung in the room.

"Most of the men were dressed nicely in black suits. On the floor leaning against the wall was a picture of Col. Leone, someone had already taking down.

"Come in my office." said one of the officers. *"We want to debrief each of you but in separate rooms."*

"Gary, do they think that we are the bad guys?"

"No Lisa," he said as he chuckled, *"that is how we do it, not to confuse the stories and see how accurate that we match.*

Just relax and tell the truth and try and remember all the details from day one."

"Day one Gary? You mean from the time that I met you and came into your life?"

"Sort of like that Lisa."

"See you in a few hours," as they took me to other room. I waved at Gary as I was leaving, *"love you."* I whispered.

"Love you too," Gary said.

In the room only I saw a large oblong table and two chairs with a one-way glass between the rooms.

"Okay Lisa, my name a Jack, and I will explain what we will be doing."

"The normal procedure is that after each 'BLACK' or 'wet' operation all persons participating in or connected with the operation are totally debriefed by a special debriefing team."

"In this debriefing with you Lisa a member of the "wet" team is required to recite to the debriefing team exactly what happened during the operation, in a precise, step-by-step, detailed manner."

"Each one, meaning Gary and you will be asked questions and is generally repeated several times—once normally, once under hypnosis, once with a polygraph, and once under scopolamine."

"Only when I am fully satisfied with all the details and that there are no glaring inconsistencies between you and Gary's different recitations, is the debriefing brought to a close."

"In other words Jack, you are trying to tell me that this will take a while."

"Lisa, you are so smart."

"Then Jack, let's get this over with."

CHAPTER 95

The debriefing went on for hours but finally it was over with and Gary and I were to meet each other in the conference room. I took one look at Gary and fell into his arms. *"Gary, I am so glad that we got that over with."* I said.

"Not so fast." came a voice from behind.

"Sit down and get comfortable we still have a lot to go over." said the Director of the CIA. He was a small man with a bald head and dressed in brown slacks and a white shirt, he must have been at least 65 years old.

"I have never in the 40 years of being in the CIA seen a debriefing that two individuals had with no differences or inconsistencies." He said to both Gary and I. *"Under both of your hypnosis and polygraph test both of you came out with the same correct details. So I am fully satisfied with you both but only one question remains and I will direct it at you first Lisa."*

"The CIA would like to induct you into our program. You would be sent to basic training camps and other including analytic tools, denial and deception analysis, and warning skills. Lisa you would also learn skills in thinking, writing, and briefing. We will teach you new languages in Russian, Chinese, and Arabic."

"Before you tell me no, I want you to think of this, here in Washington D.C. we have the best National War College in the States. Now think about it while I talk to Gary."

"Okay Gary please hear me out. We want you to be our new Assistant Director of Central Intelligence Agency, and as you are probably aware

of your job would be to report and work under the direction of the CIA Director."

We both sat there in shock at what was being offered to us.

"That is all Gary and Lisa, now go home and think about this and what I have said. The CIA would love to have you both. We hope that you will accept the new position offered to you." With that he left the room as quick as he entered it.

Before we left Gary had already talked to intelligence about Low and Mos arrest. They had surrendered yesterday without incidence and held without bail for being war lords, and espionage agents, the list was long.

We left the CIA office overwhelmed with all that we had been through in the last 24 hours between the interrogation, briefing, and job offers. I knew that the money would be good and maybe I could be with Gary more if I accepted. I was going to think about this long and hard.

"Well Lisa," said Gary as we got into a taxi, *"We need to get back to the hospital and see how our friend is doing. It also looked like the tsunami didn't make it to Washington."*

"Glad of that." I answered.

We walked inside the hospital to see how she was doing and Gary asked the nurse, *"We had dropped off a very sick Chinese lady late last night and wanted to know what room she is in?"*

"What is her name?" asked the nurse.

"Well, I think that they were calling her Ms. Freeway."

"Just a minute." the nurse said who was dressed in white and had some of her red hair in a bun and some of her hair looked like it was falling out of it. She looked about 40 years old and had a very thin body. She continued talking as she flipped through her books *"It looks like they transferred her to Georgetown University and that is all that I can tell you."*

"Thank you," Gary replied as we ran outside to catch another cab.

"Please take us to Georgetown University and step on it." Gary said.

"What are we in a hurry Gary?"

"Lisa I really want to make sure is still alright and if she needs anything?"

"I understand that Gary," as I yelled at the cab driver and said, "Yes, step on it!"

And boy did he put the pedal to the metal.

"In about 30 minutes we should be there Lisa. I will call ahead and see what room she is in."

CHAPTER 96

We arrived at Georgetown University and it was not long before we were talking to Ms. Freeway's doctor. I did wonder how they picked that name for her and when I asked Gary, he said it was because she was found under a mall near the freeway. Well, whatever at least she has a name now. *"Here comes the Doctor now"* I said to Gary

"Hi I'm Dr. Freed and I have been taking care of Ms. Freeway. Considering what she has been through she is in remarkable condition. I am not sure about her mental health yet but we will have her evaluated soon."

The Doctor looked at Gary and said, *"Who in their right mind would hold someone for over twenty years hostage and hidden in a underground cave and never knowing or seeing anyone besides her captives?"*

"Well" Gary said to Dr. Freed, *"he was a very evil man."*

"I sure hope that you capture him."

"It's already done Doctor, he is very far away from all of us, and would be almost impossible for him to escape."

"What is his name?" Dr. Freed asked?

"His name is Col. Leone, he worked for the CIA and got too greedy for his own good."

"What we believed happen to Ms. Freeway is that Col. Leone wanted this young Chinese girl for his bride, she was the daughter of an Ambassador from China and when she would not agree to go with him, he kidnapped her and held her captive."

"Well, she sure is a strong woman to go through all that she did and literally she is definitely a miracle." said Dr. Freed. *"You need to understand that she will be emotionally unstable, feel frightened and*

possibly may have suicidal thoughts. She just lost her captor and they usually form a bond with them and especially after so many years. Her long term trauma will need much therapy."

"I understand all that Dr. Freed"

"One more thing Gary,"

"Yes Dr. Freed"

"She also has what we call in the medical field PTSD meaning (Post Traumatic Stress Disorder)."

"Can that be treated Dr. Freed?"

"Yes, to some extent." he answered.

"May we see her now?" asked Gary.

"Yes, but not for long please for she needs a lot of rest."

"Thanks Doctor Freed." and we entered her room. She looked so much better already in a white gown and although she had tubes going everywhere she looked at peace. Her private room was painted a pale white and a pink spread was on her bed like the color of a pink Cadillac. I went over and held her hand and she was so cold.

"Gary why is she so cold?" I asked.

"It will take a while for her to adjust to our warmer temperatures Lisa, remember she had no heat where she was at."

"I know Gary, and if I could get my hands on Col. Leone I would take care of him."

"Hello Lisa, we already took care of him on his one way trip to space."

"Yes Gary; and I actually felt sorry for him when the space craft took off. I sure don't anymore. It was just a horrific war crime." I cried and laid my head on Gary, as he rubbed my back.

A few minutes later a nurse came in the room and said to Gary, *"Are you Gary Brooks?"*

"Yes I am." he said.

"Follow me you have a phone call." When Gary left the room I went back over and held her hands and she seem to relax when I would touch her. She is so precious I did not want to let go of her. My heart was crying for this poor lady and all that she must have been through. I knew that she needed her rest so I covered her up and gave her a kiss on the forehead and left the room and found Gary.

CHAPTER 97

"Gary, she sure will have a lot of new problems with the PTSD."
"I know Lisa; she will need to be in long term therapy."
"That is for sure Gary." I said.
We were just getting ready to leave the hospital and Gary received another phone call and this time the nurse's station paged him. He picked the phone and I could hear him talking and he said *"Hi Hua! I am surprise to hear from you. Yes, we did find a Chinese lady."*
"What? You're kidding right?"
"Okay, I will check and call you back."
"Gary" I said after he hung up the phone, *"What did Hua want? And what was he kidding about?"*
"Well Lisa, I don't think that he was kidding. He told me that many years ago when he was very small that he had a missing cousin who was kidnapped. He doesn't remember much about her because he was very small. She had disappeared. Their family kept it very secret from everyone. Hua knew that he had a cousin but his father Yao did not want to say much about it."
"Hua heard that we found a Chinese lady in the underground tunnel. It came on CNN world news."
"Gary, then why did you say that you would check?"
"Lisa, if she has a birthmark on the back of her neck shaped like a mouse then it's her."
"Wow Gary, let's get back to her room and then we will know."
A few minutes later and we were back in her room and Gary said *"Lisa, pull up the back of her hair."* I went over to her and lifted

up the back of her hair and we both looked in amazement sure enough there was a birthmark on the back of her neck and it was shaped like a mouse.

"Okay, she has relatives thank God, and of all people its Hua's cousin, and Yao's aunt. She was supposed to become the 'Empress of China.' Hua was telling me" Gary immediately made a call back to Hua and told him the news. Hua said him and his father would catch the next Maglev train that evening.

It was early the next morning when we met Hua and Yao at the train station and brought them to the hospital to meet her. Yao was telling us as we traveled there that her name was Wu Zetiana descended of the Tang Dynasty, and her first name was Wu. Her mother was the first women in Chinese history to become an Empress.

"The story goes," Yao said, *"that Wu was to take over for her mother who still was Empress but her mom's health was failing and they knew that my aunt was young but had wit, beauty, could play music and even write and all at the age of 13 years old. They were going to recruit her to the court of Emperor Tai Tsung and she was supposed to marry Tai Tsung, but my aunt had eyes for his son, Kao Tsung. Well needless to say the marriage never happened due to the kidnappers of Col. Leone taking Wu from her bedroom in the middle of the night."*

"Well the rest you and Lisa know." said Hua.

"Gary," I said, *"that is just other thing to add to the list of all the rotten things that Col. Leone has done to the Chinese people."*

"We can hardly wait to see her Gary," Hua said, *"Me either."* said Yao, *"we are so ever grateful."*

"I cannot believe you two," said Hua, *"you and Lisa saved me first from the Chinese gang then come to my Country, in China and save all my people from Col. Leone, then you go back to Washington DC not knowing that we had a kidnap cousin and find her in a underground tunnel that had a cave and almost full of water."*

"Well Hua, if it wasn't for the big wave, we never would have found her." Gary then says, *"Lets wrap it all up to a big miracle, but you both need to know that she has what they call a* **posttraumatic stress disorder.**

"I have heard about that before my friend," Hua said. *"We have already checked into help for Wu. There is a hospital in Canton, China that is called 'John G. Kerr Refuge' that can treat that disorder. It's a mental hospital our Countries very first and believe it or not the American medical missionaries build it for our people for humanity sake."*

"That is wonderful news Hua."

"Yes," said Yao, *"we are so happy and there is an old wise saying that says* **The heathens do not ask for Bibles and Missionaries but need them all the same. The Chinese did not want, but needed a mental hospital, but got it all the same."**

"Now that is a very wise saying and yes so true." said Gary.

Then Hua and Yao started quoting Bamuyita (*His name is Jesus*) Atalema (*Who never fails.*)

"Where have we heard that before Lisa?"

"You remember Gary, it was written on the wall in the cave near the room that Wu (Ms. Freeman) was in." Hua said, *"We always said that prayer every night and in the morning before we did anything . . . Through Chinese proverbs tradition she must have been taught from her mother also."*

"Well Hua, she never forgot it that is for sure. Look we are here at the hospital." I said as Gary pulled the truck up to the front door.

CHAPTER 98

We all walked into the hospital full of excitement that Hua and Yao would finally see Wu after so many years and that it would be the first time for Hua to meet his one and only cousin. When we went to the room it was empty. *Oh no! I hope she did not Shi (die) said Hua.*

The nurse in the uniform wore clothes that were too tight on her and her hair tied in a net overheard him and said, *"We just took her down for mental evaluation she will be back shortly."*

"Shang Pin (Good)" Hua said to the nurse. I asked the nurse if she was conscience now and she said, *"Yes and you will see when she gets back."*

"Please send the doctor in for us," Gary said to the nurse.

"He is on his rounds now but he should be with you shortly."

"Okay," we waited for about 15 minutes and in walks Dr. Freed

"Hello Gary and Lisa, and your friends"

"Oh sorry Dr. Freed, this is Hua and his Father Yao they are Ms Freeways cousins, or I should say Wu's is her name and she is Yao's aunt."

"Wow! Quite a surprise," Dr. Freed said to them. *"Well Hua and Yao this is wonderful, she will need much care."*

"No problem," Hua said *we will nurse her back to health.*

"Not so fast boys, your aunt may have what we call a 'Paranormal'. In Parapsychology it comes in many forms. We also describe it as an Aura like a subtle, luminous radiation surrounding a person or object. Under the conditions in which she lived she does not know what is real and what is not real."

"Can she be cured Dr. Freed?" asked Yao

"With lots of help she could get better. You both will need to understand that it's like there is a halo or aureoles surrounding her and her moods do change."

"That sounds difficult to treat." said Yao.

"Well we do have medicines that will help her out and ease her pain." said Dr. Freed.

"That is about the best news that I have heard today." said Hua, *"I was also telling Gary about the famous mental hospital in China we are so thankful for all what your Americans do for my people. I am much anxious now and can hardly wait to meet my cousin.*

"She is coming down the hall now. Please don't stay to long, she needs her rest." says Dr. Freed. We saw a nurse pushing her in a wheelchair down the hallway, we watch her come closer. Her eyes did not move around or even look at us as she went by us it was like she did not see us at all.

"I hope that we can communicate with her." Hua said.

"You can tell she's a beautiful woman," Yao said. Then the orderly came in and helped the nurse put her back in bed. After they left, Hua and Yao went over to her and held her hands and said to her

"We are your zong Hu (family) you have been Jie Yue (Saved) from the Da Hai (Sea ocean) and from Col. Leone"

"You are a Jie-Mei (your mama was our mama's) sister. We all have the same Huang Xian Yue (blood). Before you were kidnapped you were to become Huang Di (Emperies) to our country."

Gary went over to the bed and whispered to Yao and Hua *"Maybe that is enough for now for you don't want to overwhelm her any more than she is."*

"Look everyone." I said, *"There are tears coming down from her eyes, she understands what they are saying to her."*

"She is squeezing our hands," Hua said as he started crying and next Yau was shedding *Lei* (tears). Pretty soon we all had teary eyes.

Dr. Freed walked into the room and says, *"She is responding more than I thought she would."* He then walked over to her and picked up her hand and said in Chinese, *"You are Tai (safe) and will be going Jia (home) when we can get you in better Wu li (physical) condition."*

"We did not know that you could speak Chinese Dr. Freed."

"I was in Canton, China and worked as an intern there for over 5 years and was one of their first medical doctors. I only knew that someday that it would come in handy if I could learn to speak Chinese."

"To meet such a woman of her character who has endured more than ever a horrible life for over 20 years and held captive to be as sane as she is, now that is nothing short of a miracle."

"Yes," Gary said, *"that all is so true. She truly is like a magnet. Her strength is enduring."*

"Yes it is," Dr. Freed said, *"but maybe this is enough excitement for tonight for her. Can you all come back tomorrow and visit Wu?"*

"Okay," Gary said, *"I will take them to a hotel for the night and bring them back in the morning."*

As we were leaving the room her eyes followed the boys to the door and they acknowledge her and said *"See you in Chad (morning) We Chun (Love you)."* Then Wu's eyes closed and she went to sleep. Both Yao and Hua left weeping along with Gary and me. It was not tears of happiness but sorrow that she had to suffer for so many years.

CHAPTER 99

The next day was here before we knew it and we went and picked up Hua and Yao and headed back to the hospital again so they could visit Wu. We could hear someone calling us as we walked down the hall to Wu's room.

"*Oh look Gary, it is Dr. Freed.*"

"*Wait up guys,*" he said as we were walking down the hall. "*I need to talk to Hua and Yao, it's about Wu.*"

"*She is doing okay, it's just that we got some more blood work back and it seems that she has mercury poison and we need to reverse it.*"

"*How did she get that Dr. Freed?*" Hua asked.

"*It is my guess that she was fed a lot of sushi and over time that can produce mercury in her body at a high level.*"

"*What can you do about it?*" Hua asked.

"*Well it's like this Hua, we can reverse mercury toxicity but we will need to do an intravenous infusion and its called Ethylene Diamine Tetra Acutil acid that will kill the poisonous cells.*"

"*I will need you both to sign a consent form before I begin. We practice this often and it is nothing to worry about.*"

"*Okay,*" Yao said, "*prepare the paper work.*"

We continued to walk towards Wu's room. When we walked in the room here is this beautiful woman with long beautiful dark auburn hair with a pretty bow in it. It look liked the nurses-aide had washed her hair and dressed her in a Chinese robe. The aide said she had it for a costume party and brought it to work that day for Wu. She became the favorite patient of the wards.

Sitting up in the bed she looked over at us and gave a big smile and said with a very soft voice,

"*Shou Huan Ying (Welcome) I, Ji Yi (remember you) Bao Bao (babies)*"

"*Yes, my cousin (Biao Gin),*" Then Hua and Yao went over by her bed and were holding her hands. I snapped a picture with my instant camera and brought it over for her to see and then her eyes starred at the camera. I guess she never seen something so modern as this. She said, "*Xie, Xie (take more)!*"

"*She wants you to take more pictures,*" Yao said as she held and looked at the picture that I just took.

"*This went on for almost an hour just all of us being like kids. They were being silly in the pictures like making faces, and looking goofy. It was so much fun. Especially to see how much Wu was enjoying herself.*" She was showing signs of happiness and laughter.

Every day the boys went to see Wu. She was making amazing progress and all were very excited. It was not long before Hua and Yao had made plans to take their aunt back to china.

It was about a month later we were at the Maglev train station in Fernley, Nevada Gary and I stood on the platform waving good-bye to three special Chinese friends.

"*I will miss them so much Gary and I have grown to love Wu like she was my sister.*"

"*Yes Lisa, I can understand that. I feel the same towards the boys Hua and Yao; I will miss them terrible too.*"

"*My heart is heavy for her Gary, for what she had to endure all those wasted years of her life. Her life is so precious to all her people and what a shock it will be when they find out that their Empress, is still alive.*"

"*Well Gary, do you think that she will ever be well enough to lead her people?*"

"*Knowing the blood that she was born with there is no doubt in my mind Lisa. Maybe her treatments will work very fast but it is too soon to know and time will only tell us my Lisa.*"

CHAPTER 100

"Lisa, we have been through so much and now it is coming to a close."

"Maybe it is Gary, I have considered taking Jack up on his offer and go into extensive training to become a CIA agent."

"Like you didn't get enough with me Lisa? I know that you are a strong woman, and you feel deeply, and oh my, you love so fiercely."

"But Gary . . . !"

"Let me finish Lisa, your tears flow just as abundantly as your laughter. And most important my love you're soft and powerful and also spiritual and in essence you are for sure a gift to the world."

"Gee Gary that was so beautiful. I never knew that side of you before. I would say that you have been holding out on me."

"Never my love, you are just so practical and we just have had not much time with each other in the romance department. I love writing poems for you but my job with the CIA is of the up most importance as you well know. It does not leave us much time my dear. You are so terrific Lisa for your understanding. Maybe you are looking for more excitement that I can give you? I really want you to have a normal life Lisa."

"Are you kidding Gary, you've taught me so much and I don't think that I could ever live a normal life anymore."

"Well Lisa you certainly have the talent that is needed for this job and will make one experienced agent."

"You know Gary; you were with me every minute."

"Yes Lisa, but some of those minutes we were in immediate danger."

"I very well know that Gary, but we are about to put that behind us. Now tell me what did you decided on the offer presented to you?"

"*I have decided Lisa, to go for it and become the Assistant director of Central Intelligence. I have already spoke to them and will get my orders soon.*"

"*But Gary, what about us, you know you and me?*"

"*Lisa, it will work out. We will get married after you get through with your basic training.*"

"*Oh Gary I have been waiting so long to hear those words. And what about our jobs Gary? I was hoping that we may get to work together*"

"*Lisa that is one reason I took the new position. I will help decide who goes on what operation, meaning more control on what we do.*"

With that we hugged and held each other through the night. We are going to be *one* real soon I told myself. "*I love you Gary,*" I said.

"*I love you too Lisa,*" Gary said as we fell asleep.

We both reported to headquarters the next day. I was set up to go to the National War College starting in the next few days.

Then the bad news came, Gary found out that the Central Intelligence office that he was to work in was in McLean, Virginia main headquarters for his department.

"*What Gary?*" I said. "*Now we will have to be separated again.*"

"*Not necessarily, Lisa*"

"*I never knew that they would move the office back to Virginia after all these years. The CIA main office is still here in Washington D.C. and I assumed that I would be working here.*"

"*Well Gary, you're assuming too much.*"

"*Sorry Lisa, nothing much that I can do now. They want me to assist the President in making decisions related to National Security. It looks like a lot of writing of reports, research, and a lot of evaluation will end up on my desk.*"

"*I have an idea Lisa; we can fly back and forth and still be together after all Virginia and Washington D.C. are next to each other.*"

"*Yes Gary that may work so I will not stress on this anymore.*"

"*That's my girl.*" Gary said to me as he put his arms around me and gave me a kiss.

Weeks and then months went by and Gary would fly back to our apartment every day, then one day when I went to pick him up at the airport he was not on his flight that he always took. He just disappeared. I was frantic. I called into the Central Intelligence and they could tell me nothing. I lost my heart that day, for it was the day that I had planned to tell Gary, that I was pregnant with his child. I was dismissed by the Department due to the circumstances of my pregnancy and the fact I could hardly function anymore without Gary.

I moved back to Gilroy six months later and tried to pick up my life. I gave birth to our daughter and named her Tirana Brooks; she was a beautiful baby and looked so much like Gary. I decided a year after Tirana, was born and no sign of Gary showing up that I would give my baby a name. Jake, my x-husband asked me to go back to him I took him up on it and we were married for only a few years before I decided to divorce him again.

He was always so good to my daughter and I let Tirana think that Jake was her father. It was too complicated to explain about her real father Gary, and all the excitement and dangerous adventures that we had and the secrets about the underground tunnels and Maglev trains.

Now as I stood here looking at this wooden box and had all these flash-backs and memories. I just wanted to let go and read them as Jake departed and all he could say was I am so sorry Lisa please forgive me.

I went back inside my home and started reading them after I got them in order. Maybe this will tell me the answers that I have been longing for all these years. Where is Gary? And why did he disappear? Is he still alive? The letters were never opened so I got my letter opener and open another letter.

This is what it said *My Dear Lisa, I am writing this letter today* . . . It was too much for me to go on. I put the letter to my chest and just started crying. A few minutes later I went on and finished reading the letter it read,

Because memories are unforgettable,
For our love shall never be forgettable.
Though I miss your presence now
Can your love be drifting away for now?
As time passes by my love for you grows
Deeper as of now.
One Day you'll realize my love for you,
Not false but true.
Though my dream will never be
They will always linger with to be.
Although I walk through life alone
I shall not be alone for you will always be along.
If time shall heal my sadden heart
Time seems to have stood still.
Whatever you must be, my thoughts and love shall always
be of you.
For my thoughts and love are eternal now and forever.
You need to know now Lisa, that I have loved you so very
much.
I hope that this poem I wrote for you will explain my feelings
for you my love . . .'

I know you want to know what happen to me. I will start at the beginning when you dropped me off at the airport. I never did get to make that flight to Virginia. The secret service agents were waiting for me at the airport. It was all so top secret that they would not let me call you. They drove me to the White House to meet with the President. Once there I was kept in isolation. I was not allowed to call you. They were accusing me and made me totally responsible for putting Col. Leone on a one way flight into space and that was considered a war crime.

In other words Lisa, they considered it a crime against humanity therefore I was accused of degradation of one or more human beings that they the United nations consider it murder of extreme extermination and torture. They giving me no choice but to go into space to find Col. Leone and bring him back to stand trial for all he did wrong.

Col. Leone was also a strong member of The Morris Grove, in Sun De Rio, California. It's an elite group of the world's most powerful men who meet once a year. I feel that they were behind this and want Col. Leone for their own purpose. They have discussed the world problems together including some with our past Presidents, and oil barren's. It was once used in the planning of the Manhattan Project. The Grove carries dark secrets.

I knew that once I made it into space that I could land on the space station and work out of that. It would help me find the Maglev Launcher that Col. Leone was in. Is he still alive? I do not know yet. I also knew that not knowing how long I would be gone I could pre-write these letters to you and have them mailed to you once a month for 12 months. If my mission was not completed in 12 months I knew that I would never come back but you would know the truth.

I have a friend in the secret service that said that he would make sure that you received one every month per my request. I have 7 days before my departure and hope to finish the next 11 letters to you. In return they sent me on a one way mission.

More later my dear Lisa, Love Eternally, Gary.'

After reading this letter I just broke down. I hope that I can continue reading these letters later. The heartbreak is almost too much to bear.

CHAPTER 101

It was a few days later before I could bring myself to read the rest of the letters. Most of them were sad and how he did not want to go on this mission to find a very wicked man that got his just reward. In the last letter that Gary wrote to me he said that if anything happens to me and you don't hear from me within this year please contact Hua and Yao in China.

Now what could this mean I told myself? This would have been over 21 years ago that he wrote this. After all this time should I still contact the father and son in China? I had to find out what he was talking about and there was no doubt in my mind.

I packed my bags and headed to Fernley, Nevada to catch the Maglev train to China. I had heard that the tunnels and trains were rebuilt from Washington to China since the big wave had hit many years ago. The hidden train station was still underground in Fernley and looked like it did 21 years ago. Before I left home I had called Hua, and told him that I was on my way. He said that he would look forward to my visit and said to me *'The strength of a family, like the strength of an army, is in its loyalty to each other.'* He wanted me to know that he considered us family. He informed me that his father Yao had died a few years ago. I told him the world has lost a great and mighty leader and how sad I felt but I would see him soon.

I found myself alone on the train and oh how it brought back memories. I often wondered why the public never heard much about the Maglev train. Last I heard it was tied up with the environmental department saying that it would be putting all the fish and water creatures as an endanger species by the vibration from under the ground from the sound of the Maglev train, *'now how idiotic is that?'*

So they are holding the project up and even though Gary and I retrieved the patents and our Country could get so rich but now it's too late. Here it is 21 years later and all the other countries including Japan and China have the Maglev trains up and running. We now have the high speed rail and it goes all too slow. We are also a third world country now in transportation. Just maybe I thought that our environmental department is communism? Makes me wonder?

Within hours I was in China and as I was getting off the Maglev train I recognize a few of Hua's guards by the way they dressed and how they came to take me to the sanctuary . . .

We reach it within an hour and here stood Hua looking much older. His face was drawn like he had been through a deep depression. *"Lisa, Lisa, Shu-Ren (Friend, friend),"* he said as he bowed to me.

"Lisa, you still are so Mei Guan (beautiful)."

"That is all so kind for you to say. I am not as young when I saw you last." I said.

"How is your sister Wu?" I asked?

Hua answered and said, *"She is alive and well at the ripe old age of 55 now and without her I would be lost for it is said **One joy scatters a hundred grief's.**"*

"Lisa she has lived a good life after you and Gary found her and we brought her to China, she had a chance to rule with my father for a while then she took it back over with me after his death."

"I am so glad that you two have each other."

"Thanks Lisa. Now, what brings you here after all these years?"

"Well this will be hard for me to tell you this. But Gary had disappeared twenty one years ago. Just a few days ago, my x-husband gave me letters that Gary had written to me many years ago before he was sent to space."

"The President and his trolls accused him of doing war crimes and the only way he could save himself was to retrieve Colonel Leone and bring him back from space."

"The last letter that I read said that if I did not hear from him within the 12 months to contact you and Yao and that was 21 years ago."

"Wow, Shu Ren (my friend) I will do whatever you need."

"Okay," I said. *"We need to get to space and see if Gary is there still. Is there any way that your space troops can help me?"*

"Yes." said Hua, *"We have a new Dan Dao Dao Dan (Missle) that can go to space. It was just developed a few years ago, but our Country had no reason to use it until now. This is one way that we can pay you and Gary back for all you have done for us and our people said Hua."*

"We will set our spaceship to go to (Salyut 1) it was the first space station that was launched by the Russians in 1971. That would be a good place to start." said Hua.

"Yes cousin," and in walks this beautiful women with a crown on her head and a gorgeous blue and black silk Chinese gown that she wore. She went on to say, *"We can also check out the International space station it is big just like a football field and if Gary found that, he would have enough food to survive all these years."*

"Hello my friend Lisa, it's me Wu," she said to me. *"Hua told me all about you and Gary, and how you found me after all those years in the dungeon. Yao always said before he died that 'A family with an old person has a living treasure of Gold.' and he was full of tales about you two."* We started laughing then hugged and bowed to each other and she said, *"Great, but make room for me. I must go and see if I can help find Gary with you."*

CHAPTER 102

"Okay Wu, but this may be a risky mission and I hate to see you go and endanger your life with us."

"Nonsense Lisa, I want to help and be there when we rescue Gary just like you both rescued me." said Wu.

"It's okay Lisa," said Hua, *"She is thick headed like me and she rules.*

"Lisa how long before you can be ready to go?

"Well Hua I need to go back home and get a few things and let my daughter Tirana know that I will be gone awhile."

"Okay Lisa,"

"We will get the Maglev launcher ready and upon your return we will leave."

"Thanks Hua and Wu, I will be back in a few days."

I was put back on the Maglev train to Fernley, Nevada which by-passes Washington D.C. which I was happy about. I was home now after a long trip from China. I was packing my things when Tirana, walked in my bedroom and said.

"How could you mother, lie to me all those years and let me think that Jake was my dad? I found the letters that Gary wrote you. Now is he my real father or not?"

"I want the truth from you mother and for once in your life."

"Slow down Tirana, I will explain everything to you."

"How do I know that you will tell me the truth? And was he a bad guy?"

"Why no, your father was a hero and a very brave person. He saved hundreds of lives."

"*Then why was he sent to space? And where is he now?*"

"*Please dear Tirana, sit down and I will start from the beginning.*" I said,

She looked at me like her whole world was crushed. She loved Jake so very much and he was the only father that she knew, then to find out that she had another dad that was her real father shattered her.

"*Tirana it is like this,*" and I explained everything from the start.

"*I must get back to China and go with Hua and Wu to find Gary your father, and if he is still alive in space. Now I want you to stay here and wait.*"

"*Well, mother I will not wait here, I want to go to space with you and find my father. I will not let you deprive me of that one request. You have already deprived me of not knowing that I had another father that was my flesh and blood.*"

"*I told you that it was too dangerous to tell you before,*" I said "*Oh Tirana you are so strong and brave like your real father.*"

"*It will be a dangerous mission but if you insist I will let you go with us.*"

"*Well mother that is the answer that I was waiting for. When are we leaving?*"

"*We will catch the secret Maglev train tomorrow and I will tell you more of your dads and my adventures.*"

"*Okay mother I will go and get packed now.*"

"*We will leave at first dawn my daughter.*"

"*Sounds good Mother.*" she said as she walked out of my bedroom. I really hated putting my own daughter into danger but she would never forgive me if I did not let her have this adventure of finding her father.

CHAPTER 103

We drove our car from Gilroy to Fernley, Nevada the next morning. Tirana was so full of questions and could not wait to see the famous Maglev train. She liked the idea that her father and I rode on it many times with our adventures and to see the secret Maglev underground station though she said that it was rumored through the years but no one really believed there was one or if any even existed.

Though the high speed rail she knew all about. Which after 20 years was up and running, not counting the one that the U.S. put in underground and kept it a secret.

"Yes it is true Tirana, your father and I had made many trips on this Maglev and when we go in the airless vacuum tube it really goes fast then."

"I can hardly wait mother." she said.

I proceeded to tell her all about her father and how much we were in love with each other. How we were in the big wave and found Wu who had been held hostage for over 20 years. She cried when she heard that story.

I also told her the story of Col. Leone holding all those Chinese hostages and giving them all poison gas to keep them on the Maglev train. Until her Father and I came alone and zapped the guards and Col. Leone invisible so we could help all of Hua's people get their freedom. She also learned that we were held hostage on an airplane and the pilot bailed out with a parachute and lucky for us her father could fly a plane. She really enjoyed all the stories that I was able to tell her. I also felt good finally after all these years that she knew the truth.

Before long we had reach China and Hua's sanctuary where Hua and Wu met us at the door and bowed to Tirana, and she bowed back and they all started laughing.

They said, "*Shou Huan Ying (Welcome) Gong Ahu (Princess) you look like your mother so Meiguan (Beautiful)*"

Then she surprises me when she said in Chinese, "*Shu Ren my mom told me the She Mi (mystery) of my Da Ming Ding Ding (famous) father. We do appreciate your Bi Zhu (Help) you are You Ming (well known).*"

I never knew that my daughter knew Chinese. "*Well Tirana, you have a way of surprising me,*" I said.

"*I am ready mother to find my Chun (father.)*"

"*Then let's begin,*" says Hua, "*We each will have a space suit, it will be pressurized and will have an oxygen supply to support life. It will protect us from Micrometeoroid Bombardments and severe temperatures. Is everybody with me on this?*" Hua asked? "*It is very important that we understand how this all works.*"

A few minutes later Hua's guards were passing out a parachute pack, Helmets, gloves, and boots.

"*Now,*" Hua said, "*these are bladders that automatically fill air at reduced cabin pressure. Let's get on the Maglev launcher and get strapped in then I will explain more.*" This was really getting exciting now as we followed them to the launching pad.

"*Lisa, when we get to Salyut 1 and if Gary is not there we will head to the International Space Station.*"

"*Okay,*" I said, "*Hua this is your operation.*"

"*Yes Lisa it's our mission to get Gary back to you and your daughter and we will do all we can to bring you all home safe.*"

"*I do appreciate all your help from your cousin Wu and you.*"

"*I know you do my friend.*"

"*We have heard Lisa that the Yellow River may flood again and the last time it killed millions, but not to worry we will be back before it strikes.*

"*Oh no Hua, I do not want to take you away from your people now they will need you.*"

"*Lisa, no it's okay.*"

"We have heard that Russian scientists have reached a lake under the Antarctic after decades of drilling and they have found a gigantic freshwater lake hidden under miles of ice. It is our understanding that if this is true then they could divert the yellow river to flow into the hidden lake."

"Does that mean Hua that your country would be spared that huge flooding and a million lives' that could be lost from a disaster like this?"

"You have it right Lisa It's like Confucius says, **At high tides thrift is better than waste and If a man is born straight and grows crooked and yet lives, he is lucky to escape.**"

"That was great Hua, but you forgot one thing."

"What is that Tirana?"

"Well Hua, Confucius also says, **To rank the effort above the prize may be called love.**"

"You have that chun (love) right Tirana. Come now all my friends we have the Quan (power) we shall make it happen!"

CHAPTER 104

"We appreciate that Hua, but it will be a miracle if Gary is still alive. We can only pray that he is safe."

"Yes Lisa so true. Now if Gary has not weathered cosmic radiation and bone loss because of the atmosphere being made up of mainly nitrogen and carbon dioxide. It would help him with his surviving."

"What are you saying Hua?" I asked."

"With the air dry oxygen he could have pried it out of lunar volcanic rock then he could use a shadow crater for living quarters then his helmet only needs to provide air."

"I have heard that if he landed on Mars they are known to have three months of dust storms."

"Yes Tirana, you are right and let's hope we don't see one."

"Hua how did you and Wu learn so much about space?" I asked.

"Lisa many years ago Wu and I were awarded an American scholarship from the University of Virginia. We then went and enrolled in the Chinese space program of the People's Republic of China and were learning about missiles because of the threat of the soviets. We are proud to say that we were the first Country to put a space station on Mars and the Moon."

"I am very impressed," I said to Hua.

"Well Lisa, now it will pay off we pray with the finding of Gary."

And on that we took off like a rocket into space for one last finale mission. We passed Mercury and Venus and was headed to Salyut 1.

"Look," Hua said, *"It is deserted but it looks like Col. Leone's old space capsule landed there but as we got closer we saw no one around or any signs of life so will now go to The International Space Station."*

Within a few hours we orbit the station and it looked like someone had been living there with the progress supply ship that had catalogs' canisters that we could see while we were landing on the ship and one was outside of the cabin. We got inside and sure enough there were signs of life. We looked around and it was so wild to see what was done so many miles from earth.

"Mom, look over here this is awesome." she was looking at a Phantom Torso in the Destiny Laboratory.

"Hua!" she yelled, *"What is this used for?"* as Tirana pointed her finger at the suit?

"Well Tirana, that torso is designed to measure the effects of radiation on organs in our body. The P progress supply ship keeps them on hand for experimenting purposes."

"Hey mom, look here! This looks like a picture of me." She said surprised.

"Let me see Tirana?" I asked as I picked up the picture that she was holding.

"Oh my, this is me Tirana, when I was almost your age. This means that your father was here." as we all got so excited.

There was a lot of dust on the picture I thought but maybe Gary lost it or something I told myself. We looked around the room with more interest now, and found a few more items that belong to Gary. One was an old driver license from 21 years ago.

Wu said we need to look in the mobility unit (EMU) it is an extravehicular it can be used with a liquid cooling garment from spandex it will keep you cool and with head phones and microphones and a drink bag.

"Follow me" she said as we headed towards this weird looking machine. Oh no, we were not expecting to see what we did, inside of this machine was a backpack that was on this old bearded man.

Hua said, *"This is a MMU. Oh, no a body!"*

"What?" I said.

"Well it is strapped to this man, and it is a Nitrogen Propelled backpack and it lets you fly with precision, but it looks like he only partially had it on before he died."

Tirana looked over and she proceeded to rolled up his sleeve to fill his pulse, he had been dead for some time now for his wrist just went to dust when she touched it. She quickly screamed and let go of the man's wrist.

"Look Hua," I said. *"This looks like Col. Leone; this is the same suit that I remember when Gary sent him into space."*

"Yes Lisa you are right, and I remember that day also."

"He must have found this back pack suit in Salyut 1 and flew it over here to the International space center."

"He then must have run into Gary and the fight began."

"Oh my goodness, then where is Gary?" I asked.

CHAPTER 105

"My friend Lisa, remember what Confucius says, **If the family were a boat, it would be a canoe that makes no progress unless everyone paddles.** *We are all working together and we will find Gary alive and well."* Wu confirmed with me. That was so much for one day to find out about Gary, that he was here and not that long ago and we were hot on his trail.

We found some drawings of a Maglev that looked like it was made from a telescope. There was a seat inside of it and it had magnetic wheels and a guideway elevator to launch it into space. It looked almost like the Hubble craft but with a cab in it.

Wu said that she would call for other space craft with more men to come and help us search for Gary before he takes off in the Hubble craft. *"If that drawing is correct that is what he is up to."*

"We saw no signs of life over there Hua," Tirana said

"Well, he could have been on the other side where they left the Hubble Space Craft because of defects, but Gary will not know about that."

"Wait a minute," Hua said, *"is the Hubble not the one that floats above the earth with a huge telescope?"*

"Yes," Wu said, *"but remember what they told us in space class?"*

"What was that Hua?"

"They said that the components will slowly degrade and it will spiral towards earth."

"Oh No, then that means that my dad is in danger." Tirana said.

"*Gary must think that it will get him back to earth. We will have to wait until we get more men here to go to Salyut 1.*" Hua said.

"*No time.*" Tirana said, "*Please save my dad.*"

"*We will.*" Hua said, "*We just need to wait for more help.*"

An hour later I was looking for Tirana, I yelled for Hua. "*Now Tirana is missing, we must find her!*" I said.

"*Let's look first around here she could of not gotten far.*"

I went over to the mobility unit and look for the machine, it was gone and the dead body of who we thought was left of Col. Leone was spread like ashes across the area.

"*Oh! No!*" I yelled "*The Nitrogen Propelled back pack is gone. Tirana must have pushed off the body and took off in it!*" Hua yelled and said, "*She at least had the sense to put on the Phantom Torso that will help protect her from the radiation.*"

"*What do we do now?*" I asked Hua.

"*We have to wait Lisa; we have not the power to get back to the other station until we get our booster charged.*"

In the meantime Tirana was on her mission in the Nitrogen Propelled back pack machine, fighting her way back to Salyut 1. It was a very fast machine called the MMU and she remembered that Hua said that it fly's with precision.

Well the precision made her charge into the atmosphere with a huge force and acceleration. She hit the target alright but her back-pack machine fell apart as she landed on a lunar volcanic rock. When she woke up she found herself inside a shadow crater and standing over her was a grey haired man with a long beard and was trying to give her water.

He was holding her hand and said; "*My you look like someone from my past, you're so beautiful and young as he pulled off her helmet.*"

Tirana said to him, "*Where am I? Who are you?*"

"*Well pretty lady where did you come from? You show up here at my quarters like you were dropped off by a stork from space.*

Surly you have a mom and dad?" He asked.

Tirana looked up at this nice looking older man and felt his beard and stroked his face and said to him, "*Do you believe in fate*"

"Oh my," he said *"Where have I heard that before?"*

He looks at her and says, *"Well if you're not my Lisa, who only knew that saying and is as beautiful as you, who are you?"*

"I am your daughter, my name is Tirana and I have come to rescue you, my father." At that point they both embraced each other and started crying and hugging each other.

CHAPTER 106

They spend the next few hours catching up and comparing notes until reality set in. *"You know Tirana, that your mom must be worried to death over you. You are as pig headed as me I hate to admit. Tell me about your mom, did she ever get married again?"*

"Well Father, not until you didn't show back up and disappeared on her so she decided that I should have a last name and she remarry Jake, her ex-husband for a year but after a few years she then divorced him and never married again."

"Wait a minute Tirana, let's start from the beginning, how did you get here and where is your mother?"

"Mom is over at the International Space Station with Hua and Wu, waiting for more space troops to get here and help search for you."

"Where is Yao?" Gary asked

"Oh father, he died not long ago."

"Yes, he had to of been getting pretty old for he was an old man when I rescued him from Col. Leones underground cave."

"Is that where you also found the Guidewinds people father?"

"Oh yes, they were smart and well educated people they could beat anyone in a spelling bee. They trusted everyone until Col. Leone, came along and stole all their ideas then he kidnapped them and held them hostage and that is how they got in trouble, they never got their dream but they had their life's back."

"Well, thanks to you father."

"Tirana your mother was with me all the way. She was really the hero."

277

"She never said much until right before this trip to space did I find out that I had another father. I had found your love letters that she just received from Jake."

"What Tirana?"

"Well he kept them hid for 21 years and he decided finally to give them to her."

"She led me to believe that Jake was my real father, though he was like any father could be. He was kind to me and loving so I never suspected anything. But I still cannot understand why she did not tell me about you?"

"Well my dear Tirana it's like this, she knew that you could be in possible danger she had to lead a quiet life and I am sure that she loves you so much that she would give her life for you just like she did for me so many times. We need to go now; we can catch up later on all the missing years. Now we have to get to your mother and Hua and his people and get way from there."

"Tirana there is a rare dust storm that forms over that area it is called **Stardust.** The Hubble photographed it with a detail image. It has a chemical breakdown of minerals in space dust. Stars are born within the clouds of dust.

"I know all about that Father, and when there is turbulence deep in the clouds, and the clouds will collapse and the material begins at the center to heat up. The hot core gathers the dust and gas."

"Wow Tirana, you are not only beautiful like your Mother but smart like as whip."

"Oh shucks, father we have work to do."

"I am thinking Tirana that Col. Leone might have got caught in the last dust storm and maybe was incinerated a few months ago though I am not sure. We should have a few days before it strikes again."

"Did you know father that there is a dead body over at the space station. Maybe that is Col. Leone?"

"Well Tirana maybe but we had a few visitors here and it could be anyone."

"I rescue you, and then you, me, and now mother? Hey Father I like this game."

"Well I wished that it was only a game my daughter."

"Adventure runs in this family don't you think Tirana? What can I say to you after all these years, and not knowing about you, maybe that was better for it would of tore my heart in 2 places instead of one place my dear."

"I have been working on an Extravehicular Mobility Unit; better known as the (EMU) it can be reused with a liquid cooling agent. It has built in headphones and microphones. They used it for a one man suit for the space shuttle but I took their idea and built two (EMU) vehicles that work like a Maglev magnetic glide."

"They have the elevator guide ways that lead to the launching pad. I have just built two of them with a side car on each side. It can carry 3 passengers each."

"Why did you build two of them Dad?"

"Well one is for backup in case one did not start. Besides I had nothing to do with my time and 21 years is a long time to kill."

"Now Dad when can we leave to do our mission?"

"Tirana you sound just like your Mother, at first dawn." Gary said.

CHAPTER 107

"It's time to go." Gary said to Tirana.

"Already Dad? That night sure went fast." she said.

"Yes Tirana, I need to give you a crash course in this new (EMU) machine that I build."

"First thing put your headphones on and the microphones are connected. Climb inside; see the control panel on your left?"

"Yes, I do father."

"Then all you have to do to start it is push the red button that is shape like a gas can."

"Wait a minute Dad, Mom told me about all those red dot gas cans that you pushed to get inside the secret rooms."

"Well," Gary said, *"what better way than to have the escape from here the same thing as the red dot of a gas can. If some intruder like Col. Leone, 'may he rest in peace' showed up he would never know how to start this machine."*

"Oh I get it now Dad."

"To apply the brakes Tirana all you do is pull back on the steering wheel, and to go forward just push the steering wheel forward, see a kid could do it."

"Yes sir, I got it." says Tirana. *"Look Dad, things are getting windy here.*

"I know they are we must get going soon. First," Gary said, *"now that you know how to drive this machine you must listen to what I have to tell you in case the dust storms separate us."*

"Okay, Dad I'm listening."

*"Have you ever heard of **The Moses Bridge** Tirana?"*

"Yes, I studied it in college. It's a great fortress of Defense."

"And what does it do?" Gary asked.

"Well, it's lying flush with the earth then descends deeper into the ground. It then parts the water that surrounds the fort. But Dad, what does that have to do with us and our mission?"

"Everything Tirana, if we get separated by the dust storm, there is an area towards the East, towards Mars there is a gap in the atmospheres and a part that appears as a break, get inside of that break and it will allow you to pass through and puts up a wall of protection from the dust storm. This literally parts the dust storm that surrounds you."

"Wow, Dad that is a good thing to know. Just like the Moses Bridge, it allows escape."

"That is just what I said Tirana."

"I know Dad, just wanted to see if you were on your toes."

"Spoken like a true Brooks." Gary said as they both climbed into their (EMU) machines.

"Turn your craft on and follow me." said Gary, as he motions Tirana to follow him.

CHAPTER 108

"Father, can you hear me? Over and out"

"Yes Tirana,"

"The dust is getting stronger Father.

"I know it" he said, *"but just stay close to me and we will get through this."*

"Okay, but look we just passed a flying object and it went by so fast I know it was only a vapor.

"What? Oh hold on Tirana, stay to your left."

"What is it Father?"

"Nothing that we cannot handle besides they are called **The Ghost ships,** *if we leave them alone they will not bother us."*

"Who are they Father and where do they come from?"

"Watch out Tirana, now get behind me and I will tell you all you need to know. They are checking on you because they know who I am my dear. They are from Pluto which is now considered a dwarf planet. They are in a war with Jupiter, which is way too big for them to fight by themselves."

"Father, Jupiter is bigger than earth!"

"Yes and because its neighbors around the orbit they are considered the "Orbit fighters"

"What are their people like father?" she asks as she pulls up on the steering wheel to bypass an asteroid.

"That was good work Tirana."

"Thanks father but please go on."

"Okay, it's like this, the Orbit fighters want to take over the Ghost ships, and the small planet of Pluto. The poor people hardly stand a

chance. I have been working on a project with them to help them keep their planet."

"Wow Father so does that mean that you have been watching the Crimson skies?"

"Something like that Tirana, I have a radar aircraft hidden that I have been working on."

"Wow, you have been busy."

"Yes but listen we will be within 30 minutes of pulling up to the International Space Station."

As the winds got stronger and the dust blew so much sand and particles around it was hard to see anything while they were landing. They both landed their spaceships and running outside of the station Hua and Wu and I looked on in amazement. We could not believe our eyes when we saw the (EMU's) and then Tirana, stepped outside of it, I looked over at the other one that Gary was in and as he jumped out of his and our eyes met for the first time in 21 years.

"Oh my," I said, about that time the dust got so bad that you could hardly see.

"Mom," Tirana says, *"get into my side car and Father can take Wu, and Hua. Hurry not much time to make dreamtimes with Dad right now."*

"Okay Tirana, I am right behind you." as I climbed into this rare looking machine. I could barely see only a few shadows of Wu and Hua getting into Gary's side cars. In a flash we were flying in the wind, but a few minutes later we were in the atmosphere that parts us from the dust. It was like a break from the dust storm.

"How did you find this break Tirana?"

"Well father told me about it Mother; now just hang on till we get to Salyut 1."

"But there is nothing there." I said.

"Yes, Mom that is where I found my Father."

"Look," Tirana says, *"we are pulling out of the dust storm and Gary, I mean my Father, is flying right next to us and tipping his side cars. He's flirting with you mother."*

"Yes, I see Tirana; see what love does to you. Poor Hua and Wu sitting in those side cars and Dad's doing tricks. Well, at least he has not lost his sense of humor." I said.

It's been about 30 minutes now and we made the landings without any incidence. I can hardly wait to put my arms around Gary as I got off the craft. Gary had the same thought, but before he got to me he grabbed Tirana, and hugged her and then picked her up and twirled her around in a circle.

"You did it my girl, just like you were told. I see now that your Mom raised you right."

"Of course I did Gary." I said as he came running over to me and held me so tight that it almost took the breath away from me, and then he twirled me around like he did Tirana.

"Oh my Gosh," Gary said to me. *"I thought that I would never see you again when they sent me up here to find Col. Leone to bring back for a trial."*

"You are as gorgeous today as you were 21 years ago. You never told me Lisa that you were pregnant with our baby."

"Gary I had just found out and was going to tell you the day that you disappeared."

"Yes Lisa, the timing was wrong again."

"Well now Gary, there is three of us, including our daughter. Yes, and I want to thank you Hua and Wu for all that you have done to bring us all back together, and now it is our job to bring you both to . . ."

Tirana interrupted and said, *"What he means is Ba (Father) and Mu (Mother) will now Bao Wei (safeguard you both) bring you home."*

"No doubt in my mind Tirana that they will accomplish that." Hua said.

"What happen to your crew that you sent for Hua?" Tirana asked.

"Well the beams for the singles blew out with the coming of the Stardust storm."

"Guess good thing I left when I did." said Tirana.

"Not so fast." said Gary. *"That was a very dangerous thing that you did but also a very brave thing. I love you for it Tirana,"* Gary said.

"Now Gary, How did you survive all these years in space? Without food or water?" I asked.

"It was no problem Lisa, when I hooked up with the Russians Salyut 1 they have 3 parts to this and it's called the Almaz, it's for military surveillance. Then 2, is what they use for Transport. The most important for me was in their Space Station they had stored foods, and water and all kinds of supplies that would last years. Those that came here and all died going back to earth because the air escaped from their space craft."

"I have been building the second generation Maglev space launcher. It's almost completed. I have used all their supplies that the Russians left here. I did have some interference with Col. Leone."

"He is still alive Gary?" I asked.

"Yes the drugs wore off and he landed here. He was lucky in that way but then when they sent me back to space to retrieve him; it has been cat and mouse for over 21 years, until lately when he could have been incinerated."

"Well Gary, we found a man in his old space suit that was in the Propelled back pack (MMU) that your daughter took and the space suit looked like old Col. Leone's and dust from a body came out of the suit."

"Yes Dad, I took him out of the propelled back pack so I could use his machine."

"No worries my child."

CHAPTER 109

"Like I said it may not be Col. Leone for he is the only one that I know that has nine lives."

"We were worried Gary, about you getting in the Hubble craft, not knowing that the components will slowly degrade over time and then it would spiral towards earth, after finding the drawings that you left behind at the International Space Station," Hua said.

"I knew about that Hua"

"How did you find out Gary?"

"There is a new X-37 B that may be a spy shuttle. Someone is using it for surveillance but I tapped into a component when it landed over at the International Space Station. I found out all kinds of things on their black box including how to turn this Hubble craft into a Maglev rocket."

"The drawings that you all found were about my launch pad that I had planned on using for parts from the Hubble craft. It will have magnetic wheels and a guideway elevator to use for launching pad into space."

"Where is Wu?" Gary asked?

"She is checking our radio for a message that is coming in from the sanctuary back in China." A few minutes later Wu came running out from the space craft and said. *"We just got word that Huang He* (Yellow River) *may be cresting and could burst at its banks."*

"Oh Wu," Gary said, *"No worries about helping us, you two need to get back to your people. I was just going to ask you to take Lisa and my daughter back to earth and I could catch up with you when I finish my space craft but now that has changed."*

"I will not leave you again." I said as I put my arms around Gary and we held each other.

Then Tirana yelled, *"I second that motion!"* Then she comes over and all three of us are with arms around each other.

Hua said, *"The girls should stay with you. It will be more dangerous now to come back, last time it flooded it killed two million of our people."*

"Why so many Hua?" I asked.

"Well Lisa, it starts from the Mississippi river because of its load, then when it reaches the plains of North China this river carries more sediment than any major river in the world."

"When it gets here it will burst its banks into our plains, and unable to receded or return its breached course."

"Wow! What can be done to prevent these floods?" Tirana asks.

"Not much," Hua said, *"Only to get all are people to safe harbor."*

"Our great grandpa Yu was credited in taming the river and that is how he became Emperor of China."

"But remember we have the secret train in the other underground tunnel that can help my people escape. We need to be there to lead them."

"Then let us help you get your space craft ready so you can leave sooner." said Gary.

"You and Wu go back to earth; looks like the girls will stay with me."

"If you're all sure then we will leave tomorrow for our journey back to earth." said Wu.

"Yes please do not worry about us. I still have some unfinished business to attend to." Gary said.

"Alright my Shu-Ren (Friends) you can help us get the shuttle ready."

"Where do we start?" asks Tirana as she rolled up her sleeves and smiled.

"Follow me my daughter I will give you your first lesson in getting a space craft ready."

When they were walking away Tirana looks at her father and says, *"Now this is how it is done father, you put the . . ."*

"Wait a minute daughter, since when did you become an expert on spacecraft?"

"Just the other day Father I learned to fly one, so don't you think that it would be easier to learn to fix one?"

"Your right my daughter." said Gary.

CHAPTER 110

The next morning we were saying our goodbyes to Hua and Wu as they were getting into their spacecraft and to brave a great battle in saving all his people from the *Yellow River* flooding. It was fast approaching his country.

We all had worked long into the night to get his spacecraft ready for launching this morning. Even Tirana was working to get it ready for space. Gary and I both were surprised that she caught on so quickly. Just watching her and her dad working together just melted my heart. It was not before long we were saying our good-byes to Hua and Wu.

"We will see you my Shu Ren (Our Friends)," Gary and Tirana said in Chinese.

Well off in a blast they went in space. It felt somewhat lonely without Hua and Wu but we had much to do in finishing the Maglev space ship Hubble.

"Let's get to work girls," Gary said as we headed one that Gary, was

in and has he jumped

towards the launch pad arm in arm.

"I feel so helpless Gary, not to be able to go back and help Hua and his people this time and how they brought me here in space to find you."

"I know Lisa, let's just get our space shuttle ready and there really is nothing that we can do about the big flood. I bet that is probably what they were talking about when they mention the big wave years ago."

"Yes Gary, I guess they did not want to alarm anyone by saying it was the Yellow River, that was coming and all the way from the Mississippi,"

"Your right Lisa, but if we don't get busy we may have our own yellow wave. But first I want to finish up my radar aircraft that I am making for the Ghost ship riders and it just needs a few final touches."

"Tell me about this radar aircraft Gary," I said.

*"Okay Lisa, it's like this. In case of an attack from the (**orbit fighters**) this aircraft I have built will determine the range and direction and speed of objects and will pick any moving thing within 250 miles away. A signal will go off to alert the ghost ship riders."*

"Go on Father, please!"

"Yes, Gary tell us more"

"Well it goes on to use a narrow beam of light, something like we used in the operation of zapping Col. Leone's thugs."

"How does that work?" Tirana asked.

"This is how I made this to work just by using it to frequency hop, which means that it is spreading radar pulses over a wide band with a very small signal and will not stay in one place long enough to register to the enemy."

"That is genius Father."

"Well, there is more to tell you girls."

"And what is that?" I asked.

"I have made modules that I have assigned the role of radar warning receivers, so when an unidentified aircraft gets within range then the anti-air craft guns that are built inside the radar aircraft will follow the laser beam of light and shoot anything in sight."

"How much ammunition will they need Father?"

"That is the good question Tirana, and glad that you brought it up. No radar operators are needed nor ammunition. After it shoots the enemy by a slow spire and ignites, it will then just regenerate itself with light crystals off of the solar rays."

"This is astonishing Father."

"Well thank you my daughter, but we better hurry, time is a wasting.

"We just need to go to the International Space station where there is a solar wing. There are two blankets of solar cells making up the panel

and all we have to do is stretch it out tightly, then each array which measures 38ft. across and contains 32,800 silicon cells will convert sunlight into electricity. **Project done.** *Now let's get over there before another sand storm hits."* And we climbed into the EMU machine craft.

Tirana took the left side wing and Gary the middle and I was in the right side wing. *"Hold on."* Gary says as we took off in space to the International Space Station.

"I see no sign of a dust and sand storm today."

"Well mother, it's like this, (Gary knew what was coming and chuckled to himself) *sand storms hit so mostly in the summertime here in space mother, and usually starts in Mars and then quickly spreads and engulfs other planets mostly brewed in* **Hellas Basins** *to the northern Polar Caps and particles are transported by—,"*

"Wait a minute Tirana, where is all this information coming from? May I ask?"

"Let me finish mother first."

"Okay, and then you can tell me."

"Now like I was saying they are transported by saturation and suspension that causes soil to move to one place and deposited in another so the direct cause of sand storm is a gust front that blows loose sand and dirt from a dry surface."

"Oh Tirana, you sure can come up with some facts, but tell me (as I look over the top of Gary, so I could see her) *where did you learn all that?"*

"Well Mother if father was not sitting next to me I could keep it a secret, but in front of me is a screen that has all the information you can think of and I was reading it, ha-ha."

"Yes Lisa I built that in the dash for emergency's so I would be able look up anything. I found it in the Hubble machine before I tore into it and used a part from it to also build the (no think machine) that is what I call it." Gary said.

"Hold on girls I am getting ready to land this ship, yahoo we are here." And boy! did he look so happy to have us with him. He needed us to help him to work on the radar ship. It was a smooth landing as we packed up our stuff and moved off of the EMU ship.

Gary took us through this maze of moon rocks, and sand and craters. *"Well girls we are almost there."*

"Wow, father these are beautiful the way the craters are formed."

"Yes, I totally agree and they may end up very helpful to us." As we got closer to the site I noted it was hidden behind some craters.

"Oh, no it looks like someone has been messing with my radar ship," Gary said.

"But how do you know?" I asked.

"Well first of all" as he runs over to this huge telescope, *"look I made this a solar telescope from parts of the Hubble only because it would observe the hot sun."*

"And?" I asked.

"Well, it would show me a reflection like a wave traveling through air like the speed of light as in a vacuum. Then as the index of refraction increases the speed of light in the material decreases, refraction occurs because the speed of the wave changes when it enters a new material with a different density. And if you look, the array of telescopes that I had operating, well two of them are missing; I had four to begin with."

"Gary, you are not making any sense to us."

"I agree Mother, come on Father use laymen terms."

"I am sorry girls. I have been studying this for over 20 years when I found some books left in the Hubble all about the universe and planets, and how to build space ships. I now consider myself a great scientist."

"You are great my Father, but let's get on with it."

"Okay Okay, now listen." as he went on to explain to us, *"I had combined the same target simultaneously to four telescopes to operate together through a process called interferometer that combines the signals into just one. Now there is only two left."*

"Is it possible Gary to combine just the two telescopes to do the job?"

"There may be a way Lisa, give me a minute to think this out."

"Okay Gary, your minute is up." (I teased him).

"Lisa this is no time to joke."

"Sorry Gary, I just got carried away."

"What did you say Lisa?"

"I said I just got carried away."

"That's it Lisa"

"What do you mean Gary?"

"Think about it Lisa"

"We can carry away the incoming wave, such as air that bounces off a new medium in the orientation of the incoming wave."

"Yes Gary that would determine how the wave will reflect in the telescope and make a stronger signal and make sunlight into electricity."

"Gee, you two are geniuses and especially working together." Tirana sighs.

"Hey Father look over here at these footprints."

"Gary walks over and he also sees an old faded CIA badge laying in the sand and bends to pick it up and says, *"I'll be a snakes tail"*

"Oh No!" I cried, *"That sounds like bad news. What does it say Gary?"*

"All I can make out is what it looks like Col. Leone's badge only the Le is faded off of it."

"Not good, huh Father?"

"Your right Tirana, hey and the footprint is huge like a large giants foot Lisa, that can only be Leone's footprint for I had never met a man with such a big feet as he had. Remember we had trouble getting his feet inside the space craft when we sent him here."

"I remember that Gary." I said.

*"Yes father, he is a (**big foot**) more like big trouble."*

"You're right about that Tirana."

"Guess it was not him that got incinerated at the space station. But who was it?" I asked.

"It had to of been, unless it was that Russian that was killed here when they brought more supplies to the Hubble. I remember a few months ago I found a dead body, and I had a hunch that old Col. Leone was responsible."

"Gary you have not said much about the Colonel why not?"

"Well he is hardly worth talking about. Like I said before all we have done the last 21 years is play cat and mouse."

All of a sudden a grubby old man runs out from behind the rocks holding double guns in his hands pointed at us and says, *"Hey mouse, I just caught you, he-he,"* as he laugh so hard you could see all his missing teeth.

His hands were shaking and his boots had nothing left but the heel and his toes were exposed. He was dressed in an old torn black suit and his shirttail was ripped.

"I'll be a—, that's Col. Leone in the flesh, I have been playing games with you Leone for over 21 years and now I think it's time to end this."

"Not quite yet Mr. Gary Brooks."

"If you want to save that little gal of yours and Lisa, you better do as I say."

"What do you want Leone?" Gary asked.

"Well, that is not too hard to figure out."

"Just tell me and leave my family out of this, they have never done anything to you."

"Well maybe not that beautiful daughter of yours, he-he."

"You touch one hair on her head and I will kill you with my bare hands, you brute!" Gary said.

"What do you want?"

"Is that so hard to figure out Gary?"

"You tell me Col. Leone"

"It's like this, I know all about your space ship and since you have it ready to go, I want you to send me back to earth."

"Are you nuts Leone? There would be a price on your head so high China, could not afford to bail you out."

"Now you listen to me Gary, I want you to get it ready to launch by morning, I will keep your daughter with me until it's done."

"You old fart, if you touch my daughter you will pay."

"Just do as you're told and nobody gets hurt."

"Gary, do as he says what choice do we have?"

"You're still a smart lady Lisa." the Col. said.

I started crying and Tirana said, "No problem mother, I can take care of myself."

"Tell me something how do you suppose we are to get back to earth?" I said.

"I believe that will be your problem. Now come with me Tirana, let your parents get busy, he he!" as he pushed Tirana in the back and she turned around and stepped on his exposed big toes, "Ouch" he yelled, *"you wild girl, your just like your mother, and one more move like that and you will be sorry."* It was only a few minutes later and they both were out of sight.

"Now what Gary?" I said as he put his arms around me.

"Lisa it will be alright, he will not harm a hair on her head knowing that we have to get the space ship ready for him."

The next morning got here and we finished working on the craft, all we had to do was launch it from the pad. The Col. did not know that we still had the Maglev spacecraft over on Saturn 1 he thinks that this radar ship will get him back to earth. It was not built for traveling over 250 miles.

"Where are they Gary?" I asked as we fast approached the area that we left?

"I do not know Lisa." About that time we heard some noise in the brush behind the rocks and some moaning going on.

I said, *"Oh my no, he must of hurt Tirana."* as we rushed behind the rocks and was afraid of what we might see.

There pinned against the rocks and flat on the ground and bleeding on the back of his head was Col. Leone. Before we could say anything Tirana, walks out from behind holding a bloody rock in her hand and puts her leg up on a rock and said, *"What took you guys so long?"*

"I went rushing over to her and hugged her.

Gary says, *"Tirana what happened?"*

"Oh father I just pulled that old snake tail about 'I'll be a snakes tail' and when he looked over I picked up a rock and got him from behind and then I did a choke hold on him and put my knee on his backside and gave him a big push. By the way mom and dad, I forgot to tell you I have a black belt in Karate."

"So do I Tirana." Gary said.

"Good now let's take care of the Col. and lock him into the space station locker room."

What a day that was but now with Col. Leone locked up we were free to finish this mission.

"Come on crew we have a job to do." as Gary starts taking parts off from the radar ship. We worked all day and into the night on this project, but it looked like things were going our way finally.

"Tomorrow girls we will be finished with the project and I can give it to the ghost ship riders. They will be protected from the Orbit Fighters."

"Yes," I said *"and also it means we can all go home."*

"For sure," Tirana said, *"I can handle that, yippee!"* she cried.

We went back to Salute1 and all fell asleep really fast and before we knew it morning had come. One by one we got up and Gary had the coffee going that was left here on the Hubble said he had year's supply of it.

"Good morning my love." I said to him as I walked into the room.

"Good Morning Lisa sweetheart, oh how I love you so."

"You girls are my life now and I want to get us all back to earth real soon."

"Me too Gary," I said as he held me in his arms, about that time Tirana walks out raising her arms and yawning real big and says, *"Okay lovebirds no time for that lets go back we have work to do."*

"We will soon dear," I said, *"have your coffee; your father wants to explain a few things to us."*

"Go ahead;" said Tirana, *"this ought to be real good."*

"It depends how you look at it my dear daughter. I am sure that you have heard of 'dark energy' right?"

"Yes," Tirana answered, *"it is well known that 70% of the universe is dark energy."*

"Yes, you are right," said Gary, *"and so very smart."*

"Oh come on father everyone knows that."

"Anyway it is theorized that the faster expansion rate due to a mysterious dark force that is pulling the galaxies apart."

"Now we know that Pluto is the farthest from the sun and we also know that Pluto will cross the orbit inside of Neptune 20 years out of every 245 years. Well the 20 years is fast approaching and the ghost ship riders are afraid that the orbit fighters will get a hold of their people and kill them before Pluto goes into orbit with Neptune."

"Why father would they want to stop that from happening?"

"From what I can find Jupiter consists of too many gases and they know that Neptune has great geysers of liquid nitrogen and solid ground and not like their planet. If they can keep the ghost ship riders out of the way they would own Pluto and would be heading to the blue planet as it is really called, then they would move all the orbit fighters to Neptune then they could control the galaxy."

"Okay," Tirana said, *"what can we do to help them?"*

"We are doing it. That is why I built them the radar ship. When they are under attack they can stall long enough until their planet Pluto heads towards Neptune. Then their problems will be solved."

"Wow! Father I know that we can do this."

"Enough talk guys," I said, *"We need to get going."*

"Your right Lisa." We grabbed our bags and headed to the EMU machine.

"Now here is how our spacecraft will work," says Gary. *"You can see this is the size of a semi-truck. I have built pointing systems inside and they face the same direction and will zero in on our target which is earth. The reaction wheels are how we steer it. The wheels will spin the way that we point it and the Hubble will keep it going in that direction."*

"Any questions yet?" Gary asked.

"Not yet Dad keep going."

"Okay then there is flight software that commands the reaction wheels to spin, then it will start accelerating or decelerating as needed?"

"Still with me Lisa?"

"Yes Gary but what about guidance sensors?"

"No problem Lisa, I have made the guidance sensors to measure our position with precise reference to our destination."

"Sounds like you have it altogether Dad."

"Well we just need to tighten up a few lose ends today and then should ready for launch."

We had worked on the craft for an entire day and Gary felt that it was ready for launch with the magnetic wheels installed and taking it up with the guideway elevator to the launch pad. This would give us enough pressure to take off into space.

We all could not wait to get back to earth and just the three of us and all the catching up to do for the last 21 years.

The statutes of limitations were up for Gary's supposed war crimes of Col. Leone. Gary should have got a medal instead of being kidnapped by the CIA and forced into space for the recapture of Col. Leone. We never could figure out whose body was left on the Propelled back pack. Was it the Russian?

We left Col. Leone in the locker room with a key that was hid under the bunker; we figured he would figure it out in a few days. He got more mercy from us than he gave his hostages and not that he deserved it.

We finished the radar ship and gave it to the Ghost ship riders and now they had a chance to survive being killed by the Orbit fighters.

Hua and Wu made it back and the big wave made a sudden turn and lost speed as it was approaching China.

We all were walking towards the space craft Hubble and I said, *"Gary let's take a few minutes to hold hands and pray."* After moment of silence I said to Gary, *"This is the last letter that you wrote too me so many years ago."* I pulled out this old faded letter from my pocket and held it in my hand. *"I brought it with me into space and had plan on leaving it here for you in case we could not find you."*

"Go ahead Lisa," Gary said, *"read it."*

"Yes." Tirana said, *"We want to hear it."*

"Okay" I said as I started reading the letter.

Dear Lisa,
We are man and woman
Of two worlds and now different walks of life.
I have loved you eternally
We love one other.
If by remote chance God grants our wishes
Then we shall be born together, and forever.
If ever he does, He and he alone
Shall grant our desires and wishes.'

"Gary I want to leave this poem that you wrote me here in space. Maybe someday, someone else will be in our shoes and find this for hope. Everything that you wrote is so true. I see a rock over here Gary, let's put it there and put a red dot on it for a gas can."

"Good thinking Lisa." as he pulled out a red pen and made the drawing of a can.

"Yes Lisa, I never thought in a million light years that we would all be together in space with a daughter I never knew I had who was also so brave to come to space to rescue me."

"Ah Dad, it was nothing." Tirana said.

"Come my girls to a new adventure that waits." Gary says as he put his arms around each of us and we made our way into the shuttle and prepared to blast off into space.

We were all gazing at all the beautiful stars and galaxy's as we all three were holding hands as we accelerated towards earth.

"Look mom, there is Venus."

"Yes dear." I said.

I looked at Gary and he winked at me and says, *"Look girls at the solar cells it is harnessing the pressure of sunlight and the units of light are called photons that generate miniscule levels of thrust. Now, when they collide with a solar sail . . ."*

"Yes father, then it is much like a kite or sailboat that responds to wind. I remember last year father that I read that the Japanese had a solar sail mission named **Ikaros** *and successfully demonstrated solar sailing on the way from earth to Venus."*

"Well Tirana, it is used for removing retired or clogged traffic lanes like satellites out of orbit; sort of like retiring them for a less destructive reentry . . . Hey, do you see what I see? We are headed towards earth." As we got closer to entering the atmosphere and oh how beautiful it looked the closer that we got.

"Prepare for landing girls, put your gears on and close the cargo doors now we must maneuver this spacecraft into the proper position. I will fire the OMS engines to slow down the craft and I have already fired the thrusters to turn the tail first. Hang on while I fire the RCS thrusters so the bottom of the spacecraft faces the atmosphere. We have no fuel to burn so we do not have to worry about high heat so that

presents no worries. We must spin 180 degrees and that will help reduce are speed."

"Gary, slow down." I said and he answered and said *"This time honey, there is no slowing down, everything is working great."* We have now re-entered the main air of the atmosphere and we are flying like a plane."*

"Now we will deploy the parachute from the back and it will also slow us down, Tirana go to the switch that I showed you earlier and pull hard on it."

"Okay father, hey it's working." as she pulls on the switch and the parachute pops out like a large balloon.

"Take your position now Tirana."

"Oh mother look at all the buildings and houses in the distance."

"We are now landing at the Kennedy Space Station" Gary said to us *and look at the crowds over there mother and father. I think that they are waiting on us,"* Said Tirana.

When we touch down the crowds ran to the run way and the security guards tried to hold the crowds off.

"What do they want father?"

"We will see shortly Tirana."

"We one by one walked off the spacecraft, first our daughter Tirana, and then I and Gary followed."

A rash of reporters came over and said *"How does it feel to get a Hero's welcome?"*

"What did we do to deserve this we asked?"

"Did you not hear that a Chinese man named Hua and I believe his cousin Wu told the story about you and Lisa and how you saved the United States in retrieving the patents for the high speed Maglev, how your life was in danger with the criminals of Leone's chasing you and then the bad CIA director sent you to space to look for Col. Leone, after you saved China and the United States from the Colonel who wanted to rule the world?"

"And how you spent over 21 years in space alone. We all are grateful and here comes the president of the United States," the reporter said.

"Tirana who is the President?" Gary asked?

"Well father for your information it is Wu's daughter who was born in the USA. Wu just found out that she had a daughter. Her name is President Mia Weed, a woman."

The story goes that Col.Leone had Wu inseminated when she was only 14years old since he could not get her pregnant. Wu was told that the baby died after giving birth. Col. Leone wanted a son to rule the earth with him and when he found out that the baby was a girl he gave the baby away. Senator, Weed ended up adopting her and sending her to Harvard. She had a great personality like her mom Wu and smart like no other then got into politics with her step dad and the rest is history.

Wu never knew about it until recently when she met with the new President and told her story about you saving her people and then her daughter Mia, put two and two together and realized that they were mother and daughter. We all looked at each other surprised and said together **God Bless America,** *and why did you not tell me Tirana?"*

*"Well father they had the election while we were here in space."And besides I read it coming back to earth on your **(smart machine)** or I should say the **(think machine)** that you installed on the space ship. I just kept my mouth shut.*

"Okay Tirana that shows me you can keep your mouth shut when need be. Haha, and way too much excitement for today my girls." Gary said.

"I love you Tirana so much."

"And I love you my famous father."

"And I love you both." I said as we watched the crowds. We all had are arms around each other waving up a storm. With Gary in the middle and Tirana and me on each side of him.

Tirana was eating up all the press coverage and attention that we were all getting and then Jake, her step father walked out of the crowd and headed for Tirana and she hugged him and all of us held hands and waved at everyone. We could see Wu and Hua walking with President Mia Weed, as they were coming towards us.

Tirana stops waving for a minute and then whispers in Gary's ear and says, *"Father should we tell them what we did for the Ghost ship riders?"*

"No Tirana, not a word!" He whispered to her as they smiled at each other and continued to wave.

THE END

Engine House

Hidden underground room where Gary and Lisa pulled the wood from the floor and found a concrete top which they opened up they found Yao, The Emperor of China who was held prisoner

Toy soldiers who are guarding the underground caves for Col. Leone

Tracks outside of Col. Leones underground rooms.

Entrance to Col. Leone's old railroad station
where Lisa and Gary break into.

Underground tunnel where Gary and Lisa find the hidden key.

Train cars that Gary uses to rescue hostages. Key is hidden under the tracks along with underground rooms

Mountain where Col. Leone hides the Guidewinds people and Yao
shows Lisa and Gary the way to reach them underground

All the prisoners break free towards engine station.

One of the engines used for Gary to get the Guidewinds prisoners free.

Inside this tunnel is where the key is hid between the train tracks.

Mountain that hides the hostages at Treecuts Estates owner is Col. Leone

Sand Mountain, Nevada Col. Leone and his Nomad friend.
Looking for Gary and Lisa

The real Terrorist Patrol Car

AUTHOR BIOGRAPHY
"THE MAGLEV CONSPIRACY"

Mary Leone Engquist Author

Mary has written many numerous articles and manuals for the project and also was in business with her daughter Debi Devitt in their own publishing company many years ago in writing and selling "How to booklets"
Mary continues to write stage plays and sometimes performs in acting. She continues with her brother to write fiction and non-fiction books Mary Leone was the Vice President Coordinator for The Guidewinds Project, and she also holds a California real estate license.

Joseph Leone Co-Author

Joe, worked for a rapid transit company for over 28 years. President and owner of The Guidewinds Project. He wrote books for the Mission statements Environmental Impact Reports and the Executive Summary and met over the years with local State officials for the pushing of a maglev high speed train. He continues today in praying that this great Country of ours will see the importance of building a maglev 2nd generation high speed train.

"AUTHOR'S NOTES"

I never knew what was coming next in the book or the ending of it. In other words, I had no idea where the story was going. I felt all the emotions of the characters in this book. I shed tears when I wrote some scenes. I got wet when they did. I felt torn and alone when they were left alone.

I felt sad when they were abused. I cried of happiness when they were happy. When the winds blew of sand I felt it in my eyes. My heart hurt for Lisa when she thought that she lost Gary and most of all the love letters had brought so much closure to a unthinkable and remarkable romance.

A wonderful miracle happens to Joe and I while having the Guidewinds Project, Inc. web site. We had 3 brothers and 2 sisters that had been searching for us that we never knew we had. They started searching the web and they were about to give up until they came across our website. They then send us an e-mail to our company saying "we might be related" This happen in February 2011 just before we closed the Guidewinds Project, web site and the company.

Without the web site they said they never would have found us. The timing was great. We may have not got the Maglev train to become a reality but having to meet them now and because of the Guidewinds Project is the best thing that could of happen.

The Leone's

COMING SOON
FROM THE AUTHORS
OF "THE MAGLEV CONSPIRACY"
MARY ENGQUIST & JOE LEONE

"The Midnight Train Riders" Cute book clips and true stories of train operators. Nothing short of a miracle. This book has been kept secret for years and will have you laughing in disbelieve on what happens when no one is looking.

"Who's In The Army Now" If you liked the "Midnight Train Riders" you will love this well put together true clips and funny stories of basic training and what's behind the scenes? Never before dare to be told "Who would of thought that this could happen in the United States Armed Forces. A must for every fan that loves his Country. A brighter side through the eyes of someone who's been there and done that.

"The Maglev Launchers" a trailer off of the great book and future and soon to be best seller, "The Maglev Conspiracy" a continuation of the story line bringing back the unbelievable romance, action and adventure of Gary, Lisa, and their daughter Tirana from their adventures in space to the ever chasing of the old Col. Leone will for sure keep you on the edge of your seat.

How does an ordinary housewife become a strong, brave heroine and falls in love only to find out that her involvement is with a secret CIA double agent named Gary?

Running from the big ice wave Gary and her stumble across a famous Chinese woman who at the age of 13 years old was kidnapped and held hostage for over 20 years in a dungeon inside of a secret tunnel and only by chance did they find her. The suspense goes even further when a trip into space leads into danger and unexplained love shows its true course. This book is a must read for all who have dreamed the impossible dream. If you love adventure, mystery, and romance this is the book for you.

Author Mary Leone Engquist and Co-Author Joe Leone